THE DUKE'S REBELLIOUS DAUGHTER

Historical Regency Romance

THE DUKES' LADIES
BOOK 10

ABBY AYLES

This is a work of fiction.

Names, characters, organizations, places, events, and incidents are either products of the author's imagination or are used fictitiously. Any resemblance to actual person, living or dead, or actual events is purely coincidental.

Copyright © 2022 by Abby Ayles

All rights reserved.

No part of this book may be reproduced in any form or by any electronic or mechanical means, including information storage and retrieval systems, without written permission from the author, except for the use of brief quotations in a book review.

PRAISE FOR ABBY AYLES

Abby Ayles has been such an inspiration for me! I haven't missed any of her novels and she has never failed my expectations!

-Edith Byrd

The characters in this novel have surely touched my heart.

Linda C - "Melting a Duke's Winter Heart" 5.0 out of 5 stars Reviewed in the United States on December 21, 2019

This book kept me on the edge of my seat and I could not put it down.

Wendy Ferreira - "The Odd Mystery of the Cursed

Duke" 5.0 out of 5 stars Reviewed in the United States on April 13, 2019*

Oh this was a wonderful story and Abby has done it again! This storyline was perfect and the characters were developed and just had you reading to see if they get their happily ever after!

- Marilyn Smith - "Inconveniently Betrothed to an Earl" 5.0 out of 5 stars Reviewed in the United States on April 8, 2020

The sweetest story, with we rest abounding! I especially liked the bonus scene - totally unexpected engagements. Well written with realistic characters. Thank you!

Janet Tonole - "The Lady Of the Lighthouse" 5.0 out of 5 stars Reviewed in the United States on December 27, 2022

I just finished reading Abby Ayles' The Lady's Gamble and its bonus scene, and I wanted to tell other readers about this great story. I love regency romances and I believe Abby is one of the best regency writers out there!

Carolynn Padgett - "The Lady's Gamble" 5.0 out of 5 stars Reviewed in the United States on March 16, 2018

Such a great Book! So enjoyed the characters....they felt so " real"....and loved the " deleted" scene. Thanks Abby, for your gift of writing the best stories!

Marcia Reckard - "Entangled with the Duke" 5.0 out of 5 stars Reviewed in the United States on May 22, 2021

I loved this story. It took you through all of the exciting ups and downs. The characters were so honest. I could read it again and again.

Peggy Murphy - "The Duke's Rebellious Daughter" 5.0 out of 5 starsReviewed in the United States on December 3, 2022

I am never disappointed when reading one of Ms. Ayles stories. They have strong characters, engaging storylines, and all-around wonderful stories.

Donna L - "A Loving Duke for the Shy Duchess" 5.0 out of 5 stars Reviewed in the United States on December 23, 2019

A thoroughly enjoyable read! Love the complexity of the intelligent characters! They have the ability to feel emotions deeply! Their backstories help to explain why they behave as they do! The subplots and various interactions between characters add to the wonderful richness of the story! Well done!

Terry Rose Bailey - "A Cinderella for the Duke" 5.0 out of 5 stars Reviewed in the United States on October 8, 2022

ALSO BY ABBY AYLES

The Keys to a Lockridge Heart
Melting a Duke's Winter Heart
A Loving Duke for the Shy Duchess
Freed by the Love of an Earl
The Earl's Wager for a Lady's Heart
The Lady in the Gilded Cage
A Reluctant Bride for the Baron
A Christmas Worth Remembering
A Guiding Light for the Lost Earl
The Earl Behind the Mask

Tales of Magnificent Ladies
The Odd Mystery of the Cursed Duke

A Second Chance for the Tormented Lady
Capturing the Viscount's Heart
The Lady's Patient
A Broken Heart's Redemption
The Lady The Duke And the Gentleman
Desire and Fear
A Tale of Two Sisters
What the Governess is Hiding

Betrayal and Redemption
Inconveniently Betrothed to an Earl
A Muse for the Lonely Marquess
Reforming the Rigid Duke
Stealing Away the Governess
A Healer for the Marquess's Heart
How to Train a Duke in the Ways of Love
Betrayal and Redemption
The Secret of a Lady's Heart
The Lady's Right Option

Forbidden Loves and Dashing Lords
The Lady of the Lighthouse
A Forbidden Gamble for the Duke's Heart

A Forbidden Bid for a Lady's Heart
A Forbidden Love for the Rebellious Baron
Saving His Lady from Scandal
A Lady's Forgiveness
Viscount's Hidden Truths
A Poisonous Flower for the Lady

Marriages by Mistake
The Lady's Gamble
Engaging Love
Caught in the Storm of a Duke's Heart
Marriage by Mistake
The Language of a Lady's Heart
The Governess and the Duke
Saving the Imprisoned Earl
Portrait of Love
From Denial to Desire
The Duke's Christmas Ball

The Dukes' Ladies
Entangled with the Duke
A Mysterious Governess for the Reluctant Earl
A Cinderella for the Duke

Falling for the Governess
Saving Lady Abigail
Secret Dreams of a Fearless Governess
A Daring Captain for Her Loyal Heart
Loving A Lady
Unlocking the Secrets of a Duke's Heart
The Duke's Rebellious Daughter
The Duke's Juliet

SCANDALS AND SEDUCTION IN REGENCY ENGLAND

Also in this series

Last Chance for the Charming Ladies
Redeeming Love for the Haunted Ladies
Broken Hearts and Doting Earls
The Keys to a Lockridge Heart
Regency Tales of Love and Mystery
Chronicles of Regency Love
Broken Dukes and Charming Ladies
The Ladies, The Dukes and Their Secrets
Regency Tales of Graceful Roses
The Secret to the Ladies' Hearts
The Return of the Courageous Ladies
Falling for the Hartfield Ladies
Extraordinary Tales of Regency Love
Dukes' Burning Hearts
Escaping a Scandal

Regency Loves of Secrecy and Redemption
Forbidden Loves and Dashing Lords
Fateful Romances in the Most Unexpected Places
The Mysteries of a Lady's Heart
Regency Widows Redemption
The Secrets of Their Heart
Lovely Dreams of Regency Ladies
Second Chances for Broken Hearts
Trapped Ladies
Light to the Marquesses' Hearts
Falling for the Mysterious Ladies
Tales of Secrecy and Enduring Love
Fateful Twists and Unexpected Loves
Regency Wallflowers
Regency Confessions
Ladies Laced with Grace
Journals of Regency Love
A Lady's Scarred Pride
How to Survive Love
Destined Hearts in Troubled Times
Ladies Loyal to their Hearts
The Mysteries of a Lady's Heart
Secrets and Scandals
A Lady's Secret Love
Falling for the Wrong Duke

GET ABBY'S EXCLUSIVE MATERIAL

Building a relationship with my readers is the very best thing about writing.

Join my newsletter for information on new books and deals plus a few free books!

You can get your books by clicking or visiting the link below

https://BookHip.com/JBWAHR

PS. Come join our Facebook Group if you want to interact with me and other authors from Starfall Publication on a daily basis, win FREE Giveaways and find out when new content is being released.

Join our Facebook Group
abbyayles.com/Facebook-Group

THE DUKE'S REBELLIOUS DAUGHTER

Marring her for her title was his scheme... falling in love with her was his fate!

Lady Mercy is the oldest of the Duke's three beautiful daughters. She is the one who has to get married first! But her untamed and rebellious nature repels every gentleman in the Ton. Lady Mercy doesn't want a husband...and she's not afraid to show it.

Caleb Griffiths, a charming Baron with a title but no money, believes that Lady Marcy is his great opportunity.

Making her his bride, will make him the next Duke of Norfolk!

"To marry her will be easy," he thinks. "Her father expects no suitor to ask her hand and must be desperate to find a match for her."

His plan is perfect... except for one small detail... Love! Unexpected, sweet, pure, deep, true love that will turn his world upside down.

As for Lady Mercy, she will face every feeling -unknown to her- at once... love turns into betrayal in a single moment. Anger and forgiveness are fighting with each other in her mind. Her logic holds her back while her heart asks to move forward...

Will Love tame them both?

PROLOGUE

Inside the bedchamber of Norfolk Manor, fifteen-year-old Mercy White huddled close to her two younger sisters in the deep night. The middle child, Alice, was affixed by Mercy's side, as was her youngest sister, Olive, who clung to the oldest sister's arm and would not let go. Mercy stared at them fondly from above before pulling them closer.

"Have I told you the tale of the fairy and the monster?" Mercy inquired.

The two little girls' heads shook resolutely.

Mercy attempted a jovial grin and bent her head to begin the story. "In a world filled with monsters, beasts roamed the streets and raided the caverns. They were all big and smelled horrible! Everywhere they went, they left a trail of stench that made the entire village shrivel in their wake."

The two youngest sisters giggled softly.

Mercy raised her hands with exaggerated gestures. Her brows rose and her eyes widened as she dove into the story, making Olive and Alice lean closer with intrigue. "However, all the beasts cared about was strength and size. They believed their worth lay in their fists and their fat chests. Until one day, a small little fairy came flying through one of the ravaged villages. She was beautiful and smelled of daffodils. She left a trail of sparkles and a path of blooming flowers. The beasts were of course furious over this intruder. How could someone come in and ruin their hard work?"

"One beast walked toward the small fairy and asked, 'What is the name of this wretched witch?' The fairy twinkled and mused, 'This fairy has no name. I am only here to clean the mess you've all made.' The beast grew even more furious and stalked back to his other friends. They talked and talked and talked, and in the end they decided to step on the fairy! For they were enormous beasts! What could a little fairy do?"

Olive and Alice both gasped in shock, cowering behind their blankets.

"So they all marched toward the fairy and raised their feet at once," Mercy continued, a glint of pride shone in her eyes, "only to find that the fairy had flown away, weaving between the monsters. She was so fast, they couldn't even see her wings! One by one, the fairy sprinkled dust on the tops of their giant heads, and one by one, they fell asleep. Then, she flew away and left a trail of flowers and plants and grass in her wake. Remember, Olive and Alice, those mountains you see in the distance? Or in those books you two read from the library? Inside the mountains are sleeping beasts who were outsmarted by a small fairy. And those beasts dream of how the impossible can be made possible—that stinky beasts can turn into something beautiful."

When she finished, Mercy looked down at Olive and Alice's innocent brown eyes. The single candle by the bed was the only light in the room, and Mercy watched as a shadow passed over Olive's face. Her lips began to tremble, then suddenly she started to sob.

Mercy immediately pulled Olive into her lap and wiped the tears from her cheeks. She had tried to tell the story in order to make them forget, for just a moment, what was happening at present. However, it seemed that their mother's sickness was, of course, not an easy thing to overlook.

Olive continued to cry, and Mercy understood that she had to let Olive express her feelings. Because Mercy wanted to be someone that her little sisters could speak to and cry on.

So she asked Olive slowly, "Why are you crying? What is the matter?"

It took Olive a couple of seconds to stop her hiccups before she cried, "I'm scared."

"Why?" Mercy's brows furrowed. "Tell me why you're crying."

"I'm scared that other will leave us. I'm scared that we are going to live without her forever."

A broken sigh escaped Mercy's lips. She closed her eyes and willed herself to suck the tears back. She had to stay strong in front of Olive and Alice. No matter how she might feel about her ailing mother, she had to focus on the two little girls clinging to her arms right now.

"Olive," Mercy began while tucking Olive's brown hair behind her ear. "Don't cry. Thoughts are all that matter. You must think positively, and you will live positively. Do not fret over Mother. She will be all right."

Alice chimed in suddenly, "How do you know? Father said Mother is very sick! Anything could happen at any time."

Mercy was stunned speechless for a breath for a moment. Looking at her two younger sisters, she noticed how much they had grown since she peeked into their coddles after they were born. She remembered how small and fragile they were. Alice had grown taller over the years, and Olive's face had become very pretty. By now, they were old enough to understand their dear mother's condition. They had every right to know and not be lied to.

Mercy grabbed and held their hands tenderly. She

brought them toward her chest, right above her heart, as she gave them both a serious look. "All we can do now is pray for Mother's safe recovery. And if something were to happen to her...know that I will always be here. No matter what happens, I will still be your sister. I will be your mother and your protector. Know that I will never leave either of you."

Olive and Alice both nodded their heads, tears brimming from their eyes.

"Come," Mercy said. "Let's pray."

They sat in a circle and bowed their heads. Mercy glimpsed Olive and Alice squeezing their eyes closed, then gently closed her own. She prayed that news would come tomorrow of Mother's recovery. She prayed for the doctor to walk into her bedchamber and announce that her mother had become better than ever. And lastly, she prayed that she would get to see her mother's smile again and that she may see it every day for the rest of her life.

After they had finished their prayers, Mercy stood and asked the two little ones to lie down in the bed. "If you don't, the fairy might come and put you to sleep herself. Do you want to become mountains, too?"

The two fervently shook their heads and lied down.

Mercy tucked Alice in, then Olive. She gave them both a soft smile before blowing the candle out. "Goodnight, little fairies."

"Good night, Mercy."

"Night, Mercy…"

In the dark, Mercy leaned back against the wall and waited to hear their light snores.

Barely a minute passed before a soft knock grabbed Mercy's attention.

Roger White, the Duke of Norfolk, entered Mercy's bedchamber. The Duke was round-waisted in a jolly way; a brown beard and thick eyebrows covered his kind face. His small brown eyes were usually filled with joy and laughter, though right now, Mercy noticed how dark they seemed. Whether it was because of the dark bedchamber or because of her mother, Mercy decided not to dwell on the change too much.

"Father?" she asked softly.

The Duke glanced at the two little girls sleeping soundly in the bed, and a look of profound love and adoration passed over his eyes. But his look was cut short by a tug of sadness that made his face sag with grief.

He gave Mercy a small smile, kind with a hint of melancholy. "Mercy, darling. Your mother wishes to speak with you."

Surprised and filled with a sudden feeling of both elation and duty, Mercy nodded and stood from her bed quickly. Her father stepped outside the bedchamber and waited as Mercy slowly closed the door, looking at Olive and Alice in bed a final time, hoping that they were dreaming of great and happy things, that the impossible could be made possible.

Mercy and her father approached her mother's bedchamber. As the door creaked open, Mercy saw her mother's once-beautiful face smiling at her. A fortress of pillows bordered her mother's thin frame, almost dwarfing her size. A big, thick quilt wrapped around her body, shielding Mercy from seeing what she might presume to be a very sick body.

Her mother's new appearance bothered Mercy, though she tried her best not to show it. *Mother used to look so strong,* Mercy thought to herself. *How can someone like that become so small?*

She tried not to run into her mother's arms and instead sat next to the bed. Looking at her mother's face in the candlelight, Mercy ignored the slight pain in her chest. Her mother's face had become terribly thin and wan. What used to be bright and glowing skin now appeared dull and sallow. Thin wisps of hair were matted from the sweat on her forehead. And her emerald green eyes had lost the glimmer of life, but they stared resolutely at Mercy, who shared her mother's green eyes.

"Hold my hand and come closer; I must speak to my daughter," Mercy's mother croaked as she lifted a trembling hand toward Mercy.

Mercy grabbed the hand and moved toward her mother, who gently kissed her cheek. "My eldest and my bravest, Mercy White," her mother whispered. "You must know that I will not live for much longer. God is calling for me, my dearest."

Mercy could not help it. All her prayers were for naught. Tears fell from her eyes and streamed down her cheeks. She was shaking as she gasped, "Don't say things like that. Please don't say that to me."

Her mother tightened her hold on their conjoined hands with the last bit of energy she possessed and said sternly, "Mercy, we must face facts. Life is important, especially the end of it. You, my child, have a long, long life ahead of you. As the oldest, you have the most responsible. You must take care of your younger sisters and your father, all right? I trust you with this duty."

A great heave of emotion overwhelmed Mercy as she gripped her mother's hand.

"Promise me this, Mercy. Promise me that you will make sure that Norfolk Manor remains happy, even after my death."

Every word from her mother's mouth pierced Mercy's chest like a stab. She had never experienced such heartbreak in her life, and she felt, in this terrible and grand moment, that she might be dying, too.

"Mercy?"

She did not trust herself to speak, for her voice might crack and break, so she just nodded.

Her mother's shoulders sagged as if a great deal of

worry had been relieved of her. "Let me rest now, my dearest. I am growing tired." Her mother leaned back against the pillow, and Mercy morosely moved forward to give her one last kiss.

Slowly, their fingers untwined. As Mercy turned away and left the bedchamber, she tried her best not to look back toward her mother, for she did not wish to remember how such a strong woman looked in her last moments but rather how she was when she lived. Mercy recollected all the times her mother had fixed her wounds, small and large. How her mother had always sung to them and told them stories at night. How her smile could light up an entire room. Mercy remembered all of this as she closed the doors to her mother's bedchamber.

On the wall outside in the hallway, Mercy sat back and thought about her mother's words.

You have a long life ahead of you...As the oldest and as the most responsible, you must take care of your younger sisters and your father... She was right. From this moment onwards, Mercy White's life was forever changed. The fifteen-year-old child was no longer; in her place was a protector and a mother. Olive and Alice...they still needed a mother to help them grow up, to protect them. Mercy wiped away the stray tears on her cheeks with her sleeve. She could not depend on her mother's comfort anymore—rather, people would begin to depend upon Mercy from now on.

Mercy had promised her dear mother that she would

henceforth protect their family and assure their happiness. Filled with a sense of duty and determination, Mercy began to grow tired. Her eyes drooped before she could stop them.

When Mercy awoke the next morning, she found her father, the Duke of Norfolk, the great and buoyant Roger White, standing at a loss by the doors of her mother's bedchamber, appearing entirely exhausted and crestfallen. Then he said the last words Mercy wanted to hear, but knew deep in her heart, were bound to happen.

"Mercy, your mother has passed."

1

Ten Years Later

As the morning sunlight beamed into the Norfolk Manor bedchamber, Mercy White quickly rose from her slumber. She grabbed the closest gown and roughly threw it over her body—a dirt brown bodice that was as unflattering as it was comfortable. In the mirror, Mercy cursed how messy her hair looked. Overnight, her long chestnut brown hair had turned into an overgrown tree that desperately needed trimming, with a nest or two somewhere in it.

"Now, I would most certainly cut my hair," Mercy muttered to herself in the reflection. "If only Father wasn't so against it."

She could not help the laugh that tumbled from her

lips as she remembered a particular memory from three years before. Her father had only taken one glimpse at the pair of scissors in Mercy's hands, poised right by her beautiful long, luscious hair, and almost fainted from shock. She had never seen her father's face grow so red!

Mercy was trying not to roll her eyes as a long tirade assaulted her poor ears as he rambled on and on about how she must preserve her precious hair, for to cut it would be a complete waste!

"Mercy, don't cut your hair. Listen to your father!"

"You're being dramatic, Father. Don't you know how difficult it is to maintain such long hair?"

Her father was as stubborn as she. "You have the most beautiful hair! Please—don't cut it. For me."

Mercy had pursed her lips in response.

She had only wanted to cut her hair because of the effort it took to tame it down in the morning. It was more of a nuisance than an accessory, so she had decided to chop it all off.

Her father had caught her just before doing so, though, and his shock and fear at the potential loss of her hair far outweighed her desire to cut it. The duke never asked for much, but he had asked Mercy for this.

It was only due to her love of her father that she could not refuse his request, so she placed the scissors back down and kept her hair as it was.

Snapping back into the present moment, Mercy took

one last look at her tangled hair in the mirror, then quickly rushed out of the bedchambers and toward the kitchen.

A plethora of maids crowded the kitchen, promptly moving from one counter to another with a wild sense of business. Sauces and jams were hastily mixed; spoons and knives clanged against the countertops; water sloshed as a maid carried a teapot toward a waiting tray, and another swiftly brought out a batch of brioches that immediately warmed the air with their buttery smell.

Mercy clicked her tongue, dissatisfied. "Hurry up, ladies," she ordered.

The maids stopped what they're doing, eyes wide with a hint of fear. "Yes, Lady White!" they declared before returning to their tasks with more fervor.

Mercy turned her back on them and promptly left the noisy kitchen.

Walking through the halls of the manor, Mercy noticed the dust collecting on the floor, by each of the doors. There were multiple smudges on the windows. The carpets were ruffled. In the waiting room, the curtains were not drawn. With a great huff, Mercy called for the head maid, Mrs. Butter.

Shortly thereafter, a middle-aged woman entered the waiting room and immediately bowed her head. She had brown hair, wrapped into a low bun, with gray streaks running among the strands. Wrinkles covered her face, and they only deepened when Mercy said bluntly, "The house is still a mess. Pray tell me why the cleaning is not yet done?"

Mrs. Butter wrung her hands together, trying to hide her discomfort. Sweat coated her face from Mercy's penetrating glare. "I—I apologize, Lady White. Please forgive me. The cleaning will be done momentarily. I do apologize." The head maid bowed down even lower. "Please, Lady White. Forgive me!"

Holding back a retort, Mercy rolled her eyes and walked briskly out of the room. "Utterly incompetent," she mumbled to herself.

As she entered the dining room, she was distracted from her thoughts about firing all of Norfolk Manor's maids when she saw her two younger sisters' bright smiles at the table. Her father entered at the same time as Mercy, and he gave her a sweet smile that immediately melted away all of Mercy's thoughts about the inadequate maids.

"Morning, Father."

"Good morning, darling."

They all sat at the table and waited as the maids began to serve breakfast. Out came an array of pan stands, holding a batch of warm pastries: brioches, cakes, and muffins. Bowls of jam were set on the table, paired with a wooden spoon that would soon smear the red jelly onto an awaiting toasted bread. Light fluffy eggs filled half of each of their silver plates, along with sizzling hot bacon strips that made almost all of the Whites hum with pleasure.

As soon as the maids dispersed, they began their breakfast.

Duke White was the first to speak as he placed a warm brioche on his plate. "Olive and Alice, you two look lovely this morning."

The girls smiled in response. It was true. Olive and Alice White had grown into splendid women. Their brown wavy hair and beautiful round eyes, the same as their father's, fit their face with such naturalness and beauty. As the years went by, ladies from the other manors began expressing their opinions on the girls' growth, and stated that Olive and Alice White had become the most beautiful creatures in the county.

For the morning, they wore light blue and green chemises with elegantly designed corsets across their waists. Sparkling earrings hung from their ears and silver necklaces wrapped around their slim necks.

They appeared like shining jewels.

As the duke cut into the bacon, he slid a look toward his eldest daughter, Mercy White, and stated, "Mercy—you look...very fun! The brown gown suits your morning glow just nicely..."

Mercy gave him a funny look.

"I—I am just saying that...perhaps maybe a finer dress would have suited you better? Like your sisters' outfits for example. Right?"

With food still half-chewed in her mouth, Mercy

responded, "Father, let me ask you this: Why would I wear something so uncomfortable and unsuitable for such a feast?" She splayed her hands out toward the delicious breakfast.

"All I am saying is that it would not hurt to appear more elegant from time to time," the duke sighed. "It's good to remember that you are a lady."

"Yes, yes, Father," Mercy replied through the eggs in her mouth. "I am well aware that I am a lady. You don't have to worry about me forgetting."

The duke laughed softly as he shook his head. "Sometimes, it appears that you might have forgotten."

"Dressing up in the morning is too tiresome. Brushing the tangles from my hair and decorating my face with jewelry and powder is too boring of a task." Mercy smirked. "Why should I do all that if I can just throw on a gown and see all of you right away?"

Her father simply shook his head once more and continued eating.

Breakfast resumed its normal pace. Mercy was so distracted by the bread and the cake that she did not see the look passing between Olive and Alice.

"So, Mercy..." Olive began.

"Yes?"

"What will you be wearing tonight?" Alice asked with an exciting look.

"Tonight?"

"Yes!" Olive squeaked. "I personally think green would look wonderful on you—"

"What is tonight?" Mercy interrupted, a confused look on her face.

Her youngest sister appeared surprised for a second before declaring, "Mercy, please don't tell me you forgot! Alice and I have been preparing for this ball for weeks. We told you when we were invited that there would be a great ball held at Cunthor Manor!"

Mercy waved her hand dismissively. "Right, right. Forgive me for forgetting—it was just something I didn't care to remember."

"Oh, why not?!" Olive asked, shocked.

"You two go on without me," Mercy answered. "Dance until your feet ache. Talk until your throat burns. Yes...do enjoy your time at the ball. I have no desire to do such tiring things."

A frown tugged on Olive's lips.

Alice drooped her shoulders in disappointment. "I do not want to go if you do not. It will be no fun without you, Mercy."

"Me too," Olive expressed. "If Mercy does not go, I will not go."

The duke gingerly wiped his mouth with a napkin and cleared his throat. "Mercy, I think this is a great opportunity for you to spend time with your sisters. A ball! When was the last time you went to one?"

"Not long ago enough," Mercy muttered.

"You should leave the manor, darling. Look at your sisters—look how sad they are already of your absence! They only want to have some fun with you. What can be the harm in that?"

Mercy parted her lips and then closed them. She spared Olive and Alice a glance, and, true to her father's words, their frowns were deep and their eyes were filled with dramatic sadness. The last time they asked her to attend a ball, she had refused, preferring to stay in her bedchambers and read. If she rejected them again, she would not hear the end of it.

Olive and Alice both puckered their lips. "Please, Mercy. *Oh,* please!"

Mercy sighed. A few seconds went by as she tried to rationalize her options. When she finished, she said, rather hesitatingly, "All right...I'll go."

The two younger sisters' screeches rang across the entire room, and Mercy tried not to regret her decision.

"Can I take it back?"

The three sisters were all in Olive's bedchambers, with piles of dozens upon dozens of dresses and shoes and jewelry boxes. Olive sat by her vanity, leaning toward the mirror as she fluffed powder onto her cheeks, two faint pink splotches appearing over her pale face by the bed, Alice slid the wrinkles out of one of the pink Empire silhouette dressing gowns. She blushed as she twirled around, the long silk skirt swaying by her legs.

The smiles on both of her sisters' faces dropped, however, at Mercy's depressed plea.

Mercy sat on the edge of Olive's bed with a tired expression. She was playing with a loose thread in the brown gown that she had casually thrown on this morning. She had never been so bored.

"You cannot take back your words, dear sister!" Olive reprimanded without taking her eyes off the mirror. "At the breakfast table, your very words were: *All right...I'll go.*" She mimicked Mercy's voice by deepening her tone.

"I do not speak like that."

"Well, it doesn't matter *how* you speak. What matters is what you *said*."

Alice cut in. "And you said that you would go with us to the ball."

Mercy scratched her head. "I think you both are starting to lose your memories. I don't remember saying such a thing actually..."

Continuing on as if Mercy had not even uttered a single word, the two sisters resumed their tasks. Usually, a maid would assist them in dressing, but for today's special occasion, the sisters decided that they would spend some alone time together. A true sibling-bonding activity. Though,

Mercy would have much preferred to go hunting with them or something.

Alice bent down to retrieve another dress. This time, the dress was opal blue with a shimmering skirt that sparkled in the light. From under the bed, she grabbed a pair of dazzling silver heels that she quickly slipped on. Her pale, slender feet slid in smoothly, and a bright smile lit up her face.

"You are going to look very beautiful tonight, Alice," Mercy said softly as she looked at the happy look on Alice's face.

"Thank you!" Alice giggled as she twirled around to show off the shoes. She stopped suddenly, however, when she spotted something by the corner of the bed. She stooped down and grabbed the top of a green dress and splayed it out for Mercy to see. "And so will you! Look at this gorgeous dress. This is just the one for you!"

Olive spun away from the mirror, eyes widening as she gazed upon the dress. "Mercy, that is the perfect dress for you."

A grimace filled Mercy's expression. "Really?"

She felt nothing for the dress: A forest green gown, long and straight, with a low and wide neckline inlaid with gold embroidery. The high waistline gave way to a long green silk skirt that ended with golden trimmings that glimmered as it swayed. Mercy frowned. All she could think about was how scratchy it would make her feel and how uncomfortable it would be to dance and walk around in. Where were the trousers and the comfortable shoes? Why could women not wear more comfortable outfits to the ball? Surely the dances would be more fun.

Mercy frowned at the dress. "No," she refused.

"*No?*" The sisters simultaneously asked in shock.

Olive spluttered, "It's so beautiful, though!"

"Uncomfortable, more like..."

"Mercy..." Alice whined.

Standing abruptly from her seat, Olive planted herself right in front of Mercy and peered up at her dear old sister with an incredibly sad expression. "What if this is our last ball? What if something terrible, God forbid, happens to us, Mercy? Olive and I...we just want to experience one entertaining night with our older sister. Just the three of us, no one else."

"Don't forget about Father," Mercy sighed.

"*Mercy.*" Alice walked around the bed and sat next to Mercy, who was beginning to grow weak. "You always say you love us, but...how much of that is true?"

"Alice!" Mercy gasped.

"Stand up. Wear this beautiful dress," Olive said, "and join us to the ball. That's all that we ask of you."

Olive and Alice both stared at Mercy with puckered lips and doe-like eyes. As time went by, the thread keeping Mercy intact began to grow thinner and thinner, until it finally snapped. A long groan emitted from Mercy's lips until she drooped over in defeat. "Fine. All right, you two, stop staring at me like that."

Hope gleamed in their eyes.

Mercy sighed. "Give me the dress."

After a couple of tight squeezes and multiple pinches, Mercy stood in front of the mirror, trying to hide the distaste on her face. Olive and Alice both looked over her shoulder with wonder in their eyes. The green ball dress accentuated Mercy's green eyes, bringing out their light and sharpening them enough to make any man's chest burn with desire. Olive had brushed Mercy's long, unruly hair enough so that it could be wrapped into a neat, shiny chignon, exposing her entire face.

The sisters sighed, entirely in awe.

"What is it?" Mercy asked while uncomfortably squirming in place.

Olive gently wrapped her hands around Mercy's arm and squeezed with unconstrained love. "Nobody is as beautiful as you."

Alice nodded in agreement, grabbing Mercy's other arm. "You are naturally beautiful. Look at your eyes, your cheeks, your already-red lips. You do not have to put on anything else because of how naturally stunning your features are!"

Upon hearing her sisters' kind, albeit exaggerated, words, Mercy could not help but laugh. "That is nonsense! I look very plain."

Shaking her head resolutely, Olive said with assurance, "Every lady in the ton is jealous of you, Mercy. You are too busy frowning and too bored to notice the stares that they give you! But Alice and I can see them. They wish to look like you. Your beauty is the talk of the ton."

Mercy's brows furrowed as she looked at her reflection once more. She could not believe Olive's words; how could she? In the mirror, all she saw was a plain girl with plain brown hair and plain features. There was nothing to be jealous of. The ladies of the ton either had to be blind or Olive had to be lying. Otherwise, nothing of what Olive had said could be true. "Nonsense," Mercy mumbled.

"Not only are the ladies aware of your beauty," Alice said with a slight blush. "But the men are, too. Every man in the ton would file into a long, long line just to ask for your hand in marriage. If only you weren't so repelled by men and so hot-tempered."

Mercy rolled her eyes and walked away from the mirror. "I have no desire to attract a man or receive his hand in marriage. I will never marry any man, ever. Why would I? All the men in the ton are boring and much too illogical for my taste."

When Mercy finished another one of the frequent tirades of her deep hatred of marriage and men, Olive and Alice glanced at each other, a hint of pity in each of their eyes.

Before they could retort anything, there was a knock at the door.

The duke walked into the room, and the sisters all immediately stood straight and smiled—well, except for Mercy, who stood off to the side, slightly hunched over with a displeased expression still plastered on her face.

Despite her look, Duke White grinned upon seeing his daughters all dressed up. "You all look very beautiful tonight."

Olive wore a gorgeous blue gown that highlighted her slender form and petite frame. Her curly brown hair had, just like Mercy's, been wrapped in a chignon, revealing her rosy round cheeks and button nose.

Right beside her, Alice stood tall with the opal blue dress hugging her figure. Long white silk sleeves covered her from her elbows down, coupled with rings over her slender fingers. Her brown hair was strung up with two layers of curls framing her heart-shaped face.

Duke White smiled at them both before turning to Mercy. He stepped forward and held both of her hands, squeezing them gently. "May I ask for one favor?"

Mercy pursed her lips before smiling slightly. "Yes, Father?"

"Please behave at the ball: Smile; don't engage in useless arguments with anyone. And do try to at least be civil with the men."

"That sounds like more than one favor."

The duke raised a brow.

Holding back a disgruntled sigh, Mercy replied, "Yes, Father, I will try my best. Though I cannot promise anything."

"Unfortunately the last time you said the same thing before a ball, you told Lord Pembroke—who, I heard, had asked you *kindly* for a single dance—that you would rather die than accept."

Olive and Alice looked down, trying to mask their giggles with a look of disappointment.

Shaking her head, Mercy argued, "Lord Pembroke is a fool."

"He was extremely offended and thus complained to me and no doubt to the rest of the ton. Words carry, Mercy. You must remember that."

"I do not care how he feels—I hate the man entirely. Father. Instead of lecturing me, you should tell Lord Pembroke to stay away from me. That is the only agreeable solution."

Understanding that his daughter would not back down, he sighed, "Just promise me that you will behave."

Mercy fidgeted in her spot, clenching and unclenching her fists. The experience with Lord Pembroke was a nasty one and a memory that she would rather forget quickly. That such a man as Lord Pembroke would ask for a dance with her—how outrageous! The only regret Mercy had from that ball was that she had not pushed him or said something even more rude.

"Mercy—promise me."

With a deep sigh, Mercy slowly nodded her head. "I promise."

As if that response was enough, the duke smiled with relief and assisted Olive and Alice from the bedchamber to where a carriage awaited for them. Mercy followed behind with a faint frown.

Though she had promised her father to behave properly, she could not guarantee that she would. If a man like Lord Pembroke were to come up to her, the possibilities were endless, none of them good. She could not guarantee that she could plaster on a simple smile and dance with any old man. Something so tedious and boring would only give her insufferable pain.

Mercy clasped her hands together tightly as Olive and Alice hopped into the carriage, a bright, joyous expression on their faces. Her father stood by the carriage door, giving her a trusting look that could only mean he believed that she would keep her promise.

A sigh escaped her lips.

She had to keep the promise, no matter how tough it might be.

Mercy could only hope that no man would force her to break it.

2

In the Cornwall Mansion, the Baron of Cornwall, Caleb Griffiths, was preparing for the ball.

He stood tall in front of the mirror, adjusting the white cravat wrapped in an intricate pattern. His hands guided down to smooth the dark waistcoat that hugged his tight figure. Though his outfit might be neat and pristine, it was his handsome face that was the most awe-inspiring.

Dimples pierced the charming smile that split across his strong face, and his dark eyes, almost black, twinkled with allure. A sharp and bold jawline sculpted his face, making him appear hard and athletic. Shiny black hair curled over his forehead and left just enough exposure so that any lady in the ton might take one look at him and see all of their desires.

Caleb was aware of his attractiveness, and it was because of this that he smiled in the mirror, a hint of pride in his eyes.

Just then there was a knock at the door. Through the reflection of the mirror, Caleb watched as his best friend, Ben Morris, the Count of Sielle, entered the room. He spun around and splayed his hands outward, showcasing his whole attire, paired with a shining smile. "Ben, how does your dear old friend look?"

With a roll of his eyes, Ben sat down in one of the chairs. "When do you ever look bad?"

Caleb nodded his head, accepting his friend's response. He laughed as he said, "I guess the only good thing I inherited from my parents was a pretty face."

"Now, don't be so bitter."

"I was only joking." Caleb looked into the mirror once more, though any hint of his previous pride was now lost. A displeased look passed over his face. "What I meant to say is that it wouldn't have hurt to have money and a grander title to my name. Perhaps I would have had a better life with a better reputation."

Noticing his friend's change in demeanor, Ben uncrossed his legs and leaned forward, a serious look on his face. "If you work hard enough, surely you can still earn good money. I know of a few people who have been born into great wealth, and they grew up with a poor mindset. With great effort and perseverance, you are capable of being very rich, not just with money. And do not forget that you are also a baron, a good title to bear."

Hearing the last sentence, Caleb shook his head. "Baron is a good title, but I would much rather be a duke."

"Well—I cannot help you with that, my friend."

"Was it not you who just said I could achieve anything with effort and perseverance?"

"I see you did not listen closely to my words, again. I did not say miracles can happen."

Caleb sighed before nodding his head once. "You're right. I know."

"Though if you marry the daughter of a duke with no brothers, there may be a chance," Ben said rather offhandedly.

Caleb turned around briskly, a new and inspired expression filling his face. With wide eyes lit with hope, he exclaimed excitedly, "Ben, will I be able to inherit the title of a duke if I do that? If I marry the daughter of a duke?"

Ben paused for a moment, slightly alarmed by his friend's exhilarated face. Slowly, he said, "Well, yes. Only if the daughter is the oldest and there are no brothers in the family—no heirs to the fortune and title. If you marry her, there is a possibility that her father will pass the dukedom to his daughter's husband."

That is it, Caleb thought. This was the perfect way to achieve the title of duke, a wish that he had had for so long. All he had to do was find the eldest daughter of a duke, with no heirs in the family to inherit the father's fortune and earn the dukedom by marrying the eldest girl. It was a clear path ahead of him, and Caleb could not help the determination that surged through him. He could not believe that he had not thought of this sooner! What a splendid, brilliant plan, and he had only just thought of it now. This was what he would do. Caleb Griffiths, the Baron of Cornwall, finally had hopes of becoming a duke.

"Tell me you are not actually thinking about it?" Ben asked, worried. "About something so foolish."

"Ben, it is not foolish. It is a brilliant plan!"

"I should not have opened my mouth," Ben cursed himself. "Caleb, listen to me. This is cheating. Marriage is a beautiful thing, and I want you to experience its beauty. Do not marry for money or for a title—you will only be alone in the end. Marry for love, my friend. For *love*."

Caleb waved his hand dismissively. "Those are all ancient notions. Money is the most important thing in my life right now—my *main* priority—not a wife."

Ben tried to argue once more but was disrupted by Caleb's dragging him up from the chair. "Come on, Ben. Let's not quarrel. We do not have the time; we must hurry to the ball!"

Looking rather dejected and concerned, Ben followed Caleb through the halls and out of the manor. Caleb, on the other hand, looked livelier than ever. A bright, mischievous gleam glinted in his dark eyes.

He would need his good looks tonight.

Upon arriving at Cunther Manor, the two men, Caleb and his friend, Ben, walked inside and were immediately bombarded with the extravagant flourishes that usually accompanied a ball. A grand chandelier hung from the high ceiling, lighting up the entire room with shimmering shades of yellow and white. The gentlemen all conversed with one another, adorned in their richest coats and trousers, a drink in their hands. The ladies, in their corsets and frilled dresses, giggled behind their white-gloved hands, their curls bouncing around their petite faces. Conversations echoed throughout the ball, along with a soft orchestral accompaniment in the background.

"What a grand ball!" Ben exclaimed.

"Yes, yes..." Caleb flippantly answered; he was too busy scouring the entire room, from one corner to the next, with only one goal in mind: To find a duke with only daughters and no male heirs. "Shall we mingle with the guests, then?"

He marched toward a small group of ladies, Ben hurriedly trailing behind him. Upon seeing these two men, the girls perked up and straightened their postures. When they snuck a glance at Caleb, however, they blushed and grew a little shy.

Caleb bowed. "Good evening, ladies."

The girls all curtsied.

"You all look very beautiful tonight." The ladies all expressed their gratitude. Caleb turned to the girl closest to him, who stood shorter than him by half a foot and was currently staring at him with wide eyes. When he caught her staring, she looked away, embarrassed. "May I ask for your name?" he asked, voice lowering.

Her response was quiet. "Annabelle Kent, Lord Griffiths."

"Of course—a beautiful name for a beautiful lady."

Annabelle's face grew as red as a tomato.

By deep into the evening, Caleb had left a trail of more and more ladies who grew red and flustered. One girl almost spilled her drink on his coat. Another was so awed, that she could not stop hiccupping. Another lady could not stop smiling at him, which made Caleb slightly uncomfortable, such that he had to leave immediately. All of the ladies' blushed faces and attentive eyes fueled Caleb's flirtations. He understood this folly of women, how they might easily melt under the influence of a single conversation with an attractive man. A prolonged look or a gentle smile could go a long way. It seemed that Caleb had perfected the art of flirtation, knowing the ins and outs of what a woman desired.

He had talked to almost every lady in the room, smoothly transitioning from one group to another. His looks granted him this talent. The girls flocked to him with intrigue. Caleb saw all of it, and he was not afraid to take advantage of the power he had over all of the ladies.

Ben, who had been trailing behind Caleb the entire time, had finally had enough of it and grabbed Caleb's arm before he could approach another group of ladies. "Stop! I beg of you—stop!"

Caleb turned, brows raised. "Is something the matter?"

A look of apprehension filled Ben's bright blue eyes. His blonde hair was slightly disheveled due to him traipsing after Caleb's long gait. "You are taking this too far. Several of the ladies here are being escorted by their fathers," he reminded Caleb. "And the fathers do not take kindly to your...dalliance with their daughters."

Caleb released his arm from Ben's grasp and sighed. "If their father is not a duke, I do not care."

Suddenly, everyone dispersed toward the wall, leaving the dance floor open. The orchestra switched to their next piece, one more jovial for dancing. The men turned toward their ladies and asked for a dance. As people began to float towards the dance floor, Caleb glanced around the room, looking for a partner.

Just then, his eyes fell on the Duke of Norfolk, who stood with his three daughters. Caleb paused to think about Lord White's family. He remembered how there were no sons in the family, only three beautiful girls, who the duke cared for deeply. The eldest one, Caleb recollected, was Mercy White. Through the talk of the ton, Caleb had heard quite interesting things about her. He had once overheard how offensive she could be and that she had a difficult temperament. Quite an impossible woman to be with. He had also heard that she was without a husband. Caleb paused for a moment, anticipation slowly building in his chest. *Could this be...?*

"Ben," Caleb asked for his friend without taking his eyes off the Duke of Norfolk. "Have you met the Duke of Norfolk and his family?"

"Yes, I have..."

"Brilliant. Who is the sweetest daughter?"

"Oh, that would be Olive White, the youngest. She has a very lovely disposition."

Caleb nodded once. He knew what he had to do. His long legs strode across the room, heading toward the duke and his daughters. He quickly adjusted his tie and made sure that his coat was without any wrinkles. With a quick sweep of his hand through his otherwise perfect hair, he finally stood before Olive White, a charming grin already on his face.

"Lady Olive," Caleb greeted with a gentle bow. "May I have this dance?"

Without hesitation, Olive nodded quickly and took his hand.

He led her to the dance floor with a poised posture. When he let go of her hand, they assumed their respective positions. Caleb took the time to observe her appearance.

She had beautiful and shiny brown hair and small, kind eyes. He was not sure if it was powder or a natural blush that dusted her cheeks. Her nose was small and quite adorable; they scrunched when she smiled. Caleb was not too presumptuous to admit that she was a pretty woman. A couple of seconds went by before the strings moved and the song began. Caleb, very efficient and dominant, led Olive through the dance, holding her hand just so, and supported her back with care.

A smile lit up her face. "Thank you for this dance, Lord Griffiths."

"It is my absolute pleasure."

They spun and twirled, his hand gripping onto hers. Then suddenly, he dipped her, and she giggled. "You are a very good dancer!"

"A dancer can only be good if his partner is beautiful."

The dance continued, and Caleb was appreciative of Olive White's beauty and grace. She was kind, her words sweet and gentle. When he held her hand, she was careful not to hold it too tight. When he spun her, she greeted him with a soft and shy smile. Though she was amazing, she was not the duke's eldest daughter.

"Do you frequently attend these sorts of balls?" Caleb inquired smoothly.

Olive nodded. "Yes, I do."

"And your sisters accompany you?"

"I come mostly with my older sister, Alice; we do almost

everything together! Although sometimes it seems like she has two left feet when she dances. Do not tell her I said that!"

Caleb laughed gently. "Your secret is safe with me. How about your other sister?"

"My oldest sister is not often interested in these types of events."

"Lady Mercy?"

"Yes! I do not think she understands the appeal of dances and dresses." Olive laughed and a look of complete adoration covered her face. "She was adamant about not attending this very ball. It took a few pushes before she finally relented. People might presume her to be rude, but she is very funny and kind when she is with us."

"You must love your sisters very much."

"More than anything."

The song reached a crescendo as Caleb twirled Olive once more, her pink dress swirling with her movement. He asked, "You said Lady Mercy is uninterested in balls. Why is that?"

Olive pursed her lips, contemplative. "They just don't make her comfortable is all. I think she much prefers to spend time without the constraint of a fancy dress."

"I see... Pardon my bluntness, but why is Lady Mercy without a husband?"

Olive blushed slightly. "She is currently looking for a

potential match, the right man suitable for her disposition and interests."

Caleb nodded. "And what are her interests, and her disinterests?"

Answering in great detail, Olive began to list Lady Mercy's favorite activities. Caleb learned that the eldest daughter quite enjoyed her time outdoors, either hunting with her father or simply riding through the woods. Olive expressed that sometimes when she could not find her sister, she usually had to take only one look outside of the window to find Lady Mercy walking down a pathway. As for disinterests, it was apparent that Olive was being lenient. She stated that Mercy abhorred uncleanliness and disobedience. She was very strict with others, but more so with herself. Everything had to be in order. But most of all —she hated when people asked her to change.

When the music ended, Caleb bowed, and Olive curtsied. He held out his arm for her to take, and escorted her back to the duke.

"Thank you for the lovely dance and conversation, Lady Olive."

Olive smiled and tipped her head.

Caleb looked at the duke, who regarded him with neither interest nor indifference, and bowed low. Then he spun around, walking away toward his best friend, who looked at him with raised brows. Hope lit up Caleb's face, and a feeling of faith overwhelmed him, an emotion that he had not felt in a long time.

Tonight had been a miracle in and of itself. It could not have ended in a better way.

"How was the dance with Lady Olive?" Ben asked. "It looked as if you were interviewing her rather than dancing…"

"It went perfectly," Caleb murmured.

"I do not like that look on your face," Ben said. "It always means you're up to no good."

Caleb did not respond; he was too busy looking far off into the distance, a plan already forming in his head.

3

The birds twittered as the sun rose the next morning. Norfolk Manor was quiet, save for the crisp turn of a page and an occasional sound of needles in fabric. In the drawing-room, the three White sisters relaxed, soaking in the peaceful ambiance of the morning, which was very much needed after an intense night of dancing and talking.

Mercy and Alice sat next to each other on the same couch while their youngest sister Olive sat in an armchair, knitting a yarn blanket that seemed to be growing longer and longer by the second.

With a small quirk of her lips, Olive glanced at her two sisters and asked with an air of nonchalance, "At the ball last night, who did you two meet and dance with?"

Mercy raised a brow as she put the book down on her lap, noticing an interesting smile on Olive's face. Before she could ask why Olive looked like she was hiding something, Alice answered with passion.

"*Oh*, I danced with several fine gentlemen last night! There was Lord Morris, the Count of Sielle, who was very gentle and kind. He had charm, and his blue eyes were very pretty, but, unfortunately, he was not my type. Then, I danced with Lord Curzon, the Earl of Carligh. My darling sisters, come closer…"

Mercy and Olive both leaned forward from their seats.

"He is everything I've ever wanted and more! *Oh*, he is just my type! His eyes, his dark hair, his height, his strength. He was a very marvelous dancer indeed! I simply floated across the floor. He held me, and I melted. What is even better is that Lord Curzon is not only gifted with looks and movement, but he is also very smart. I cannot remember how long we stood by the wall, simply conversing with one another about all of our interests! For instance, we both love to read; he even went so far as to recommend me a book, written by someone whose name I can't even pronounce—which is what I am reading right now." Alice giggled as she brought her book close to her chest. "Last night was magical."

A soft smile appeared on Mercy's lips as she watched Alice blush and grow flustered from just the thought of

Lord Curzon. She was very glad that her sister had a wonderful time at the ball. In other words, she was quite glad that at least one of them had had a pleasant night out.

"How wonderful!" Olive squealed. Then she cast Mercy a Cheshire-like grin. "How about you, Mercy? Did you meet anyone like Lord Curzon?"

"Of course not. Unfortunately, several men did approach me and ask for a dance."

"Brilliant!"

"How foolish of them to even try and ask," Mercy said with disdain.

"Oh."

"I simply told them that I refused to step on the dance floor. And when they pestered me some more, I confessed that I have two left feet, and if they do not wish to be stepped on and bruised for the duration of the night, then they should leave me be."

Olive and Alice both rolled their eyes at the same time. Mercy's behavior was not a surprise to them. To presume that Mercy would ever accept a man's request for a dance was foolish! Every time they convinced Mercy to go along with them to a ball, something disagreeable occurred. When a man dared to approach Mercy, she would not be afraid to put them down, her outright disgust plain on her face. She would not try to hide it either. Sometimes, she would catch Olive and Alice watching the incident and panic, rushing forward to apologize on her behalf. But their efforts were all for naught, as Mercy would only just shield them behind her back and go on offending the men some more.

"Mercy," Alice began. "You are a very talented dancer. You cannot use that poor excuse to reject all of these men."

Mercy pondered for a moment. "Indeed, I am a great dancer, though I would rather perish than dance at any of the boring celebrations of the season. People only dance because they have a hidden incentive, not purely for the pleasure of dancing. They want something more. And they have no problem moving their feet just as much as their mouths! It seems their lips are always running; there is only gossip at those balls."

Alice and Olive both shook their heads, unwilling to quarrel with their adamant older sister. Thus, it became Olive's turn for answering the inquiry.

Alice turned toward Olive and asked excitedly, "Well, how about you, Olive. Surely your night turned out much better than Mercy's?"

"It was quite an interesting night indeed." Olive smiled with an odd glint in her eyes. "I danced with Lord Griffiths."

A squeal flew out of Alice's mouth, so loud and shrill that Mercy flinched. "How could I forget?! He asked you first out of any other lady in the room!"

"He did!"

"Do not spare any details, sister! Tell me—tell me how was it?"

After composing herself from Alice's squeal, Mercy straightened and asked with a confused look, "Alice, why did you make that horrible noise?"

"Because Olive, *our sister*, danced with *Lord Griffiths*!"

"And?"

"*And*?! Lord Griffiths is the most handsome man in the entire ton. He is the Baron of Cornwall, single and absolutely perfect in all of his features. His hair, dark as the night, and his eyes even darker." She sighed. "Every lady in the ton wonders what thoughts occur behind those mysterious eyes. When he speaks, Mercy, *oh* when he *speaks*, it is a gift for all of our ears."

Mercy raised a brow. "What happened to the handsome Lord Curzon?"

"You cannot place Lord Curzon and Lord Griffiths on the same pedestal. That is too rude."

"Well," Mercy began with an eye roll. "I'm sure that Lord Griffiths is not the most handsome man in the entire ton. I will admit that there are more pleasing-looking men."

Mercy had seen the famous Lord Griffiths in passing several times at an occasional ball or two. They had never had a conversation together, and she did not plan on starting one anytime soon. He stayed in his own world, so Mercy would gladly stay in hers. When she did spare him a single glance, though, she never really focused on his appearance. She was too busy wishing to be somewhere else, either bored or exhausted, praying in her head that the Lord would not ask her for a dance or try to engage in pitiful conversation. Lord Griffiths had never once been the object of Mercy's appreciation. So it was because of this that she could not relate to her two sisters, who seemed very, very excited about the dance the previous night.

Olive shook her head ferociously. "Alice is right, Mercy. There is *no* other man more handsome than Lord Griffiths. It is difficult to even try and name one."

"Well, there is—"

"*Very* difficult!" Alice and Olive both shrieked.

Mercy sighed and leaned back against the sofa, playing with a stray thread on her chemise. There was no arguing with the two passionate girls.

Seeing that Mercy had backed off, Olive pushed onwards with determination. "Lord Griffiths is not only handsome, but he is kind, polite, charming, and an excellent dancer." She joked, "Perhaps a better dancer than you, Mercy."

Mercy rolled her eyes. "Impossible."

"Will you court him, Olive?" Alice blurted suddenly.

There was a brief pause in the drawing-room, where Mercy and Alice stared at Olive with curiosity. Could this be Olive's future husband, an addition to their family? How would their father react? Would he be a suitable man for the family? Of course, these were all mainly Alice's questions; Mercy simply sweated at the thought of her little baby sister growing older.

All of these musings were cut short when Olive burst into laughter.

"We danced, but it was obvious that Lord Griffiths was thinking about someone else."

Upon hearing this, Mercy suddenly stood from the couch, her book tumbling to the floor. A look of complete anger and distrust overcame her face. Her fists clenched by her sides. "*What?* He dares to ask you for dance even though he was interested in someone else?!" Of course—*of course*, this would happen! Men were not to be trusted. They were completely despicable and deceitful, selfish in every way possible. Her dear baby sister had been lured in by Lord Griffith's looks, and she would be the one to suffer in the end. Why would he even ask her for a dance to begin with? If he was so distracted throughout the dance that Olive had noticed, then he was not a very kind or smart man at all! Mercy could not stop the anger from growing by the second.

She continued her tirade. "Olive, you have to be careful with men like him. They ask you to dance, then they ask for your hand in marriage. They are always scheming with ill intentions, and you will be hurt in the end. You will be trapped in a prison with a terrible man as a husband. I do not want that for you, Olive."

Seeing how angry she had become, Olive tried to calm Mercy down. "Now, Mercy, hold on a second. Let me finish."

Mercy clenched her jaw before slowly sitting back down.

"Lord Griffiths was thinking about someone else. It was apparent that he was interested in someone other than me—someone who obviously would reject him if he asked for a dance. So it was through me that he had to get to know that girl."

Mercy's brows furrowed with confusion. She did not understand. She was confused why Olive was looking at her excitedly. And when she turned to Alice, she saw that Alice, too, was looking at her with excitement, eyes widening as if something in her head had clicked; a suspicious smile also split across Alice's face.

"I don't understand," Mercy said.

Alice began to laugh, almost hysterical. Her eyes squeezed shut as she covered her mouth to temper her outburst.

Mercy was more confused than ever.

"Mercy..." Olive started slowly. "Lord Griffiths, the most handsome man in the ton..."

"The one he is interested in..." Alice piped in.

"...Is you!" They both screamed joyously in unison.

The two girls erupted in laughter as a look of complete bewilderment dawned on Mercy's face.

"During the entire dance, he only asked about you! 'What are Lady Mercy's interests and disinterests? Do tell me! I must know or I will simply die!'" Olive exaggerated with a dramatic flourish of her hands.

Mercy was completely silent as her two younger sisters erupted in another bout of laughter. It seemed as if her mind had entirely shut off, leaving her to stare blankly at the wall. It took a couple of seconds for her head to match up with her ears. And when it clicked, she was left completely stunned. She did not know whether to scream or cry.

Lord Griffiths was interested in her?

How was that possible?

She tried to remember every single time they had ever crossed paths. After struggling for a few seconds, she found herself at a loss. There was no spark of interest on his behalf. This simply could not be true. A man like Lord Griffiths...?

Finally finding her voice, Mercy mumbled, "You are lying."

"I am not!" Olive argued. "His hand was on mine, but his eyes were on you!"

"Why would..." Mercy spoke slowly. "Why would someone as handsome as Lord Griffiths be interested in someone like me?"

Olive and Alice stared at her blankly, almost in shock. After a moment of stunned silence, they both said at the same time: "Because you are the most beautiful lady in the ton!"

Mercy reared back, confused.

In the few moments when she glanced in the mirror upon waking up every morning, she briefly saw a head messy brown hair and a face with normal features. She wore neither makeup nor any sparkling jewelry. Her fashion was mediocre at best. She had grown up hearing that she was an exceptional beauty, but she had never thought too much about that. The only beautiful aspect about herself was her green eyes. The same green eyes she had inherited from her mother. Now, her mother was an exceptional beauty, through and through. She was the most beautiful woman Mercy had ever seen. Mercy had always thought to herself that she could never be as pretty as the former duchess of Norfolk Manor. And now this? Suddenly Lord Griffiths—the most handsome man in the ton, by her sisters' accounts—was intrigued by Mercy?

That could not be! Surely, Olive had misread the entire situation. He was probably only curious about Olive's family, about her sisters. And Mercy was frequently the center of everyone's gossip. As a man-repeller and a single woman of twenty-five years, Mercy was always talked about in a negative light. Lord Griffiths was surely just asking harmless questions about Mercy, to satiate his curiosity, such that Olive took it as him being interested in Mercy!

With this final thought, Mercy looked at Olive and said resolutely, "You must be mistaken. Lord Griffiths would never be interested in me."

4

Mercy had never felt like this before. It was all so confusing and strange! It was only just this morning that she had woken up with thoughts of frustration and annoyance toward her sore feet, but now there were worse things to worry about.

Such as Lord Griffith.

Just the name gave her a migraine.

Only a few minutes had passed, and Olive and Alice were still staring at her with wide eyes, a look of complete excitement plastered on their faces. They seemed to be waiting for Mercy to say something —*anything*—about how she might feel about this whole ordeal.

Mercy frowned and stood abruptly from the couch.

Her sisters looked up at her with anticipation.

"I must go...out," Mercy mumbled, slightly disoriented. "Yes, I must go to clear my head."

"Where will you be going?" Olive asked as Mercy walked toward the door.

"I'll be riding."

Without allowing Olive or Alice the time to say anything more, Mercy marched out of the drawing room, out of the Manor, and toward the back garden.

At times when she needed to think., her legs always lead her to the stables. She entered through the gate and walked to her horse; Apple was a strong horse, with light brown matted fur, glistening under the heat of the sun, and big, muscular legs. Mercy could not help but smile as she caressed the horse's neck and gently pet her snout. A feeling of calm washed over her.

Grabbing a saddle, she quickly and efficiently threw it over the horse's back, tightening and clipping the leather until it was secured. Mercy had done this so many times that she felt as if she could do it in her sleep.

She remembered the first time she had entered the stable and how her father had taught her how to saddle a horse.

"Mercy darling," he had said, *"saddling a horse is one of the most important skills a person must learn in life!"*

"Really, Father? Even for ladies?"

Her father had nodded his head resolutely. *"Of course— even for ladies. Your mother rode horses all the time when she was younger, and she loved it. I want you, my first child, to learn how to ride a horse as well."*

"Yes, Father." A large smile completely overtook Mercy's entire face. She was so excited to see her father's excitement. So she stood by her father the whole day, plastered by his side in the stable, as he taught her where to hold the horse and how to buckle the saddle. Though her legs were too short to reach the stirrups, she still felt like an adult, learning adult things.

When her father picked her up and placed her on the saddle, Mercy felt like she was on top of the world. The ground seemed farther away and the sky seemed closer. And when she first started riding the horse, she felt as if she was flying.

When her mother passed away, Mercy began riding horses almost every day. She remembered how she would always sneak away into the stables whenever she felt the beginnings of a migraine. Then she would ride out into the woods with her horse. The feeling of the wind whipping her hair and the leaves caressing her cheeks made her feel alive. Unlike the suffocating rooms of the manor, where Mercy could almost always feel the absence of her mother, the outside world felt like a welcoming embrace, where Mercy could simply close her eyes and breathe.

Once, in the morning of a terrible, dreary day, Mercy had run out of the house after seeing her mother's empty spot at the breakfast table. She had never saddled a horse with such speed before, but at that point, it felt like second nature. She then hopped onto the horse, without the help of her father, and soared through the stable gates and into the woods. Mercy did not remember how long she stayed out there, but the day dragged on, and she traveled deeper and deeper into the forest. Time escaped her. Her surroundings calmed her down and quieted her rampant thoughts. Hours seem to go on until she heard her father's voice calling her name in the distance.

"Mercy! Mercy—where are you! Mercy!" His shrill shrieks rang through the forest; a flock of birds flew from the trees.

When he had finally caught up to her, he was so worried that there were tears brimming his eyes. Mercy remembered feeling completely shocked. He embraced her, begging her never to run off like that again without telling him.

She could only nod, her voice escaping her.

Since that day, she had always been careful, though her love of horse riding had never changed.

There were times when Mercy desired to spend some time alone with herself and to clear her head. And a nice horse riding always calmed Mercy down. That would never change.

So, with her foot in the stirrup, Mercy pulled herself up and over, landing on the horse's back with practiced ease. Grasping onto the cantle, Mercy urged Apple forward, leading them both out of the stable and into the fresh air.

She immediately turned in the direction of the woods.

Mercy closed her eyes briefly as she focused on her senses. The sound of the horse's hoofbeats, the leaves crunching on the ground, and the wind rustling through the swaying trees cleared her head almost instantly. There was an occasional twitter of a bird. Or a crinkle of the straw patches of grass. No loud noises, no overbearing ladies of the ton, and no voices telling Mercy about things she could not understand.

She would much rather spend a peaceful day of riding horses than a gallant night out at some extravagant ball, with glittering, scratchy dresses and sore feet.

In one of the trees she passed, Mercy spotted a small nest perched in the branches. Three little eggs nestled together inside. If she were a talented artist, Mercy would paint the image on a canvas and have it framed.

Just under Apple's hooves, a sprightly frog hopped from one log to another, so fast that Mercy almost missed it. She smiled down at the insects burrowed in the ground of the forest. There was an entire ecosystem underneath the ground she walked on. Though it might sound disgusting, the thought comforted Mercy.

Mercy had once taken Alice and Olive horse riding, just for fun and to show them how nice and enjoyable it could be. It had only lasted ten minutes before the two sisters had started screaming with fright and disgust.

"Help, Mercy—help!" Olive had shrieked. "There's a bug on my sleeve!"

Alice had shielded her eyes with her hands. "Quick! Get it off!"

It was, in fact, not a bug but rather a dead brown leaf that had floated down from one of the trees.

They promptly returned home.

After the short ride, Alice and Olive told Mercy that she may do as she pleased, so long as the two of them weren't pulled into it. The woods, they claimed, was not the most desirable place to be in, and that if they were forced to venture into such a place again, they would want someone else to steer the horse for them rather than make them do all the physical labor.

Mercy, at the time, had shaken her head with pity. "Now you understand how I feel when you beg me to attend those measly balls," she wanted to say but ended up keeping the thought to herself.

They were missing out on such a peaceful activity.

Since then, she only went horse riding by herself or with her father. Mercy hadn't complained too much about it.

As Mercy laughed softly to herself at the memories, her horse suddenly stuttered to a complete stop.

Mercy's brows furrowed. Apple puffed a breath of air and stepped backward. Mercy began to grow wary, knowing that her horse acted like this only when something unusual occurred.

"What's wrong, Apple?"

In the next second, the answer came.

The sound of another horse's hoofbeats could be heard in the distance.

It came closer and closer; Mercy clenched the cantle with trepidation.

Who else could be in the woods at this hour? At the same time as Mercy herself? Usually during this time of day, the woods were empty for miles and miles. Rarely did she ever see anyone else enter the forest for a simple horse-riding excursion. Mercy's brows pinched together with annoyance. Everything was so calming and peaceful! Who dared to disrupt the quiet?

Just then, a horse emerged through the lush trees, revealing a brilliant white stallion. On its back was a man with impossibly black hair, even darker eyes, a handsome physique, and a countenance that made Mercy's breath stutter.

It was none other than Lord Griffiths himself!

She grit her teeth in exasperation. What were the chances! She had escaped into the quiet woods, looking for a bit of peace and quiet, away from the talk of a man named Lord Griffiths who was apparently interested in Mercy, only for her to bump into that exact man!

Mercy had to stop herself from urging the horse to retreat back home.

"Good morning, Lady Mercy," Lord Griffiths said, his lips quirking slightly in a presumably timid smile.

She did not respond and tried to hide the shock on her face. A hoard of questions bombarded her head: *Why was he out in the forest at the same time as her? Had Lord Griffiths always taken this route? What were the chances? Had he been following her?*

With increasing suspicion, Mercy gave Lord Griffiths a guarded look. "Lord Griffiths, what are you doing out here in the woods, especially at this hour?"

If he was surprised at her blatant question, he did not show it. He appeared entirely unconcerned and answered with ease. "I came here to ride, as I usually do."

"I see," Mercy replied curtly.

He smiled.

The breath almost instantly left her lungs. She remembered her sisters' words, about how Lord Griffiths was the most handsome man in the ton. In the moment, Mercy could not believe such a thing. The most handsome man in the ton! What a grand thing to say. However, now, as she stared at his face and the way he sat upon his horse, she could not help but agree. His smile was bright, so much so that the rays of the rising sun seemed to pale in comparison. His black hair rested casually, almost disheveled but purposefully so, on his forehead, right above eyes that were so brown they appeared black. They stared at Mercy without any shame at all, and Mercy began to feel her cheeks warm, just slightly.

A battle surged in her mind as she tried to remember any other man in the ton who was more beautiful than the man in front of her. There was that one man at that one ball...though his breath did smell a little odd. *Oh*, there was that interesting fellow at the feast thrown in her manor, who had a cute smile with friendly eyes...though he did sweat profusely through the night. How about that one man who smiled at her in the plaza? Though, as Mercy thought back on it, he did have a large wart hidden just under his chin.

Mercy groaned internally.

Her sisters were right. There was no other man in the ton who was as handsome as Lord Griffiths! No one else had such a sharp, chiseled jawline and dimples that pierced his cheeks whenever he smiled; his dark eyes were beguiling as he gazed at her from under his long lashes, in a way that no other man had ever looked at her.

This revelation did nothing to appease Mercy's prior frustrations; it only reinforced her confusion. Yes, Lord Griffiths was a very handsome man, but why would the most handsome man in the ton be interested in Mercy, going so far as to dance with her youngest sister to ask question upon question about Mercy. Something was entirely not right!

"Lady Mercy?"

Mercy snapped out of her thoughts. "Yes?"

"I asked you a question, but you seemed to have drifted away."

"What was your question?"

He cleared his throat. "And you, Lady Mercy? Why are you out here in the woods at this hour?"

Mercy instantly stiffened. Did he dare to be suspicious of Mercy? Her patience snapped, and she spoke without thinking. "I am here because I always ride here, as well. And since I always take this path, I do not remember ever encountering a man such as you. So, if what you say is true, then I should have at least seen you before. However, I have never, which only means that you are lying. Tell me the truth this instance on why you have been following me!"

Lord Griffiths' eyes widened, surprised at Mercy's outburst and blatant accusation.

Mercy expected him to retaliate in the same manner, yelling at her or even threatening her for saying such obtuse things. However, his posture remained relaxed and poised. Though his face showed his shock, he did not appear either angry or offended.

His voice was calm as he finally responded. "I could say the same to you, Lady Mercy. I, too, have never seen you ride on this path. Does this not mean that *you* might be the one following *me*?"

Mercy was stunned. Before she could hold back her

words, she retaliated. "That is not true! We are not the same—I am not a liar and a compulsive flirt like you."

She knew that she was being too harsh on him, allowing her anger to speak for her. But she did not care. The day had been so stressful, and it was only the morning. Her younger sisters' words had put her in such an uncomfortable state, and she had been on edge for some time now. Then the only place where she could find some peace of mind had been infiltrated by the one and only person who could make the entire situation worse.

Lord Griffiths stared at her for a couple of moments longer, making Mercy feel restless. She waited for him to say something rude or give an offhanded remark, but he only laughed softly.

Mercy was silent as he bid her farewell. "Good day, Lady Mercy." He bowed his head slightly before steering his horse away and disappearing back into the trees.

She did not understand why he had not said anything in retort. She would much rather he yell at her rather than leave her in an awkward state of confusion.

Without dwelling on Lord Griffiths' words and quick departure for too long, Mercy beckoned her horse to turn, and she slowly headed back home.

5

As Caleb rode his horse out of the woods, he couldn't help but think about Mercy White.

He must have done something amazing in the past to be rewarded with such a coincidental meeting! That very morning he had woken up with quite a sore back, perhaps from all the dancing and mingling he had to endure at the ball the previous night. Looking for a brief breath of fresh air and a nice stroll, he decided to ride his horse out into the woods. Rarely had he ever rode into the forest; however, after the ball, Caleb did not mind a change in scenery.

Then, the miracle had been bestowed upon him!

He had accidentally stumbled into Mercy White herself.

Unbeknownst to Caleb, his plan had already begun.

Their meeting was spontaneous and advantageous on Caleb's behalf. When she sat there, mounted on her horse, an expression of complete shock on her face, he could not help but be amused. Initially, he had half-expected her to sit in that uncomfortable silence for the rest of the day. However, when she soon opened her mouth, Caleb understood the rumors about Lady Mercy.

"*Careful of Lady Mercy,*" Caleb remembers hearing a guest say at a ball a long time ago. "*I would not ask her for a dance. If she does not outright refuse initially, she will make sure both of your feet are broken by the end of the night!*"

Another man had said, "*She is not only violent in her manner but also with her words! Lady Mercy is unafraid of putting you down...I am deeply and utterly disgusted by her disposition and her offensive ways. I pray for the man who is forced to tame such a beast.*"

One time, as Caleb had been drinking from a champagne flute, he overheard a rather loud man speaking with exaggerated hand gestures: "*What a pitiful creature! She is quite beautiful but that is only a facade. Lady Mercy will never find a decent man for herself. She will stay alone forever.*"

The gentleman he was talking to replied, "*You are right. If she continues to reject every single compliment or offer for a dance, she will surely end up alone. How shameful.*"

"*Maybe then she will yell obscenities at herself and understand how it feels to be on the receiving end of her words!*"

Those harsh opinions echoed in his head as Lady Mercy yelled at him in the woods. Caleb should have anticipated her harsh reaction, but he could not help but be stunned. She was quick to defend herself, even when he was only just trying to poke fun.

They were right, he thought. *She is quite intense.* However, such quick and sharp words would not stray him from his true goals.

The title of a duke hung before Caleb like a taunt. Living life with such luxury and power meant more to Caleb than a woman who spoke too freely. On the bright side, perhaps it would make the whole plan at least a little entertaining. Although it would have been easier if the duke's eldest daughter had been timid, poised, and charming, Lady Mercy's fierce character would be quite an obstacle and make the end result of achieving the dukedom that much more victorious!

As his horse trotted forward, Caleb smiled to himself.

Lady Mercy would pave the way to his dreams—that much was certain. The chance encounter with her in the woods had only reasserted that idea.

Filled with renewed vigor, Caleb turned his horse, away from the direction of his home, and toward Sielle Manor.

He needed to talk to someone about his plans.

And there was only one person who would lend him an ear.

The doors opened, and the butler greeted Caleb with a single bow.

"Good morning," Caleb began. "Is Ben home this morning?"

"Yes, Lord Griffiths. He is currently in his study. Shall I—"

"No need!" Caleb interrupted before making his way inside the manor. "I will go to him myself." He marched through the halls, his eyes set on the double doors of Ben's study.

Without knocking, Caleb charged through the doors.

As always, Ben's study room was kept very clean. A large ebony desk was placed in the center of the room, and a large, expansive window was behind it, showcasing the wide landscape behind Sielle Manor. Long rows of bookshelves lined each wall, filled with books that seemed to be overflowing. Paintings of Ben and his family framed any empty space that the bookshelves missed. Couches were placed before the main desk, along with a table with drinks and glasses already out. It was a very homely environment, perfectly embodying Ben Morris and his ways.

Caleb immediately walked toward the couches, sitting down and making himself quite at home.

Ben did not flinch or scorn at the sudden intrusion; he

only smiled brightly and readjusted his vest as he greeted his friend. "Good morning, Caleb! I'm happy to see you."

"As am I, Ben." Caleb reached over and grabbed a wine bottle from the table, picked up two glasses, and poured himself and Ben a drink. They would both need it after Caleb was done telling Ben everything. "Here, have a drink."

Ben accepted the glass, slightly wary now as he noticed Caleb's antsy manner. "Thank you…"

Caleb moved next to Ben, sitting beside him on the sofa. He cleared his throat, contemplating where to start. His plan was great, but the longer he pondered over it, the more cautious he became of the ending. Lady Mercy was the perfect beginning to Caleb's hopes and dreams. She would help him gain the title of duke and a dukedom, something he had wanted for so long. It was perfect. However, sudden intrusive thoughts flooded his mind.

What if he was being too bold?

Was he making any sense? It made sense in his head—but would it be the best way to earn the title of duke?

Should he seriously go through with this plan?

Was this too good to be true?

These thoughts bombarded his head, and they began to make Caleb feel entirely unassured. He was glad that he had changed course and rode to Ben's manor. He needed his best friend to tell him if his mind was right.

Caleb must have been silent for too long because Ben

suddenly grasped his shoulder and shook it gently. "Are you all right, Caleb? Why do you look so...tense? You look as if you are divided about something." Ben's lips twitched into a smile as he bumped his shoulder against Caleb's. "Or maybe you just need to use the restroom."

"I'm fine." Caleb waved his hand dismissively. However, Ben still looked concerned, his brows pinching and his mouth pursing a little. Caleb had known Ben for years now and counted Ben as his dearest friend; he was smart, wise, and capable. He would always advise Caleb when he asked for it, and always without judgment; Ben listened and stayed attentive, paying attention to Caleb's every word before coming to a sound solution that would help Caleb. He had been there for Caleb countless times. Therefore, at that moment, Caleb knew that Ben was the only person in the world who could give him advice about his plans.

Caleb took a deep breath. "Actually, I am not fine. I need your help."

Without pause, Ben placed his glass down on a nearby table and leaned over, appearing very serious. "What is it?"

"It is about Lady Mercy. I met her in the woods just now."

Ben's jaw dropped a little in shock. "Did you go to call on her?"

Caleb waved his hand in denial. "No, no. We stumbled upon each other accidentally. She was riding her horse, as was I. Completely coincidental."

"I see..."

"We exchanged a few words," Caleb continued. "Though, *she* did most of the talking. She openly called me a liar and a compulsive flirt; I could tell that she did not care for me, not one bit. She was very rude."

Ben shook his head. "Lady Mercy is known for her rudeness and temper. You have heard of the men speaking about her; they were never positive. She repels every civil man. It is not a surprise that she called you such crude things." Ben paused for a moment before holding his chin with his thumb and finger, pretending to think, and joked, "Actually, now that I think about it, maybe she is the one in the right..."

"Yes, well, I must learn to accept the truth about her, because I plan on courting Lady Mercy."

Silence. Ben stared at Caleb, mouth slightly open from shock. His brows furrowed deeply, and complete bewilderment crossed his features. Caleb couldn't remember the last time he had seen his best friend appear at such a loss for words. Perhaps there was that one time he had accidentally ripped his suit right before a ball. Or when he had cooked dinner for the both of them one night, only to burn the meat to black crisps and ashes. Other than that, Caleb had not seen Ben look so entirely in shock that he could not say a single thing for a long time.

"Ben, please say something."

That seemed to snap him out of his stupefied daze. Ben

pressed his fingers to his temple and squeezed his eyes shut, no doubt contemplating what Caleb had just said. "Are you insane? Have you entirely lost your mind?!"

"I am guessing you do not like my plan…"

"This is a lost cause, Caleb. This is not right." Ben moved to face Caleb fully, staring at him directly. "Listen, I…understand, to an extent, why you plan on courting Lady Mercy. *However*, it will not be as easy as it might seem now. She will never fall in love with you. As I said before, Lady Mercy is rude and offensive and stubborn—she will never become your wife. And even if there is a slim chance of her marrying you, this will not be a happy marriage and thus, consequently, you will not have a happy ending."

Caleb paused, pondering over his friend's words. He was correct, as always. But what he was saying had already crossed Caleb's mind. Of course, it would be difficult to woo the stubborn Lady Mercy into accepting his hand in marriage. But Caleb was nothing if not stubborn. He would find a way. And if she did miraculously accept him, he understood that it would not be an ideal marriage, with a happy husband and a happy wife. But that was not what Caleb was hoping for. He wanted to be a duke. And he would gladly sacrifice anything else to secure that title.

Caleb nodded his head. "I understand what you are saying, Ben. I do. I know you just want me to be happy in the end, but you must understand that being a duke is what will inevitably make me the happiest. Not a wife. *Being a duke.*"

Hearing the certainty in Caleb's words, Ben shook his head and stood up from the sofa. He began to pace the study, his face contorting into an expression of concern and worry. "How are you so confident about this? Tell me your reasoning. How would this ever work–this plan to court her? As far as I know, she is not the type to agree to such a binding deal as a marriage."

Caleb had thought about this as well. As far as he knew, Lady Mercy did not have many suitors lining up to ask for her hand in marriage. Based on the men of the ton's perception, Lady Mercy was unsuitable, disagreeable, and untamable. There would never, in her life, be a man who would utterly fall in love with her and take away Caleb's chance to be a duke. It just would not happen!

Thus, this sad fate for Lady Mercy would deeply sadden her father, Roger White, Duke of Norfolk. The man was in his fifties, growing older by the day, and his eldest child still had not married. Surely, that would tarnish their family image in the ton. People already talked so much; if Lady Mercy were to never find a husband, the White family would simply be hopeless in the eyes of the people.

Not to mention, there were two other sisters to think of as well. Olive and Alice White. Caleb knew that they had neither husbands nor suitors either. So far, the sisters did not have a bright future ahead of them.

However, if Caleb were to swoop in and ask for Lady Mercy's hand, the duke would be elated beyond all measure! From the duke's perspective, he would be handing off his eldest daughter, the repeller of all men, to a *very* capable man—Lord Griffiths himself—and soon, there would be a flock of men lining up to marry the two other sisters.

It would be a win-win situation for everyone.

Caleb explained this to Ben, who listened to his every word in silence. When Caleb finished, Ben paused to think. He looked almost convinced.

Confident now, Caleb continued. "Do you get it now? I am not only helping myself, but I am also helping her and her family! I will be helping the duke get out of a very tough situation. If anything, they need me."

Ben pursed his lips. After a moment, he parted his lips and spoke for the first time since Caleb started his long explanation. "I see you've thought a lot about this since yesterday. And you seem confident of yourself. That is great and all, but I still stand with my point: Lady Mercy will not fall in love with you. She is a tough stone to crack. The only time you have conversed with her alone, she insulted you."

Caleb looked aloof, not bothered by Lady Mercy's tough exterior. "I am not *too* worried about that. You know me, Ben. You know me more than anyone else." He sat straighter and tilted his chin up, appearing sure of himself. "I am very charming. You've seen me at the balls. Women flock to me. They simply cannot help it! They fall for me easily, and so will Lady Mercy. Sure, she can be uncivil and irritating, but she is still a lady. She will warm up to me."

He did not tell Ben that he expected it would actually take quite a long time for her to warm up to him. It was apparent from the start that Lady Mercy would be difficult to please and woo. The meeting in the woods solidified that thought. But Caleb was still proud of himself and sure that he was capable of attracting any and all women in the ton—Lady Mercy being one of them.

Based on what Olive had said during the dance, the sisters loved one another very much, meaning that Lady Mercy had to love them dearly as well. Therefore, if Lady Mercy could love her family, she could love Caleb, or *at least* accept him.

Because who could ever resist Caleb's charms?

Ben sighed deeply, breaking Caleb out of his thoughts. He said in defeat, "You have completely lost your mind. This plan will most definitely fail."

"It will not!" Caleb exclaimed. "I will show you myself. You'll know I've succeeded when I invite you to our wedding."

Ben seemed to acquiesce because he did not argue any longer. He picked up his glass and drank the wine in one gulp.

Caleb gripped his glass and stared at the dark red wine with determination. He had come to Sielle Manor looking for the guidance of his friend. Although he may not have gotten what he hoped for—a forceful push in the direction of his future—he still felt confident in his plans.

He would charm Lady Mercy and woo her until she finally begged for his hand in marriage.

6

On the other side of the woods, Mercy trotted on her horse towards Norfolk Manor. She appeared distracted, her brows pinched and lips pursed, as if in deep thought; her encounter with Lord Griffiths replayed over and over in her mind.

She did not know why she had said those things to him and been so rude. Perhaps it was because of the irritable morning that she had snapped completely and been so blunt. Seeing him—at that specific moment out of *all* moments—was the last straw for her. So, at the time, she did not care about how she acted.

However, what was currently nagging at her mind was the fact that Lord Griffiths had barely said anything.

She was not ashamed to say what was on her mind, neither sugarcoating things nor appearing fake. The usual response from men was an angry response back, yelling, or even a direct complaint to her father. Her ill-mannered attitude usually resulted in a man's blatant disgust.

But with Lord Griffiths—he appeared entirely calm. He did not say anything at all, only laughed softly, as if he understood Mercy's irritation. Then he left, without a single word, leaving her alone. That was what she had wanted, and he had given that to her.

Mercy felt disturbed.

There was a weird feeling in her chest, something she did not feel comfortable with. When she thought of him, she tried not to feel too guilty for what she said and how she acted. In retrospect, Mercy felt slightly embarrassed for her dramatic attitude and his aloof demeanor.

As she approached Norfolk Manor, Mercy shook her head and willed all of those thoughts to fly away. What had happened had happened. It was over now. It was time to think about the present.

After leaving her horse in the stable, she walked into the manor and reached the drawing room, looking for her sisters.

When Mercy cracked open the doors, she paused.

To her great surprise, the room was filled with gentlemen! No longer were her sisters alone in the room, but a plethora of men hung about, conversing with another, a couple of them drinking from flutes of champagne. Her father lounged in the room as well, talking to a few gentlemen. The most important thing to note, though, was all the men's unabashed attention on Olive and Alice. Everyone seemed to be deeply attentive to and engaged by Mercy's two little sisters, hanging onto their every word.

They were all here to call upon Olive and Alice!

Mercy raised a single brow as one tall gentleman with long, curly brown hair sat down next to Olive. He did not hold back how he felt. His posture showed everything. His legs were tilted toward Olive's, his body turned just slightly. He did not once look away from her eyes, talking so that he may hold her whole attention.

"You are as beautiful as the stars, Lady Olive," Mercy heard his compliment and tried not to laugh out loud. *How could men say such embarrassing things so easily?* she thought to herself.

Olive lowered her eyes, looking at every part of the sweet, shy girl. Her voice was soft as she responded. "Thank you, sir. You are too kind."

Another man appeared by her side, and Olive turned to him. The previous man looked upset, but Olive did not notice. With the new man, she exchanged more pleasantries.

Olive seemed to relish in the spotlight, though she blushed every few minutes. Mercy shook with silent laughter; her dear little sister had grown up so much!

Another man approached Mercy's other sister, Alice,

who seemed distracted by something on the other side of the room. This man sat down and stuck by her side.

Mercy leaned forward slightly so that she could hear what the man was going to say.

"Lady Alice, it is a great pleasure to meet you." His voice was high-pitched; it sounded like nails on a chalkboard. Mercy tried not to wince. "For so long I have yearned for this conversation. I have heard that your voice is the sweetest in the ton, and your words even sweeter! Lady Alice, would you grant me the gift of a simple conversation?"

Alice flipped her hair. "Perhaps another time, Lord Oran. I am quite busy at the present moment. There is another gentleman who I wish to speak with. I do not want to be rude and fix my entire attention on you alone."

"It would not be rude! They all want the same thing anyway. Why don't I deserve your time since I approached you first?"

Alice covered her mouth as she laughed. "Nonsense! You are very funny, Lord Oran."

Mercy slowly closed the door as she rolled her eyes. She did not want to enter the room and interrupt her sisters. They were very social beings. Mercy wondered to herself: *How could they spend their time engaging in useless, unnecessary conversations with even more useless, unnecessary men?* Such a quiet, peaceful morning had turned into a completely tiring one indeed!

She walked away from the drawing room, deciding that she would take a short nap. Perhaps then she could wash away the exhausting day that was her morning.

After entering her bedchamber, Mercy flopped into her bed without changing into her sleeping gown, closed her eyes, and immediately fell into a deep slumber.

Mercy woke up in the evening, feeling something heavy on her bed—or rather *someone.*

She blinked until her vision cleared and saw that her two little sisters were both sitting on her bed. She smiled, but it slowly dropped when she noticed the apprehensive look on their faces.

Alice was biting her lips, looking away so that she wouldn't make eye contact with Mercy. Olive, on the other hand, stared directly at Mercy, though her hands were wringing together nervously.

There was something off. They looked nervous as if they had something to say but were too scared to say it. Mercy's brows pinched together as she asked slowly, "Is everything all right?"

Both of them opened their mouths at the same time, but the bedchamber remained silent. They looked away, feeling slightly shy.

Okay—something was definitely wrong. Mercy sat up in her bed. "What is it, you two? Is something wrong or do you just need to tell me something? If so, tell me now."

Olive is the first to speak. "We *do* need to talk to you..."

Mercy nodded, prompting her to continue. "All right, what is the matter?"

"This is very important, so..." Alice tentatively said.

Mercy realized that she was still in bed, half-asleep and confused. She got out of the bed and entered the powder room to wash her face. Fully awake now, she came back into the bedchamber, seated herself by Olive and Alice, and told them to continue.

"So, this morning," Olive began, "we had a bunch of men come to the manor."

"So we could get to know them and talk to them," Alice said.

Mercy nodded, keeping it to herself that she had, in fact, known about the men and spied on their visit.

"Well," Olive said, taking a deep breath. "Several men want to ask for our hand in marriage."

"We have plenty of suitors now," Alice exclaimed.

Mercy's eyes stretched wide in surprise. This should have been expected! There were many men visiting this morning, all vying for the two girls' attention. She had seen it herself. But who knew that they would be so quick to ask for their hand in marriage? This was amazing. Mercy knew that Olive and Alice had always wanted to get married, and now their wishes were coming true.

A genuine smile appeared on her lips as she stared at her two baby sisters. "How exciting for you two! Have you already picked which ones you want to accept? Do you need my help with choosing? I understand how difficult it can be to find a worthy man these days. Do not fret—I can take one look at a man and see if he is deserving of either one of you."

Olive and Alice immediately shook their heads. "No, no. Thank you for the offer, but seriously: No thank you."

"Fine. Well, how may I help both of you then?"

Olive and Alice gave each other a look before Olive stood up from the bed and began pacing the room. She looked nervous, eyes wide and cheeks slightly pink. Her brown hair looked a little disheveled as if she had run her hands through it multiple times in agitation.

Mercy remembered when they were all very little, Olive had accidentally ripped one of Mercy's favorite walking shoes. The next day, Olive's hair looked like a bird's nest, unlike her usual perfectly-styled chestnut hair. Apparently, she had been grabbing her hair in guilt and concern.

Remembering this, Mercy squinted her eyes in suspicion. Alice looked a little guilty as well. She would not maintain eye contact with Mercy, which could only mean that she had done something wrong, too.

Olive began speaking before Mercy got too impatient, "Alice and I cannot get married unless you do."

The bedchamber became suffocatingly quiet.

Mercy's jaw dropped slightly.

How absurd! Why would they ever say such a thing?! It made absolutely no sense; what did she have to do with the happiness of their lives? Mercy was at a loss for words before she managed to get out how she felt. "What are you talking about? That is completely illogical. You know I have no desire to marry!"

Alice finally looked into Mercy's eyes and said firmly, "You are the eldest daughter in the family. If the youngest sisters were to get married before the eldest, would that not make our family look scandalous? It would stain our reputation—especially yours. Do you know how bad the ton would speak of you, knowing that you have no suitors when your two younger sisters are already married? Really bad!"

"We do not want that for you, Mercy."

Mercy blinked, her head beginning to hurt.

This was all so confusing. She put her head in her hands as she thought for a second. Were her sisters right? She had never pondered how people might view her or her sisters' affairs for too long. If they were to get married and Mercy stayed single indefinitely, how would that reflect on their family?

She honestly had never taken that into consideration and did not know what to say.

After a few minutes of silence, Mercy sighed. "Don't worry. We will find a way out of this problem."

Alice groaned. "Mercy, there is no way out of this problem! We already have the solution, and it is for you to get married. That is the only way."

With resolute eyes, Olive nodded. "Alice and I really wish to get married. We are already of age, and it is our time. Mercy, you must understand—this is why we wish for you to get married as well."

Mercy's lips parted, but nothing came out. She truly did not know what to say! Her sisters had always dreamt of this moment. They had even gone so far as to attend almost every ball imaginable, conversing with multiple men and dancing with them until their feet grew blue and purple! Now, their dreams were becoming a reality. Suitors were lining up for them, waiting for their hand in marriage. Mercy could not tarnish Olive and Alice's desires purely because of her own selfish opinions.

True—Mercy was not the slightest interested in marrying.

She would rather attend all of those dreadful balls than accept a man's hand in marriage!

However, looking at their desperate faces, Mercy could not help but think to herself: Would it be *too* bad?

If Olive and Alice were happy, wouldn't she be happy as well?

She would be happy—to an extent. She would still have to come home to a man she did not love and spend the rest of her days catering to a man she did not desire. Could she live like that forever? There would be a violent battle every single day.

To become fettered to another person...Mercy could not imagine it.

She felt incredibly divided.

Growing tired, Mercy gave Olive and Alice a small smile and said, "I will consider this matter. Don't worry too much. Olive, stop pulling at your hair. Alice, there's nothing to be worried about. I'll make sure to not disappoint you both. I will never let you suffer because of me."

With eyes shining with gratefulness, Olive and Alice dove forward and engulfed Mercy in a tight embrace.

They shuffled out of the bedchamber, looking better than when they appeared on Mercy's bed.

Mercy sighed deeply in the now empty room.

She had to make a choice, but she had no idea which side to choose.

7

The next morning, a loud knocking awoke Mercy from her sleep.

From the other side of the door, a voice called. "Mercy, it's your father."

Still half-asleep, Mercy slowly rose from her pillow and croaked, "You can enter."

The door opened, and her father entered the room, a joyous expression on his face. His eyes shone, and his lips were split into a great, big smile. He looked immensely excited, and Mercy was momentarily stunned by the sudden outburst of emotion from her father this early in the morning.

"Good morning!" he declared in a loud voice.

Mercy smiled and quirked a brow. "Good morning?"

"How would you feel," her father began with an excited

gleam in his eyes, "about going hunting with me this fine morning?"

Mercy's eyes widened slightly, and a huge grin lit up her face. She could not contain her excitement as she sprung her bed, the blankets almost slipping to the floor. They had not gone hunting together for some time, and she was beginning to feel worried. Hunting was something Mercy and her father enjoyed doing together, and it was a sport that bonded them. The fact that her father asked her to go hunting again made her feel warm and happy; how could she say no?

"Of course!" she practically shrieked. "We haven't gone hunting in so long."

Her father clapped his hands. "Yes, yes—dress quickly so we may get started."

After he left the room, Mercy dove for her wardrobe, digging out her hunting outfit, which she had last worn a long time ago.

When she was a child she had never felt comfortable with the normal activities of a fine lady. Her mother used to dress Mercy and her sisters in the most beautiful dresses; teach them how to style their hair; and show them how to appear gentle, kind, and sweet: all the traits of an agreeable woman. Although Olive and Alice took great interest in all of that, Mercy always hung back, awkwardly shifting on her feet, discomfited by all the dresses and powder. At the time, her sisters had told Mercy that she would grow up to be a beautiful princess, but Mercy could not see it.

Then one day, her father asked her if she wanted to join him for a day of hunting. Her mother was a little apprehensive about Mercy going, but eventually, she agreed. When Mercy and her father went out into the wood, he had taught her how to hold a rifle, how to position it so that she wouldn't recoil and hurt herself, and how to perfectly aim at a target.

Mercy had never felt so comfortable.

Her father was a patient man. He did not yell or scold Mercy if she made a mistake. He understood that she would eventually learn and become a very skilled hunter. When she would begin to doubt herself, he would tell her that he could see potential in her and that, one day, she might even become better than him.

Mercy enjoyed hunting but, most importantly, she loved hunting with her father.

Whenever she appeared sad or distressed, her father would miraculously appear and ask her if she would like to go hunting. It was as if he *knew* she needed it. For instance, after one of the many extravagant feasts in the ton, Mercy had retreated to her bedchamber, grumbling about the trivialities of events such as these and how they were just a waste of time. It always seemed that everyone around her enjoyed these events, except for her. She could not understand it. Then, the next morning, her father had asked if she would like to join him for a hunt, and it was like a ray of sunshine had lit up her dark thoughts.

With the gun in hand, eyes on the target, next to her father, Mercy felt that she finally could do something she loved.

And her father understood that.

He had told her once as they hid behind the bushes, *"Mercy, you are my eldest child. I could not be more proud of who you are and the woman you will grow into. In all my days, I have never met someone as strong as you, both in the mind and spirit."*

Mercy could not stop smiling for the rest of the day.

She knew that her father loved her very much—that much was true. Despite all of her shortcomings, specifically her stubbornness, he would always care for her. After all, she was his eldest child, his first daughter. Nothing could ever change that.

This morning, Mercy quickly dressed into a pair of white breeches with a wool frock coat. She then slid on boots with spurs and boot garters. Putting on this attire made Mercy feel pleased. Wearing men's attire was simply more efficient and comfortable than wearing those long dresses that could easily be tripped upon if one took a single misstep. Sometimes Mercy thought to herself, *Why can't women wear this all of the time?*

The only time this attire was acceptable was when she was hunting. It was the only time nobody could object to her wearing pants and boots, because what would be the alternative? Wearing a long gown in the dirt? Absolutely not.

So, in consequence, Mercy also enjoyed hunting because she could wear such an outfit and not be criticized for it.

When Olive and Alice had first seen her in the man's attire, they had pursed their lips, obviously not excited about a pair of pants and dirty boots. Olive had said as she observed Mercy up and down, "Though you might dress like a man, you could never appear as one. You still have the face of the most beautiful woman in the ton. And an exemplary figure that could never be mistaken for a man's body."

Mercy had rolled her eyes in response.

Walking out from her bedchamber and into the hallway, Mercy met up with her father. He stood with a giant smile on his face, holding two guns. She walked up to him, and he gave her a rifle. It felt heavy in her hands, but she had held one so many times before, it did not burden her too much.

Afterward, they approached the stables, and her father caressed one of the horses who huffed in a breath. "For today, should we get rid of the saddles and ride bareback?"

Mercy immediately nodded, smiling as she answered, "That sounds like a great plan."

So, they hopped onto their horses without using a

saddle. Just them and their horses. Riding bareback was an immense skill, one where the rider would have to completely trust in their ability to steer and hold onto the horse without using any equipment that could keep them secure. Mercy was confident in herself—her father knew this as well—so she did not hesitate to ride bareback.

They both rode out from the stables, heading toward the woods where they usually hunted together. With a rifle in one hand and her horse's mane in the other, Mercy allowed herself to breathe. It felt like she was back in her youth, with no worries in the world, just her and her father out in the woods, their only concern was if they could shoot prey. No men, no marriages, and no reputations in danger of being ruined. Breathing in the open, fresh air made her feel like all of her troubles had vanished. Mercy felt her shoulders ease of their tension.

She needed this desperately.

Trotting beside her horse, her father suddenly asked, "Are you all right? Why do you appear so stressed?"

She clenched her hand tighter around the rifle, stiffening slightly from his question. She lied, "I'm fine, Father. I'm not stressed at all."

"Do you think I'm so old and foolish? I know when my daughter lies. Tell me the truth—why are you stressed?"

Mercy exhaled a long breath. She did not want to burden him with her troubles, but he would not relent, she knew this. Plus, her problems involved the entire family. It was only right that he should know. He would find out sooner or later anyway.

With that, she told him the truth. "I saw Olive and Alice talking with the gentlemen yesterday morning. And in the evening, they came to me and said that they now had multiple suitors asking for their hand in marriage."

Her father smiled with delight. "I'm glad that it worked out!"

"I was happy for them. But...there is one condition."

"What is it?"

Mercy frowned slightly. "They want *me* to get married, too. They told me that it would not look good for the family and me if my younger sisters were to get married before me. People already talk so poorly of me; this would push them over the edge. It could possibly ruin all of our reputations as well."

There was silence for a couple of seconds. The only sounds were the horse's hoofbeats, the leaves rustling, an occasional bird singing, and sticks cracking. Her father seemed contemplative, his brows furrowing and lips pursing.

He thought for some time before he said, "I have to agree with your sisters."

Mercy tried not to look too shocked. "You do?"

"Yes—I believe that your lives will be greatly improved if you found a husband deserving of you. That being said, I also believe that you should follow your heart. As your father, I will never force you into a match that you would never feel comfortable in. I want to give you the freedom to make your own decision."

Mercy slowly nodded her head. Her father was supportive of her, no matter what she chose. That gave her a great deal of comfort she hadn't even realized she needed.

Her father eased the horse forward, looking for a target to shoot. Mercy followed behind him. She would not be alone at the end of all of this. For the first time in a long time, she finally felt content.

Caleb Griffiths decided to ride his horse out into the woods again.

He needed to act quickly and put his plan into motion. This morning, he had woken up with the full intention to stumble into Lady Mercy again. And the only place he knew that she spent most of her time was the woods. So he dove onto his horse and ran the animal back into the woods, ready to see her again.

In order for her to fall in love with him, Caleb needed their encounters to appear entirely accidental. If they continued to see each other unknowingly, she would soon start to believe that perhaps their relationship was ordained by destiny and that they were soulmates. Caleb knew that he had to keep showing up, to show his face in her presence so that he would always be at the forefront of her mind. She would think to herself: *Why do I keep seeing Caleb? Why is he everywhere? Is this the universe telling me that we are meant to be together?*

He would manifest himself slowly into her life until Lady Mercy would finally acquiesce and accept his hand in marriage.

It was perfect!

As Caleb continued to go deeper into the woods, he began to hear talking in the distance. He slowly steered the horse forward until he could finally hear that there were two people conversing.

When he heard who they were, his eyes widened.

Caleb had to be the luckiest man alive!

Through the space between the leaves, he saw Lady Mercy and the duke mounted on their horses, huge rifles in their hands. *They must be hunting*, Caleb gathered. Lady Mercy wore breeches, a men's coat, and long boots that almost reached her knees. She dressed like a man, but anyone could tell that she was, in no way, a man.

Her brown hair was tied back in a low ponytail, looking as if she had simply thrown it up without a second thought. Rather than a fashion statement, the styling was more for convenience.

Caleb shook his head. *What a woman*, he thought.

Before he could approach them directly, Caleb stopped himself. In order for this to appear coincidental, he had to make it look like Lady Mercy had found him instead of the other way around. Besides, it was only yesterday that he had approached her first. This time, it was her turn to come to him.

He racked his brain for a plan.

What was something that could immediately grab her attention? Caleb thought for a few moments before an idea popped into his mind. He was a genius! In order for Lady Mercy to approach him first and focus solely on him, he had to have an injury! They were all already in the woods and she was hunting, so an injury would not be entirely outlandish.

So with this, before he could think twice, he grabbed a stone and threw it into the leaves of a nearby tree. Lady Mercy's head snapped in his direction, but he hid before she could see him.

She rose the rifle and aimed in his direction—Bingo! Caleb grinned. Just as he had predicted, she thought he was an animal.

Then with great precision and accuracy, she pulled the trigger, and the bullet grazed the leaves that Caleb had rustled merely seconds before. The shot rang out. Birds flew from the trees. A bunny in hiding strode away.

And from the trees, Caleb moved forward from his hiding place and made sure Lady Mercy and the duke saw as he fell off his horse, his face pierced with unadulterated pain. He clutched the side of his arm, acting as if he was injured.

He heard two pairs of footsteps bound toward him.

It seemed that they had seen him quite clearly because Caleb soon felt a large hand on his shoulder and heard the duke speak to him, worry evident in his voice. "Lord Griffiths! Are you all right?!"

Caleb made sure to let out a groan before he responded. "I think I am all right. The bullet only grazed past my arm. Luckily there's no blood, but I think my arm has been impacted. It hurts very much." Of course, he was nowhere near the bullet, but Lady Mercy did not need to know that.

All of a sudden, Lady Mercy appeared right before him. She reached her hands out, tentatively touching his arm. Upon contact, Caleb flinched dramatically and made a sound of intense anguish. Mercy's eyes widened.

She looked incredibly concerned: her brows were deeply furrowed, her green eyes serious and slightly scared. Her voice wavered as she apologized, "I am so sorry. I thought you were an animal!"

Caleb shook his head dismissively. "No, I should be the one apologizing. I should not have been in your way."

"Don't be ridiculous!"

"It's true," Caleb declared. "You are a very skilled shooter, and I am clumsy. This is my punishment for being unaware of my surroundings in a place where hunting is commonplace."

Mercy shook her head ferociously. "That does not excuse you for getting injured by my bullet. As a hunter, I should have been more cautious. I am so incredibly sorry, Lord Griffiths."

Pretending to look immensely guilty, Caleb frowned deeply and said, "Lady Mercy, *I* am sorry!"

They went on like this for a very long time before Mercy finally relented and reached for his arm. She tried to move it gently, but Caleb cried out in pain, throwing his head back, acting as if he was dying. Mercy immediately let go, scared of hurting him even more.

"Mercy, take Lord Griffiths to Norfolk Manor so we can treat his wound. He looks to be in incredible pain. The poor man. We must hurry—hurry! This could be life or death!"

The duke rushed over and helped Caleb stand up, but Lady Mercy grabbed Caleb and insisted on supporting him the whole way home. She clutched his waist tightly, allowing him to lean on her entire body. Caleb was surprised to feel her strength. She neither grunted nor strained from his weight.

Even more surprising was that she grabbed his horse's reins with her other hand, guiding both him and the big horse forward.

The duke grabbed the reins of his own horse and Lady Mercy's as he led them to Norfolk Manor.

As they all trudged out of the woods, Caleb couldn't help but smile slightly to himself, making sure that neither the duke nor Lady Mercy could see his devilish grin. He could not believe that his plan was successful! Perhaps the plan would escalate quicker than he had imagined.

The title of duke was so close now he could almost touch it!

8

As they began to near Norfolk Manor, Caleb squirmed slightly in Lady Mercy's hold. It had been several minutes now, and her hands only tightened around his waist as she led him across the plains. It seemed that she was genuinely worried and planned to help him.

For a brief moment, Caleb could not help but feel a little bad. The duke was marching quickly, both his horse and Lady Mercy's reins in his hands. Lady Mercy was quick on her feet too but made sure Caleb could keep up. They both appeared startled and concerned, as if they had committed a terrible deed.

To see them both look ill at ease on Caleb's behalf caused him to feel awful about faking the entire ordeal.

But that guilt shortly dissipated. Physically, his body was in great shape; he could prance around the field right this moment, outrunning the horses! Though, that was just his ego talking.

He was thrilled. The plan was finally getting underway. They had fallen for his ruse so easily, perhaps this whole marriage thing would come sooner than he expected.

Caleb had just granted himself some more time to spend with Lady Mercy. He knew that they would have to spend time alone together in order for Lady Mercy to truly fall in love with him. If they got to talk with one another, allowing her to see Caleb's charm, then the rest would be easy. He would simply have to propose once, and she would fall all over him, exclaiming: *"Yes, yes! Of course, I'll marry you! I've been waiting for days for you to ask!"*

A simple plan, really.

Just then, Caleb could make out a huge building in the short distance. He realized that they had made it to Norfolk Manor. For a brief moment, he thought that he would be led inside of the house, but Lady Mercy steered him in another direction.

She was leading him to the stable.

The duke walked over and grabbed the horse's reins from Lady Mercy's hold, thus allowing her to completely hold all of Caleb's weight, focusing solely on him. The duke then walked away, securing each of the horses at their respective gates.

Caleb smiled inwardly. Now was their chance to be alone.

Lady Mercy helped him walk to a door inside of the stable. When she opened it, Caleb saw that it was a spare room with a single bed.

The room smelled a little off. Of course, since they were right beside the horses and the place where they defecated, the room would not smell like roses and soap. There were sparse strands of hay littered across the floor. A small window was centered in the wall, allowing a beam of light to shine through—the only source of light in the room. The bed was small; only a thin sheet and a faded blue quilt were tossed over the mattress. In conclusion, the room did not fit Caleb's ideal location for his and Lady Mercy's first time alone together.

She carefully laid him on the bed, making sure that his head was positioned comfortably, and even went so far as to bring the quilt over the bottom half of his body, warming him just so. Caleb did not remember the last time he had ever been treated with such care.

"How are you feeling?" she asked, her voice soft and worried.

Caleb faked a wince, trying to appear as if he was still in slight pain. "It might take some time, but I'll be all right."

She still pursed her lips, brows furrowing, and looking more worried than before.

Just then, the duke appeared in the doorway, his hands wringing together with nerves and his face mirroring Lady

Mercy's expression. "Is there anything he might need? Water, food, medicine..." He asked his daughter.

Lady Mercy looked back over her shoulder. "We should call for a physician."

"No," Caleb croaked. "No, there's no need. I'm not so severely injured that you should trouble a physician needlessly. There's no blood, and I can move my hand freely. See?"

She did not look convinced, but she did not argue any further. She looked to her father once more and said, "Can you get water and some pain relief tonic or ointment from the cook? I know that he has some stored."

"Yes, I can. I'll be right back," the duke said. "And Lord Griffiths, don't move too much. I don't want your injuries getting any worse."

As he turned to leave, Caleb nodded his head. "Yes, sir."

Caleb heard the gates to the stable closing as he rested his head back onto the mattress. The room was filled with silence. *This is the perfect time to talk with her*, Caleb thought to himself. Here they could talk, alone in a room where no one else could interrupt. It was the perfect situation to completely woo her. He was injured and wounded—though, of course, there were no external marks—but a vulnerable man was still vulnerable. No lady in the ton would ever take this moment for granted. Women loved it when they had to care for men, and they fell most ardently in love when the man allowed himself to open up and submit to the woman's care and worries.

He remembered how once, when he had fallen from his horse during a ride in the fields, Caleb was taken back to Cornwall Mansion. One of the house nurses, Miss Shelley, took great care of him; she was a young woman with strawberry blonde curls and a pretty face—a sight for sore eyes.

He was bedridden for days, stuck in the confines of his bed chamber, with only a book and a sprained foot for company. That was until Miss Shelley dropped by, insisting that she could keep him company during his breakfast, lunch, and dinner. She would check his foot and elevate it with a mountain of warm pillows fluffed by her own hands.

Caleb watched her as she did her duties—and even tasks that were totally out of her responsibilities. He knew that she only wanted to spend time with him, even if that meant just checking on him. They never engaged in conversation, but still, Caleb could tell with just one look that she was completely infatuated with him. She would blush when he asked for her guidance. When he stood up from his bed for the first time, she assisted him without hesitation.

Whatever he asked for, Miss Shelley would bring in a single blink of an eye.

It was astounding.

Now, as Caleb rested on a single bed in the stinky, dirty stable room, he felt like he was back in that moment.

However, the only similarity between Lady Mercy and Miss Shelley was their concern for him. Other than that, Lady Mercy did not blush or look flustered in the slightest from his close presence. She was too busy tightening the quilt over and under his body and making sure that his arm was resting in a proper position.

He knew that he had to change the atmosphere in the room. Currently, it felt as if Lady Mercy was more the maid and Miss Shelley the true lover. It had to be switched. He needed Lady Mercy's complete focus and attention. So, in order to gain that, he would have to confess his feelings to her.

That's it! Caleb lit up like a candle. If he could just find the moment to confess to her, she would definitely melt for him in a single second. Ladies loved confessions. Who would not enjoy hearing that they were loved and adored?

With that thought in mind, Caleb cleared his throat. He had to tread carefully so that his confession seemed true. "Lady Mercy," he began. "Do you normally go hunting?"

She did not respond for a few moments, only focusing on his arm, looking for any signs of bruising or internal bleeding.

Caleb opened his mouth to ask again, but he was interrupted by Lady Mercy's soft glance. "You should stay quiet and just rest," she said. "You don't have to engage in unnecessary conversation just for the sake of it. Rest is what you need, so you can get better faster."

For a second, Caleb was stunned. With all the rumors of her being offensive and outwardly rude, and based on their previous brief encounter in the woods, he could not believe that this was the same feisty woman. She looked like a completely different person. Her eyes were softer. She did not look strained like she was completely disgusted by the conversation at hand.

Back in the woods, he recalled how annoyed she had looked. When she talked to him, it felt as if she desperately wanted to be doing anything else—as if their conversing together was the worst possible situation that could ever befall her. Caleb could feel the palpable distaste in the air between them.

However, at the present moment, there were none of those harsh feelings.

She genuinely appeared worried for him. Guilt was clear on her face. And Caleb felt warmth in his chest. He was delighted! Now there was a chance that she could develop feelings for him, especially since he now knew that Lady Mercy had the ability to feel something other than anger and annoyance. She could perhaps begin to feel affection for him!

She sat next to him, close so that she could assist him with anything. She made no move to leave. In all honesty, Caleb felt relieved. When they had walked into the room, he had thought that she would place him in the bed and depart with her father for the medicine. However, she had stayed right by his side.

If anything, it made Caleb feel overjoyed.

With this feeling in his chest, he leaned up and supported himself on his elbow. Lady Mercy startled, surprised that he was getting up. Before she could say anything, however, Caleb moved forward and brushed a few strands of hair from her face.

Her green eyes widened as she immediately pushed herself away from him, jumping back and sticking herself against the wall. A look of complete confusion dawned on her face. Her mouth opened and closed, trying to say something but not knowing what to say.

"Lady Mercy," Caleb said, sitting up now.

"What are you doing?" she asked, her brows pinching together, cheeks slightly pink.

Caleb knew that it had to be now. The moment of his confession had to be done, and he could not figure out a better time to say it. She looked frozen, paralyzed to the spot. But he had her full attention. Before, she had not held eye contact for one second. She only looked down, her long eyelashes brushing over her cheeks. Caleb had stared at her from the moment they had entered the room, but she did not spare him one glance.

Currently, however, he had her full attention. Her forest green eyes were locked on his. Her chest rose and fell in sporadic beats, and her fists were clenched so hard that her knuckles turned white. He knew that she was flustered based on her pink cheeks and the disheveled brown strands of hair that fell in her eyes, but she was too preoccupied to brush them away. When he had touched her hair, in that split second, he thought to himself that he had never felt anything softer.

Without wasting another moment to think, Caleb stood from the bed. He faced her directly, though she was shorter than him, so he had to bend his head to gaze into her eyes fully. Then, he parted his lips and made sure to sound convincing. "Lady Mercy, I am in love with you."

Her jaw dropped slightly.

Before she could say anything in retort, Caleb continued, speaking with conviction and passion in his voice. He moved forward with a hand over his heart with an unabashed look of vulnerability in his expression. "Since the moment I saw you in the ball at Cunthor Manor, I had fallen in love with you. Not a second has gone by that I have not thought of you. Lady Mercy, you have taken over my entire life. At first, I tried to let it go, thinking that perhaps this was just a small infatuation that had no substance…but as the hours go by, day after day, I realize that I cannot ignore this feeling any longer."

Caleb took a deep breath. It was completely silent in the room; he could not even hear her breathing. It was as if he had completely robbed her of breath. He had to keep going or else he would lose her attention. So, he pushed forward and said with his eyes closed, focusing on the tone of his voice, "I love *everything* about you. Everything! I love...your strength! Yes, your strength and your...smile." Caleb stuttered for a second, losing his momentum as he tried to name another agreeable trait of hers. "Just—Just know that I really do love you. And I want to make you a part of my life. The only true way I know how to make that happen is if you would marry me.

"So...would you, Lady Mercy, give me the permission to court you and to please understand my feelings and love me too?"

9

Mercy had to blink multiple times before what Lord Griffiths had said resonated in her mind.

Lady Mercy, I am in love with you.

None of it made sense. Mercy turned and walked a couple of steps away from Lord Griffiths, trying to steady her breathing; she needed to get away from him to think about what he had just confessed. *That was a confession!* Mercy was not so foolish to admit that it was a full-on love confession. From Lord Griffiths himself.

She recalled her sisters' words from the day before: *The one Lord Griffiths is interested in is you!*

At the time, she had completed rejected the idea. To her, he was a simple man in the background, insignificant in every way possible. They had barely conversed and were not even acquainted with each other. Thinking back on it, Mercy could not remember a single moment when they had properly introduced themselves to one another.

In his confession, Lord Griffiths claimed to love everything about her, but truly, what did he know of her? He had danced with Olive at the ball, and she claimed that he had asked about Mercy's interests and disinterests. Surely Olive did not explain *everything* about Mercy to him. Therefore, there was no possibility that Lord Griffiths could love her.

He did not even know her.

Mercy clenched her fists in her hand, suddenly angry. She did not believe him one bit. This had to be a sick joke —a game where Mercy was the one being tricked. Because there was no way, in any world, that anyone could fall in love with Mercy White.

Lord Griffiths was crazy. His love confession—if one could even call it *love*—was not only unexpected, but completely stupid.

His voice sounded from behind her. "Lady Mercy, please say something…"

Mercy turned away fully, showing her back to him. She tried to drown out his voice, but she couldn't. How could she? She had just suffered minutes of listening to his voice saying incredibly outlandish things!

How dare he say such unspeakable and idiotic words?!

Mercy could feel her face growing hot. Anger coursed through her veins, overwhelming her entire body. She was so furious with the man behind her, who claimed to know everything about her and her ways, saying that he had fallen completely in love.

Another feeling settled in her chest, but she did not want to dwell on that too much. It did not make sense. So, she decided to focus on a feeling that did make sense to her: Fury. Mercy gritted her teeth, trying to stop herself from cursing at him.

Never in her life did she ever expect a man to confess his love to her, with so much passion too! Lord Griffiths was idiotic and hurt in the head. That such a man would ever dare to claim that he could fall in love with Mercy was annoying.

Perhaps after she had accidentally shot near him, he had fallen and hurt his head.

That was the only possible reason for his insane behavior at the present moment.

Mercy took a couple of deep breaths, holding onto the feeling of anger. Ever so slowly, she turned to face Lord Griffiths. She saw his serious dark eyes and his lips set in a straight, nervous line. When she looked at him, she saw his eyes moving sporadically, inspecting every feature on Mercy's face, as if he was desperately trying to find something positive in her expression.

Unfortunately for him, she would not grant him that gift.

She opened her mouth to say something, but nothing

came out. Lord Griffiths' brows rose, anxious for her response. But that was the problem—Mercy *didn't* know what to say. He had truly left her speechless.

Mercy always had a smart retort, especially to men who had offended her.

She was known for her wit. Anyone would know that if they listened to the gossip in the ton. Mercy White was known to be the man-repeller, a fierce woman who was not afraid to speak her mind and verbally attack men who dared to approach her.

With Lord Griffiths, however, she struggled.

And this struggle made her frustrated. She normally knew what to say. But nobody had ever made a love confession to Mercy; this was her first time. *How does one respond to such a confession?* She wanted to shout at him, to completely tear him apart with her words. She wanted to make him feel the exact same way she did at that very moment.

The tight feeling in her chest expanded until she finally parted her lips. Lord Griffiths' eyes widened as Mercy began to speak, her tone furious. "*Repeat yourself.*"

To her utter disbelief, Lord Griffiths actually began to repeat his earlier words: "Lady Mercy, I am in love with you. Since the moment I met you, I've fallen completely in love."

"Stop."

"I love everything about you, and I want to cherish you forever."

"Please—*stop*."

"Let me court you. Marry me, please."

"*Stop!*"

The room was silent. The horses in the stable were shuffling around in their stalls, the hay crunching under their teeth and hooves. A bird sang, and the wind whistled. The outside world continued, even when such a tragic event was happening right beside them.

Mercy squeezed her eyes shut tight before opening them, glaring at Lord Griffiths with such pure, unadulterated anger that she could not miss his slight flinch. Before she could think of how to appropriately respond, she screamed at him. "Have you lost your mind?! Everything you said is stupid. Completely stupid! It is impossible for you to love me. You don't even know me! What—my strength and my smile? Are you crazy?! You can take your confession and leave because I do not care for you at all!"

Lord Griffiths was shocked at her outburst; his brows rose to the top of his hairline, eyes wide with surprise. It appeared as if he was not expecting this response, which seemed even crazier to Mercy because—did she not look distressed? She had never accepted a love confession, and she would most definitely not start now.

She continued with her tirade. "You would be crazy to think that I would ever accept your feelings and fall in love with you. To be truthful, I would rather die than marry you. So, you should not even consider courting me. Unless you want to be rejected for the rest of your life."

For a minute, Lord Griffiths wore a complicated expression. He bit his lip, trying to scrounge up a response. Mercy could tell that she had given him an unexpected reply. Her patience was running very thin. If he did not say anything in the next second, she would storm out and curse him with every expletive she could think of.

Luckily for him, he responded, "I understand what you are saying. And it's true. I do not know *everything* about you. That's why, if you allow me to get to know you and to spend some time together, I truly believe that you will fall in love with me. Don't all great relationships start with a simple conversation? Can we not try that?"

A loud, humorless laugh exploded from Mercy. She felt crazed and incredulous that this man would ever think that she would give him the time of day.

"You really do not know me," she began, her voice dripping with venom, "if you think I would ever want to spend time with you, *voluntarily*. Trust me when I say this: You will not be in love with me if we had any more conversations. In actuality, I can assure you that, if anything, you will run away and pray to never see me again!"

Lord Griffiths shook his head, opening his mouth to no doubt retaliate, arguing that he would never feel like that. Mercy scoffed. He was too easy to read. An idiotic man who said baseless, foolish things. It was true: She could never fall in love with him.

"Listen, Lord Griffiths," she said. "I do not have the desire to marry, now or ever. Especially not to someone like *you,* who flirts with every woman of the ton."

In the brief moments she had seen Lord Griffiths during numerous balls—when she was forced to attend by her sisters—she had noticed him talking to large groups of ladies. She was not too stupid to understand what he was doing. The girls' faces were all bright red, and they acted flustered. A big, cheeky smile was on his face. When Mercy saw this for the first time, she had no idea who Lord Griffiths was, but she knew he was up to no good.

Since she had seen his interactions with the other ladies, she quickly made up her mind that he was a nobody —that he would always be an insignificant person in her life. She pretended like he did not exist.

So, to hear that exact man say that he was interested in her and actually wanted to marry her was outlandish! How had her life progressed negatively so quickly? It seemed like it was just yesterday when she had awoken from her nice, deep slumber and had no worries in the world—at least no worries pertaining to men and love.

Mercy quivered with what she believed was disgust.

There was a movement in front of her, and Mercy snapped her head up in surprise. Lord Griffiths was moving toward her, a look of complete determination on his face. "Lady Mercy, the impression you had of me before is true. But my impulse to flirt has been gone since the moment I laid eyes on you. I have never felt like this with any woman I have ever talked to in the past. But since I've known you, I find myself vying for your attention. Since the very beginning, I have looked at you only, but you have not spared me a single loving glance."

Mercy's lips parted. She wanted to clamp her hands over her ears to block out everything he was saying. But it was like her entire body had been paralyzed. She did not want to believe anything he was saying. However, as she observed him from a distance, she saw how serious he looked. His eyes never left hers, trapping Mercy in place. His posture was ramrod straight as if he was a soldier standing before his official, reporting something very, very important. He spoke quickly but with conviction. His deep voice sounded assertive as if he was completely sure of himself. Mercy was stupefied. She had never heard a man sound so...sure of himself.

"You've changed my entire perspective on life," he continued, each word landing like a blow to her chest. "Every conversation I have had with a woman in the past was unnecessary. Utterly trivial. But with you, I *beg* for just an exchange of a few words. Lady Mercy, you have taught me the value of true love."

A strange feeling coursed through Mercy's heart after he finished. It was not anger, and it was not annoyance. It felt weird, and it made Mercy feel awful. She wanted to shout at him again, but all her prior energy had left her. She could threaten him or shriek obscenities and offensive words to him, but, for some reason, she knew that Lord Griffiths would not budge, not even a little bit. The strange feeling in her heart filled her senses until she couldn't breathe. Each of his words pierced her chest, but it did not hurt; it was only a slight disturbance. As if everything he was saying was merely a hindrance, obstructing her from what she had always wanted: to never be married and to live life by herself without a man.

Mercy sighed. Whatever this feeling was—she decided to ignore it. If it was not anger or annoyance, it was not important. Surely, it didn't matter. So, Mercy flicked her head to the side, deciding to pretend as if she was not affected by his amorous affections. "You...should return home," she grumbled. "I do not wish to spend another second in your company. I do apologize for the incident earlier in the woods, but that will be our last encounter. Please leave."

With that, she turned on her heel and left the room. Her steps were quick as she marched toward the mansion, wanting to separate herself from that suffocating atmosphere where Lord Griffiths' gaze never left her face.

Her heart was beating rapidly, but she did not know why. *It is just hatred*, Mercy tried to convince herself. *Just anger*. Because what else could it possibly be? This was an entirely foreign situation, and Mercy had never felt so uncomfortable and out of place.

In the beginning, she had truly felt bad for him. She did not mean to aim her rifle at the trees and shoot blindly. Her father had always told her to be patient, to make sure to keep an eye on the prey before pulling the trigger. She knew she had acted brashly. And when she had spotted Lord Griffiths on the ground, writhing in pain, her mind had blanked.

At the end of the day, she truly did not expect him to confess to her!

A simple *thank you* would have sufficed.

True, Mercy had injured him, but she did not deserve to be punished with these confusing thoughts plaguing her head!

No matter how hard she tried to forget them, his words kept ringing in her head.

Lady Mercy, I have fallen in love with you.

I am in love with you.

I love everything about you.

Marry me, please.

Lord Griffiths had looked and sounded truthful, but she barely knew him. How would she know if he was telling the truth? Based on his unflinching gaze and serious countenance, Mercy could understand if he was being honest. However, on the contrary, there was just no way that a man could possibly fall in love with her. She would not believe it. For so long, she had heard of the gossip surrounding her; she was not dumb.

At the balls and during celebratory events, Mercy had seen the ladies staring at her with apprehension and even pity. She had even heard their voices: *There's Mercy White. Which man is she going to reject tonight? Oh, you think a man will actually be brave enough to lose his dignity?*

The men were loud, too: *Mercy White? That's Mercy White? She is pretty but I would never approach her. Have you heard that she told multiple men that she would rather die than dance with them? And that she would bruise their feet if they forced her to dance? How barbarous!*

With this in mind, Mercy could not believe that a man would actually take the time to appreciate and love her—much less marry her! Thus, with her mind plagued with confusing thoughts and unsatisfactory endings, Mercy moved further into the manor, trying to create a bigger distance between her and Lord Griffiths.

10

*L*eft behind to his own devices, Caleb stood silently in the now-empty stable room. He should have expected that kind of response from the infamous Mercy White—a verbal attack and a slew of offensive words that carved into his chest, wounding his pride—but for some reason, he still felt shocked.

Lady Mercy was an interesting woman. Caleb could not predict her actions. Usually, with other women, he could easily observe their subtle actions and interpret the type of lady they were. With Lady Mercy, he could conclude that she was a rude, blunt woman who did not shy away from shutting down men. But he tended to underestimate her character.

With his confession finally out in the open, he did

expect her to reject the idea. Of course, he did not think that she would jump up and down in delight, accepting the marriage so easily. But he also did not expect her to scream at him so, and to look at him with such contempt and unease. Was he that repelling?

She had run out of the stable without another look back. He caught her expression and saw how wide her eyes opened as she fled the room, and how her mouth was slightly curved into a sneer. At that moment, for a split second, Caleb felt hopeless. No woman had ever looked at Caleb the way Mercy had looked at him as he confessed. He had put all of his energy into the words, and, truly, he thought his performance was very believable. However, Lady Mercy was so disgusted she could not say a word—at least that was how Caleb interpreted it. She had her fists clenched tight and her body positioned far away from his. She was not attracted to Caleb—that truth he was very much aware of.

This revelation made Caleb ponder. Would this plan be as easy as he had hoped? How long would it take until she finally accepted him? To finally fall in *love* with him? After her explosion of utter confusion and deflection, Caleb could not see her ever willing to spend time with him of her own volition.

But that was exactly why he had to confess. Time was of the essence. They did not have an infinite number of days to simply talk with one another. They had to get married quickly so that he could earn his title and live a long life as a duke.

Although Caleb did feel a little bad about confessing so suddenly, with such great passion, that Lady Mercy had been left completely stunned and speechless. He had never seen a woman so paralyzed with confusion. However, though he might feel guilty about saying such things, he had no other choice. They would not have many chances to be alone together—what with the inelegance of a woman conversing with another man in an empty room. So, as he managed to secure a very secluded space with Lady Mercy, he had to take his chance.

I love everything about you... Thinking back on his words, Caleb cringed slightly. His confession was very out of the blue, and if he were Lady Mercy, he would be absolutely stunned too!

But Caleb had to say that he loved her, so that idea would be out in the open and so that she would know how he felt. From there, Lady Mercy could slowly adjust to the notion of his love and give him some time to effectively make her fall in love with him as well. Now that she knew how he felt, perhaps she would look at him a little differently. The next time she saw him, maybe she would slightly blush or pay more attention to his words and watch him wherever he went. As outlandish as it seemed—Lady

Mercy actually feeling shy towards Caleb—it seemed impossible thinking about it now. It was better than her not feeling anything at all for him. This was the first step.

As for the next step…Caleb was a bit unsure.

Trying to brainstorm another way to get Lady Mercy's affections, he suddenly noticed

that he was not the only person in the room.

Looking up, he froze before bowing.

The duke had entered the room, a glass of water in his hand. He looked very confused, his brows quirked as he turned his head, no doubt looking for his eldest daughter.

"Where did Mercy go?" he asked Caleb as he handed him the glass of water.

Caleb thanked him for the water and stared down into the cup. He was unsure of how to respond to that. If he told the duke the truth, how would the man respond? Surely if the duke found out that his daughter had run out of the room because of Caleb's outlandish confession, then the duke would side with his daughter and reject Caleb as well.

However, as Caleb continued to think about it, that response seemed unlikely. As far as Caleb knew, Lady Mercy had not had any suitors recently—or at all. The duke must have heard of all the talk in the ton: How she still was without a husband and would not be getting proposed to in the near future. In everyone's eyes, the White family's future was looking bleak. If the eldest daughter did not get married, then what would that look like for the younger sisters? If the younger sisters could not get married as well, then the duke would have a family of single daughters.

That would be a deep stain on their reputation.

Realizing this, Caleb knew that he, in fact, *did* have to tell the duke the truth. As soon as he found out that his eldest daughter was going to be courted, then, of course, the duke would accept Caleb's plans.

Therefore, Caleb quickly placed the glass of water on a nearby surface and looked into the duke's eyes seriously. "Duke White, I am in love with your daughter, Lady Mercy."

The duke's eyes widened; his face was covered with complete surprise. It appeared as if he could not believe what he had just heard. Caleb was slightly surprised by his sudden confession, too. Perhaps he should have eased into it first—a bit of a preamble. But it was too late for that; Caleb *needed* the duke to know.

The duke blinked a couple of times before asking, his voice dripping with shock, "Excuse me?"

Caleb gulped before repeating, "I am in love with your daughter. And I would like to ask for your permission to court her...and marry her."

A look of complete shock dawned on the duke's face, his eyebrows raised to the top of his hairline, his jaw slackened slightly. He appeared to be at a loss for words, as Caleb had expected. This was the second time in the span of thirty minutes that he had confessed his supposed feelings. All in the spare room inside the horses' stable too—how romantic.

It took a couple of moments before the duke schooled his expression. Caleb could tell that he was thinking very deeply about Caleb's confession. Besides, the duke had left Caleb and Lady Mercy alone and came back to hear that such things. It wouldn't be outlandish to surmise that something inappropriate had occurred here. Caleb cringed inwardly. He should have waited to tell the duke, but it was too late now.

The duke cleared his throat, and it was obvious that he was hesitating to speak.

Seeing the hesitation, Caleb surged on, "I had just confessed to Mercy—when you left to retrieve the water. I told her that I loved her, but…I'm afraid that she got offended by my words. She left in haste. I showed my sincerity to her—I truly love her, I do—but I do not think Lady Mercy considered my feelings. The reason why you do not see her in this room with us now is that she stormed away before I could stop her."

The duke nodded his head as if he had expected such a response from Lady Mercy. He then responded, "Are you sure of this, Lord Griffiths. These feelings you have for my daughter—are you sure that you would like to marry her?"

"I have never been more certain of anything else."

Scratching his chin, the duke replied, "As nice as that is, I highly advise you to get to know my dear Mercy first. I am not too sure that she would accept your proposal with ease. She is a...fairly complex woman and deserves a man who would do anything to earn her love. Therefore, I would suggest that you spend some time with her, talk to her, and dine with her. You should do all of these things, Lord Griffiths before you reach a decision."

"I understand," Caleb answered, but then straightened his posture and stared at the duke directly, showing his seriousness in his stance and face. "But with love, there is no second-guessing. I do not have to think any longer to reach the same conclusion. I do not have to spend another second idly talking to her, to know that I have fallen in love with her. Duke White, I love your daughter, and decisions made from the heart are final."

The duke took in Caleb's words and seemed to dwell on them for a long while. Caleb had said them with conviction, knowing that whatever decision the duke came to would be final. He needed this push toward Lady Mercy. He needed all the support he could get.

When the duke didn't seem to find the words to respond, Caleb surged forward, exclaiming again, "I will not back down from this. My feelings for her are real and final. Duke White, I just need your help to convince Lady Mercy that she too can fall in love with me. She is a strong-minded woman—that I know. Because of how she is, I know that she would continue to reject me without allowing her feelings to fully blossom. If she had just one push in the right direction, I truly believe that Lady Mercy will find her happiness, and I am fully willing to give her that."

A couple of seconds of complete silence ensued. Caleb had said all that he needed to say. Now, it was all up to the duke. As time seemed to pass, Caleb felt the gravity of the situation dawn on him. Whatever the duke said next would decide his future. There would be a huge weight to the duke's words—and Caleb tried not to throw up from the anticipation; that would definitely not look good for the duke's future predecessor.

Just then, a large, bright smile lit the duke's face. His eyes pinched closed as his face completely brightened with pleasure. It seemed that whatever he had decided on was very good.

Caleb took a deep breath of relief.

The duke clapped his hand as if he was completely sure. He nodded his head once, then a second time. After seemingly talking to himself in his head, the duke finally looked up at Caleb and gave him a very large smile, and said vibrantly, "Don't worry. I will talk to Mercy. I will make sure that she understands and takes into consideration your feelings. Truly, I am so glad that a man has fallen in love with my dear eldest daughter. And to go to such lengths to ask for her courtship. Today is a beautiful day, isn't it?" The duke leaned forward and patted Caleb on the shoulder. "Do not fret; I will make her agree to this match. You will be a happily wedded couple in the end!"

Filled with a sudden influx of exhilaration, Caleb bowed and said brightly, "Thank you so much!"

The duke stared at him with great happiness before he finally gave Caleb permission to leave the stables. He did not ask about Caleb's nonexistent injuries, and Caleb was very happy about that. The emotions in the room had surged to such a high degree, that the duke, no doubt, could not think of anything other than the soon-to-be engagement of his first daughter.

Caleb went to retrieve his horse from one of the stalls and mounted it before leaving Norfolk Manor. As he tugged the reins to go back to Cornwall Mansion, Caleb could not help smiling to himself. He had gotten the approval of Lady Mercy's father, the duke himself! His dukedom would soon pass down to Caleb, and Caleb would finally get the title he always wanted.

He imagined Ben's face as he treaded home. How would he react? He was the one who had proposed the idea in the first place. That Caleb had not thought of marrying the daughter of a duke with no sons before was astounding! Ben Morris had thought of that proposition.

When Caleb had jumped forth at the idea, Ben had rejected it completely—because *why*? Because one should get married for love? Though that could be the case for certain marriages—perhaps the duke hoped for the same for his daughter—Caleb only had one goal in mind, the dukedom. If he had to fake his love to get it, he would.

And he had successfully accomplished a huge task.

To get his marriage proposal accepted by the duke.

11

"This cannot be true; this *cannot* be true," Mercy mumbled to herself as she paced around her bed chamber. She had been walking in circles for a long while now, biting her nails and clenching and unclenching her fists, not paying attention to Alice, who was sitting on the bed, watching Mercy without saying anything.

Alice was unable to say anything without Mercy answering back in a blubbering mess.

Mercy felt completely at a loss for words. No matter how many times Alice had spoken and asked for an explanation, Mercy could not respond without wanting to tear the hair out from her head.

When she had barged into her bed chamber a while ago, she had felt Alice's presence trailing right behind her.

She heard Alice's tentative voice as she asked, "Mercy?

What's wrong—are you all right? I saw you pass by the drawing room, but you ignored me when I called for you. My word, your face is so pale; it's as if you've seen a ghost!"

There was no way to reply to Alice's bombardment of questions. Mercy could not even answer without having to relay to her younger sister what had just happened in the spare room in the stables.

It was embarrassing to have to say what Lord Griffiths had confessed to Mercy much less relive those memories. Alice would no doubt call for Olive, and they would both explode in a fit of giggles, humiliating Mercy even further. Even thinking about it made Mercy's face turn red; she felt her warm cheeks as she pressed them with the back of her cold hand to try to cool herself.

However, it was all for naught. Mercy realized that it was not embarrassment that made her face blush. In reality, it was from the pure, unabashed anger that still coursed through her.

It was anger that confounded all her thoughts.

That's what it was.

She was neither flustered nor shy about this entire ordeal. A man could never make Mercy blush like a damsel or a maiden; she would never want to stoop so low.

Especially for a man like Lord Griffiths who flirted with every woman in the ton, and who, based on Mercy's recollections, was so full of himself, he would believe that every woman that he had flirted with would fall for his charms immediately. He was the type of man who could easily fool others and took advantage of his looks.

Back in the woods when they had first stumbled upon each other, Mercy had thought that Lord Griffiths was attractive. He was very handsome, and, at that moment, she had admitted to him being the most handsome man in the ton. Thinking back on it now, Mercy could not help but feel annoyed with herself. Like those women, she had fallen for his appearance. But she would never truly fall for *him*.

She would not allow herself.

For her entire life, Mercy had tried to appear entirely uninviting and repelling, so that no man would try to approach and get to know her. She had done well, too, based on the talk of the ton. No one wanted to marry her, and that was exactly what Mercy wanted.

But Lord Griffiths was ruining all her efforts! Despite Mercy's rude disposition and offensive words, he continued to pursue her, as if he did not care for her displeasing antics. He was a very difficult person to unravel, such that he would not give up, even though Mercy was incredibly forthright with how she felt towards him.

"Mercy?"

Still, he had looked at her with such grave seriousness, as if he was unleashing a great flood of his emotions toward her, and she felt as if she was drowning from it. His eyes never strayed from hers; it was like his mind was completely set on her. Despite Mercy trying her best to reject him and show him how much she did not care for his feelings, he appeared unaffected. He did not yell or throw a tantrum from her words; he did not cry or threaten her. He promised her love, and that made Mercy feel much worse.

To top it all off, everything he had said was too embarrassing to repeat, yet he had done so without any humiliation, which made Mercy aggravated. That Lord Griffiths would go to such lengths in his confession made Mercy feel disconcerted.

"Mercy?" Alice's voice came from behind her. *"Mercy!"*

Snapping out of her thoughts, Mercy looked over her shoulder and saw Alice with an exasperated expression. She had leaned over and there was a crease between her brows as she stared at Mercy, worry written all over her face. She asked, concern in her voice, "Mercy, what is wrong? You've been muttering to yourself this whole time. Did something happen?"

Of course, something had happened, but Mercy could not force herself to say the words. She briefly imagined how Alice's face would change from confusion to excitement; in the drawing room the other day Alice had been so happy to hear that Olive had danced with Lord Griffiths. How would she react if she heard that he had asked Mercy for her hand in marriage? It would not be good.

Shivering from the thought of that reaction, Mercy decided to keep her mouth shut. She was much too angry to have to deal with Alice's enjoyment of her suffering.

"Nothing—nothing's wrong," Mercy replied.

Alice obviously didn't believe her because she continued to pelt Mercy with questions, "You're lying! What's the matter? I've seen you angry *plenty* of times, but I have never seen you look *this* angry."

She was right. Mercy was always the angriest after a man would try to ask her for a dance or when they would try to engage in meaningful conversation with her, only to be a bumbling fool with the same temper as Mercy. The last time she had thrown a fit, it was when Lord Pembroke had insisted on dancing with her, but she had been completely thrown off by his pride and arrogance. It was obvious that he loved himself more than anyone else, much less Mercy. He just wanted to dance with her because she had a record for rejecting every man in the ton; he wanted a challenge, and she had given him that. Unfortunately for him, he *was* a man so of course Mercy rejected him, too.

She only had to tell him that she would rather die than dance with him and he had scurried off, tattling on her to her own father, which made her hate the man even further. Lord Pembroke claimed to be a strong, brave man, but he had run to her father for help instead.

After that ball, Mercy had been angry with Lord Pembroke. But it was not close to how she now felt towards Lord Griffiths. It was a different type of fury. Because no matter how much she tried to make him repelled by her, he would not relent. He never told her father about what she had said in the woods, and he had not threatened her after she had injured him on her hunt.

Lord Griffiths had broken the precedence of how every other man had acted towards Mercy, and she did not know how to feel about it.

So of course, she would channel all of her emotions toward anger, which was why Alice was looking more worried by the second.

Alice was about to say something else when there was a knock at the door.

Mercy and Alice both turned their attention to Olive, who had just entered the bed chamber.

Mercy was shocked to see the look on Olive's face. She was completely in shock. Her eyes were wide as if she had seen something she shouldn't have; her cheeks were slightly pink, and her jaws were slack. A piece of her curly brown hair fell from her bun, falling into her eyes, but she made no move to brush it away.

Silently and with slow movements, Olive shut the door and walked toward Mercy, without ever breaking eye contact. Olive stared at her with suspicion in her eyes, a little wary and hesitant.

Then she turned, realizing that Alice was there, too. She asked, "What's wrong with Mercy. Why does she look so angry?"

Alice shrugged. "I don't know! I asked and asked, but she won't tell me anything."

Mercy did not say anything, knowing that now that Olive was here, it was even more imperative she did not tell them the truth. But Olive looked on edge, biting her lips to keep something hidden within her lips. Mercy's anger slowly dissipated, and her wariness over why Olive was acting so secretive increased.

After everything that had happened today, Mercy could not handle any more surprises. Also, it could not be a coincidence that Olive was behaving so abnormally after Lord Griffiths' confession. Could it have something to do with that? Mercy desperately hoped not, but with the way Olive was staring at her, Mercy had a slight suspicion that she might be right.

So, she decided to ask. "Olive...what do you know?"

Mercy's heartbeat quickened as Olive slowly sat down on the bed beside Alice. She was looking at the wall, zoning out, but her words were resolute. "I was downstairs, knitting on the couch. Everything was fine until I saw Father rushing out of the house with a glass of water and a tonic. I...didn't understand because he looked really worried, and so I thought something had happened to you when you both went hunting. But I heard you walk into your room, so I knew it couldn't have been *you* who was hurt. Curiosity got the best of me, so I...."

Mercy's eyes widened slightly. She could guess what Olive had done next because it was precisely what Mercy would have done if one of her sisters had gotten hurt.

"I followed after him," Olive said. "He went to the stables, and I thought to myself: *Why the stables? Why is our father bringing medicine to the stable? Did something happen to the horse?* I went inside to check, and I saw him go into the spare room. I hid behind one of the hay bales so I could listen to what was happening inside the room, to see who Father was taking care of. To my surprise, it wasn't Mercy who was hurt…it was Lord Griffiths."

Olive tilted her head then, a look of shock dawning on her face as if it was the next part that had shaken her to the core. "He…he was talking to Father about Mercy. Lord Griffiths was telling Father that he had asked court Mercy, but she had reacted very harshly."

Hearing this, Alice covered her mouth in surprise. "*He what?!*"

Olive looked away from the wall, focusing back on Mercy. She asked, "Mercy, is this true? Did Lord Griffiths really ask to court you? I didn't hear wrong, did I?"

Mercy closed her eyes and took a deep breath. She had wanted to hold this conversation off for a while, at least until her anger had completely washed away. But it seemed that her luck was gone these past few days. "What else did you hear?" she asked.

Olive let her own questions go unanswered and responded to Mercy with a relay of everything she had heard in the stable. "Lord Griffiths seems deeply infatuated with you, Mercy. He wishes to marry you and apparently confessed all of his feelings to you. He said that you ran away, which I wasn't surprised at. In reality, I was surprised at Lord Griffiths' words. That he had confessed to you so soon! He said that he was in love with you and wished to be with you. He begged for Father's permission."

Mercy's face grew red. "What did Father say?"

"Father told him that it would be difficult to court you. But Lord Griffiths persisted, saying over and over again how he loved you and that his heart's decision is final. He seemed very adamant; I did not have to see Father's face to know that he was shocked. As was I. I mean—I knew he was interested in you; I told you this the other day. When we danced, he would only talk of you. It was easy to see that he was very interested. However, I just did not know that his feelings...had escalated so quickly."

When Olive finished speaking, Mercy felt her stomach drop. She had never felt so humiliated in her life. It was already bad enough that Olive had eavesdropped on the entire conversation, but the fact that Lord Griffiths had told her father everything made her feel so embarrassed. This whole time, Mercy had planned on keeping his entire confession a secret. So far, Lord Griffiths had kept their interactions to himself. No one in the ton knew anything about them together.

But it was a proposal, and she was not stupid to think that they could ignore this

confession altogether. She just had not expected it to be

revealed so soon—not even an hour had passed! How would she face her father? It was only just this morning that he had come to her room asking her to join his hunt. Now, the next time they would meet, they would have this barbarous confession over their heads.

Mercy wanted to bury herself under her pillows and stay there forever.

However, it would be quite difficult since her two sisters were crowding the bed, staring at her with wide, expectant eyes, waiting for her to say anything at all!

"So, it's true…" Olive muttered after a couple of seconds of silence. It was not a question but a quiet declaration.

Mercy took in a deep breath before nodding her head, trying to hide her unabashed embarrassment. "Yes…Lord Griffiths confessed to me."

Alice gasped loudly.

Olive tightened her lips, but her eyes widened. She looked as if she wanted to screech but wouldn't. Mercy guessed she was thankful for that.

She continued, "We accidentally met each other in the woods the other day when I left the drawing room after you both told me that he was interested in me. Though, I don't believe it was an accident. We spoke for a few seconds, but I made him leave. I was suspicious of him, especially after everything you both said. I did not wish to spend another moment with him. He did not fight me; he left promptly."

Mercy had to turn away and look out the window. It

troubled her to tell her younger sisters all of this, but the truth about his confession was already out. She could not stay silent any longer. They paid complete attention, their postures straight, leaning slightly toward Mercy so they could hear everything she was professing.

Mercy tried to ignore their expectant expressions as she said, "Then today, we met again in the woods. Father had asked me to hunt with him. I heard something in the bushes, and I didn't think; I shot blindly, thinking it was an animal. Then I saw Lord Griffiths. He was on the ground, in pain. I had hurt him. But he wasn't bleeding. The bullet had only skimmed him—thank goodness. But he still looked to be in pain. I was so…scared.

"Then Father and I hurriedly took him to the stable room, so that Lord Griffiths could rest and get his medicine. Father left to go get water and a tonic, which was when you saw him, Olive. It was just Lord Griffiths and me in the room. To be honest, I tried not to think about that too much. I felt nothing for him, but it was still a little awkward. I had hurt him, so I couldn't just tell him to leave."

Truly, at that moment, Mercy had felt uncomfortable. It wasn't because of Lord Griffiths' overbearing and strong presence in the room, but because she could not argue with him. She could only speak to men if she was either rejecting them or arguing with them. But in that instance, it would have been entirely inappropriate for her to be rude to him, even by her own standards.

Alice whispered, "And then he took that chance to confess? What a man..."

Mercy scoffed. "Yes, he did. I was taking care of him, and he took advantage of my vulnerability. He told me that he...loved me. Which I cannot believe. It cannot be true. He said that he loved everything about me, but he does not even know me! I told him that I would not reciprocate his feelings, nor did I care for them. I said everything that I could to repel him. It would have worked for any other man...but based on what you said, Olive, I cannot believe that he is continuing to pursue me. And to even tell Father! *How embarrassing...*"

When she finished recounting her tale with Lord Griffiths, she looked back to see how her sisters would respond. Alice looked stunned, but based on her brightening countenance, Mercy could tell that she was trying to hold back her excitement. As for Olive, she was desperately trying to hide her exhilaration. Apparently, her shock from before had disappeared, and she was now thrilled to find out that she had been right all along.

Before giving them a chance to explode, Mercy asked Olive, "You said Lord Griffiths

asked Father for permission. How did Father respond?"

Olive bit her lip, looking a little nervous now. "Well...he sounded very happy."

It seemed as if the world had stopped spinning. Mercy's face blanched.

"Father said that he would help Lord Griffiths," Olive continued. "He would try to

convince you to marry him."

Mercy could not hear anything else. Olive seemed to have continued talking; based on her hand gestures, it appeared that she was trying to defend their father's words and that she was very excited for Mercy. But Mercy truly could not hear anything else. Her father sounded happy? She was shocked. So shocked, in fact, that she had to sit down to let the betrayal settle in her heart.

12

Shortly after Mercy heard about her father and Lord Griffiths' conversation from Olive, she followed her sisters down the stairs like a ghost, her expression one of confusion. *Father said that he would help Lord Griffiths.* Mercy slowly took one step after another with those words echoing in her head and wondered how she could even move in such a state. Eventually, they went to the drawing room to wait for their father. They all sat down in the lounge: Olive and Alice sat close together, giving each other a look of excitement, though there were traces of worry. On the other side was Mercy, who sat rigidly with a complicated expression.

Mercy guessed that their father was still outside in the stable with Lord Griffiths, and just that thought alone made her feel uncomfortable. She wondered if, after Olive had left, Lord Griffiths had said anything more, something to embarrass Mercy further.

Heat warmed her face as she thought about it. She needed to talk to her father about this—though confronting him after he heard everything was the last thing she truly wanted. The shock was still there in her heart, and Mercy wanted to know if what Olive had said was accurate. Did he truly wish for her to marry Lord Griffiths? When they had gone hunting earlier, he had told her that it was up to her if she wanted to marry, that it was *her* decision; he would not steer her in either direction. But apparently, he had told Lord Griffiths that he would try his best to help, to advise Mercy to accept him. That alone made her feel like everything her father had said during the hunt was a lie.

Just as she expected, her father walked into the drawing room. A huge smile was on his face; he was glowing. He looked as if he won a grand prize that he had wanted for a very, very long time.

When he spotted the sisters, he paused for a brief moment before smiling warmly again. His round cheeks were pink, and there were creases by his eyes that crinkled when he smiled. At that moment, the Duke of Norfolk appeared to be the jolliest man in the ton, Mercy thought.

"Hello, darlings, how are—"

Before he could finish, Olive stood up and asked without warning, "Where did Lord Griffiths go?"

Their father paused, a little surprised at her abrupt question, before responding. "Lord Griffiths has gone home."

Mercy waited with bated breath for him to say something—*anything*. Expecting him to ramble about the proposal and the forced engagement, Mercy tried to stop bouncing her knees from the anticipation. Surely her father would say something to her now. But there was nothing out of the ordinary with him, other than the fact that he looked very happy. A couple of moments passed and, still, not a word out of him. He moved from the entrance and sat down in front of them, leaning back against the couch. He puffed out a breath and made himself comfortable. It appeared as if he was not going to say anything at all.

Mercy gritted her teeth as the silence dragged on. If he was not going to bring it up, she would have to talk first. "Father, what conversation did you have with Lord Griffiths?" Her voice trembled about halfway through; anger was slowly taking hold of her sanity.

Her father sat up a little straighter and gave Mercy a direct look. "I'd like to ask you the same thing: What did you and Lord Griffiths talk about?"

"Father, I'm serious. I need to know what you and he talked about," Mercy said; her voice trembling about halfway through as her anger began to slowly take hold of her.

He gave a short sigh before nodding his head. "Lord Griffiths told me that he wishes to court you and to ask for your hand in marriage. He wanted my permission."

Trying not to show that Mercy had already heard about this from Olive, she remained still. She wanted to hear it directly from her father: Everything he had heard and talked about. Because then she would know if he had really decided to go against her and help Lord Griffiths.

Alice pulled Olive down to sit next to her, and they stuck close together. Mercy could feel their stares on the side of her face, but she ignored them. She ignored everything and focused on her father, who sat in front of her with a joyful face, appearing not to notice that he angered her more with every passing moment.

"And what did you say, Father?" she asked, her hands wringing together.

"I, of course, gave him permission to court you."

That was when Mercy's heart dropped, and she stood up from the couch, unbridled fury taking over her. Her father's words were quick and casual; how he would sound when listing out ingredients for a cake. It was effortless, as if he was not hurting Mercy with every word.

In her bedchamber, Mercy had thought, for just one second, that Olive was wrong. She hoped for it. The fact that her father would accept a proposal, that he knew Mercy did not want, was unfathomable. Besides, they had just talked about it in the woods when they were hunting!

He told her himself that it was up to her. It had seemed to Mercy that he would play little part in her romantic life, which she was very grateful for. At that moment, she felt free. But now, she felt as if she was locked right back into place with the foreboding shackles of marriage looming over her. And it was her father who had put her in this place.

Mercy quivered with anger as she stared at her father. "I have *no* desire to marry Lord Griffiths!"

Her father reached out a hand to placate her, but Mercy stepped back. He sighed. "Calm down and sit. Listen to what I have to say."

Mercy did not sit.

"Well, at least listen to me: I think you should get to know Lord Griffiths before making any rash decisions. Let him court you first. He is a well-mannered man and very respectable, and I believe that his interest in you seems true; he deserves a chance to prove to you that he is the one."

Hearing her father say this, Mercy felt constrained. She could not move or say anything.

"There is a possibility," he continued, "that after getting to know and talking to him, you could fall in love with Lord Griffiths. You should give him a chance, not for his sake, but yours."

Mercy could not believe it. He was actually, at this very moment, trying to persuade her to accept Lord Griffiths' courtship. He had already begun to help him and go against her.

Fueled with shock and disdain, Mercy stormed out of the room without a look back. She heard her sisters call after her, but she surged through the house, pounded up the stairs, and barged into her bedchamber where she could think.

She sat on the edge of her bed and covered her face with trembling hands. Anger pooled in the pit of her stomach as she thought about what her father had said.

You should give him a chance, not for his sake, but yours...

It felt like a stab to her chest. Earlier, her sisters had told her that Mercy needed to marry before they could marry. That, in and of itself, felt as if a mountain of pressure had descended on her shoulders. When she heard that, she had thought, for the first time, about her reputation and what it would mean to remain unmarried indefinitely. Would she be terrorized by the pitiful eyes of the ton? Would she be the main topic of gossip for years to come? Would she ruin the lives of her sisters—and the respectability of her father?

All those tempestuous thoughts loomed over Mercy for hours and hours, until she felt stuck. For the first time in a long while, she was unsure of herself. For the entirety of her life, Mercy wanted to be independent. She did not want to live in submission to her husband. She wanted to be her own person and do whatever she wanted.

Mercy wanted to be free.

But that wish slowly began to look burdensome. Because if she wanted to pursue her own wishes and live the rest of her life unmarried, she would undoubtedly hurt her family.

And it was because of this that Mercy knew what her father had wanted to say: *You should give him a chance, not for his sake, but ours...*

It appeared as if her father felt the same way as Olive and Alice. When they had gone hunting this very morning, Mercy believed that her father was on her side. He had made her feel better by saying that she should do whatever her heart desired.

Obviously, her heart chose to never get married.

But now that it was confirmed that her father had agreed to help Lord Griffiths, it felt like he was accepting the marriage on Mercy's behalf. And it made her feel like she had lost control of everything.

In the solace of her bedchamber, Mercy felt entirely alone.

Just then, there came a knock on the door.

"Mercy?" It was her father's voice.

"Please leave me alone," Mercy said.

Despite her request, the door slowly opened, and her father walked inside.

She did not say anything and instead looked away. She did not want her father to see the pained look on her face.

Anger had pulled her legs from the drawing room, but that anger had slowly dissipated into an uncomfortable feeling of pain and loss. Mercy did not want her father to see that she had almost started to cry.

"What do you want?" Mercy grumbled after clearing her throat.

She felt the bed dip, and she turned to see her father gently seating himself beside her. The vibrant look of joy on his face that she had seen earlier was gone. His eyes looked softer; his brows were slightly tugged downwards; cheeks that used to be pink had now lost their color; he was no longer smiling. This was the Duke of Norfolk's guilty appearance.

He turned to give her a sincere look, and Mercy could feel something within her softening. He genuinely looked upset by her outburst. "I meant what I said this morning. I will not force you to get married; that is still your decision."

Mercy opened her mouth to retort, but he quickly continued, "I know I said that I would help Lord Griffiths with his courtship. But at the end of the day, Mercy, it is entirely up to you if you accept it or not. I did not and *will not* force you to marry him."

A small sigh of relief escaped Mercy's lips. A little part of her loosened up. Her father could be difficult, but he did not lie, at least to his family. Now that she thought about it, he *did* say that he would help Lord Griffiths, but that did not necessarily mean that she had to accept his advice.

Mercy felt a bit guilty for thinking so far ahead and losing track of her father's words. But the feeling of betrayal remained. In a way, her father had still accepted Lord Griffiths' proposal, and that was real.

"However…" her father began, and he looked slightly apprehensive of what he was about to say. Still, at the end of the day, he was a duke, shouldering responsibilities. He needed to be realistic, and Mercy wished she did not have to understand that. "Your sisters still wish to get married. And, in order for them to accept their suitors, *you* will have to get married, too. Now, I understand how unfair that may sound, but this is the reality of our world. Sometimes, sacrifices must be made in order to fulfill our duties. Your sisters have already talked to you about this, and I am sure you've thought very deeply about your decision. I know you'll come to the right conclusion."

Mercy hung her head, her eyes fluttering shut. Of course, it was her duty to marry for the sake of her sisters' happiness. She had promised to protect those girls. What would it mean if she broke that promise and lived a life for herself? What would be the cost? Her younger sisters would never get married and be lonely forever. And they would be shamed alongside Mercy.

"Lord Griffiths seems like a good man," her father said. "I think he is someone that is well suited for you. I mean, it could have been an old, despicable man who wished to court you, but Lord Griffiths is well perceived and kind.

Mercy, I think this is a great chance for you. Just get to know him and see if he is worth the trouble or not. *Try before you decide what you want to do. There is nothing to lose.*"

Her father gave her an expectant look when he finished speaking, and Mercy sighed. He was right, she knew it. Perhaps, she knew this whole time that giving Lord Griffiths a chance was the correct decision to make. It was her duty to do so, but she was blinded by the selfishness of her own desires. She was stubborn, through and through, and she did not like having a man ruin all her efforts. Lord Griffiths was the first gentleman to ever pursue her despite her misdoings. Maybe it was time to finally relent and give him a chance to see if he was truly a good and kind man.

Plus, her father was right on another note. She would give Lord Griffiths a chance to prove himself as worthy, but that did not mean that she had to immediately fall in love with him and accept his proposal. If she continued to dislike him, then she would make the decision. At least for now, she could make her father and her sisters happy.

At the end of the day, that was all Mercy ever wanted.

Slowly, Mercy nodded her head, and she watched as her father's eyes regained that glow from earlier. "You're right...I'll...give him a chance."

A look of unadulterated happiness overwhelmed his face, and he gave a little cheer that made Mercy puff out a little laugh.

It did make her feel a bit better that Lord Griffiths had a face that didn't hurt to look at. He *was* the most handsome man in the ton, based on Olive and Alice's speculations. And, though she would never admit it out loud, Mercy agreed.

It could have been worse. He could have been an unsightly man, who was incredibly disagreeable and pitiful. Mercy did think that Lord Griffiths was an upgrade.

I should take this chance now, Mercy thought to herself. *Before I am doomed to an ugly, old man like Lord Pembroke.*

13

When Caleb returned to Cornwall Mansion, he pranced into the lounge room, adjusting the cuffs of his shirt with a bright smile on his face. Sunlight streamed through the opened window; the wind blew the curtains, and Caleb could hear the birds chirping faintly in the distance.

The day seemed brighter, and it did nothing to dampen his already-happy mood.

Just then, one of his maids opened the door and alerted him that Lord Morris had come to see him. Caleb's best friend, Ben, walked in soon after and greeted Caleb with a sweet smile.

Caleb answered back with an even fiercer grin, pulling Ben down onto one of the couches. He walked over to the table and poured himself and Ben a drink.

Ben quirked a brow. "What's with that smile on your face? You look as if you've won a thousand pounds."

With pep in his step, Caleb moved to sit next to Ben. "I have great news, my dear friend. *Fantastic* news."

"Out with it!" Ben pushed, his body positioning toward Caleb, giving all of his attention. The smug, yet entirely ecstatic look on Caleb's face must have provoked the unbridled curiosity in his good friend.

"I went to the woods this morning, hoping to bump into Lady Mercy and the duke. And, just my luck, I saw them hunting together. I knew that I had to seize this chance before I'd lose it, so I came up with a plan…" Caleb rehashed the story to Ben with fervor. He explained everything that had happened just this morning. From him faking his injury to asking the duke for permission to court Lady Mercy.

"I told her that I had fallen in love with her," Caleb said. "You should have seen me, Ben, I performed quite splendidly. I think she believed everything I said because she looked so shocked. Honestly, I was a little shocked, too. I mean, I know I was only faking the whole thing, but, for a moment, hearing myself say such things felt surreal—as if perhaps I actually meant it. My experience with all the ladies in the ton really paid off. Oh, and the duke certainly believed me. He gave me permission to court Lady Mercy. He agreed to help me!"

Ben listened attentively, but he did not appear as joyous as Caleb would have liked. His lips were tugged down in a slight frown, and his eyes were glued to the floor; he seemed to be thinking deeply about something, and Caleb had a gut feeling that the thought wasn't in his favor. But when Caleb had mentioned the duke and his acceptance of Caleb's asking for permission, Ben's eyes snapped to his, and his face morphed into an expression of shock.

His friend blinked rapidly before asking, "The duke himself gave you permission?"

"Yes!"

"Lady Mercy must be very angry about all of this…"

Caleb sighed before assuring Ben. "It's all right. I will make sure that Lady Mercy falls in love with me. We can spend some time together and get to know one another. I will do everything I can to charm her. And gradually, she'll begin to favor me and soon forget about all the negative emotions she harbors toward me. She will be too busy fawning over me to stay angry."

"That will not be an easy task."

"I know," Caleb replied. "But I assure you that I can do it. You've seen me interact with all those women at the balls. Remember Lady Michelle; she was a little wary of me at first—unlike all her other lady friends. But by the end of the night, she was practically glued to my side. She went from ignoring me to practically hanging off my arm. Yes, I vaguely remember finding handprints on my arm the next morning," Caleb joked.

Ben shook his head. "Lady Michelle and Lady Mercy are entirely different people. Lady Mercy is assertive and confrontational. If the two ladies were to engage in an argument, I am willing to bet that Lady Mercy would win in the first ten seconds."

"Wow—that long?"

"See?"

"Yes, all right, I understand. But I can do it. I managed to get the support of her father today. If anything, I am one step closer to obtaining the dukedom. I will not stop now; I will only work harder."

Seeing how adamant Caleb was being, Ben relented for just this moment. He leaned back against the couch and brought the glass of wine to his lips. Caleb drank, too, and the two men sat in silence, one savoring the sweet taste of the drink and the other savoring the sweet victory that he had earned this morning.

Ben's wary response did not deter Caleb from his goals. He had already half-expected Ben to be worried about the entire plan. Since the beginning—even though it was *Ben* who had brought up the plan in the first place—Ben had not been entirely supportive. This whole time he had warned Caleb about the difficulties of wooing a woman like Lady Mercy, and though he wouldn't admit it out loud, Caleb already understood that.

Lady Mercy's was undeniably stubborn. Based on the limited interactions they'd had in the past few days, Caleb had analyzed how rigid and strict she was on herself. Even as he implemented some of his most charming moves—and his good-looking face should have helped as well—the woman did not budge one bit.

But when she had brought him to the spare room in the stable, Caleb glimpsed for the first time a shadow of something sweeter coming into light. Lady Mercy's worried face was etched in Caleb's mind. Her brown hair looked disheveled; a few strands swayed perpetually in front of her green eyes. Her cheeks were slightly sunken in as if she were biting the inside. It was obvious that she was nervous and concerned. And the fact that it was on Caleb's behalf made him feel hopeful for the first time.

When she wasn't angry, Lady Mercy appeared thoughtful. Her face was a little more relaxed, and Caleb saw how pretty she could be. Having a temporary peek into that side of her made him think of how beautiful she would look if she were happy.

Caleb was intent on seeing her happy side. And if he could manage to move past her angry phase, everything else seemed possible.

"I have something to say, too," Ben said after a few moments of comfortable silence.

Caleb placed his drink down. "Ah, right. I shouldn't

have assumed that you wanted my presence simply to lend me an ear. What do you want to say?"

"I am planning to court the youngest daughter of the Duke of Norfolk, Lady Olive. I will be calling upon her soon and will ask the duke's permission to court her properly."

Caleb raised his brows in surprise before beaming. *I've been selfishly thinking about my own affairs. I've failed to remember that Ben has been plotting the same thing!* He patted his friend on the back and laughed, "That's great! We can get married together." He raised a glass. "To us, future husbands to the White sisters—hopefully."

They both drank the rest of the wine in their glasses. Soon after, Ben released a long breath before sitting up straight. Caleb prepared himself because he could tell, with the serious expression dawning on Ben's face, that his friend was about to warn Caleb yet again.

"Since I am planning on courting Lady Olive, I ask that you tread lightly with Lady Mercy. Because, if you mess up anything with her, then it might also ruin things for me and Lady Olive. I cannot have that."

That should have added pressure onto Caleb, but he did not feel that he would mess up in the first place. He was fully confident in his ability to obtain Lady Mercy's hand in marriage. Therefore, Ben's request was an easy one to agree to.

"Don't worry, Ben," Caleb said. "Like I've been saying, I

assure you that everything will go as planned, and we'll both be married by the end of all this. I won't do anything to ruin your courtship with Lady Olive."

Ben nodded his head, but he didn't look completely appeased. He still appeared slightly apprehensive about the whole thing, so Caleb parted his lips to assure him once more, but they were interrupted by a knock on the door.

When Caleb called for him to walk inside, the butler stepped into the room. Caleb saw him holding an envelope in his hand.

"Sorry to interrupt, Lord Griffiths. But this is a letter from the duke. It is an invitation to dinner at Norfolk Manor tonight."

Caleb's eyes widened as he took the letter from the butler. He opened it and read the contents, and saw, true to the butler's words, that he was indeed invited to attend dinner at Norfolk Manor. Pride bloomed in his chest as he passed the letter to Ben. "Look! An invitation from the duke himself!"

Ben looked very surprised, too. "I heard!"

"Didn't I tell you? I already have support from the duke. And this dinner will help plenty." Caleb's face was practically glowing. The duke had said that he would help Caleb and convince Lady Mercy to agree to the courtship, but to have it happen so soon was surprising! It felt as if the world was finally on his side. The dinner tonight would be a grand opportunity for him to slowly ease his way into the

White family. He would need to formally introduce himself to his future family, after all.

"Wow…" Ben muttered as he read the letter.

"This is tangible proof that the duke wants me to marry his eldest daughter," Caleb exclaimed.

"Caleb, you must try your best to make sure that Lady Mercy *does* fall in love with you—not just her settling and admitting defeat. She must *truly* love you for this to work. The duke, I heard, is very protective of his daughters. If he notices that Lady Mercy cannot, under any circumstances, have any feelings for you, then this won't work out in our favor." He let out a deep sigh and muttered, "Let's hope that perhaps you can fall in love with her, too. Falling in love might be your only hope to change."

Choosing to ignore the last sentence, Caleb swiftly nodded his head in response to the bit about the duke. He had also heard of Duke White's protectiveness over his family. Although Caleb did have his support in this now, that did not mean that he would have it forever. If Caleb hurt Lady Mercy in any way, it would come to the duke's attention, and Caleb could possibly lose the duke's support. That could not, by any means, happen.

Caleb was confident that it would not ever get to that, but it still made him feel a little nervous.

"Everything will be fine," Caleb said resolutely, wanting to make Ben believe him a little more. "I *will* succeed in this plan. And you will be able to marry Lady Olive with few problems."

Ben muttered to himself, "I hope there are *no* problems, really."

Ignoring that comment, Caleb stood up to quickly get ready. Night would fall in a couple of hours, and he needed to be absolutely prepared. Ben wished him good luck before departing, and Caleb rushed into his bedchamber thereafter. He rummaged through the best-fitted clothes. Standing in front of the mirror, Caleb tried his best to look presentable for the duke and the two sisters while also trying to look pleasing to Lady Mercy.

He ended up with a pair of pale trousers that accentuated his long, toned legs, and a white linen shirt layered under an obsidian-black coat with glossed buttons trailing up into a wide collar. He styled his dark hair in a way that appeared as if he had put little effort into it—but, in a way that made it casual more so than lazy. Caleb did not want to seem overeager.

Taking a final look at his reflection, Caleb felt that he was almost ready.

He had prepared his appearance, but he needed to prepare emotionally. If he were to win over the infamous Lady Mercy, he would have to be resilient, patient, and calm. He could not only rely on his charms with her.

So, he spent the rest of the time until dinner practicing what he should say and how he could successfully woo the entire family. Slowly, the little nerves he had started to fade, and he began to get excited about what tonight would bring.

Caleb admitted to himself that he was excited to see Lady Mercy again—and to seize this great opportunity to claim another victory.

14

Outside the window of her bedchamber, Mercy could see the sky darkening. The setting sun cast a warm orange glow on the three sisters: Olive and Alice were fumbling around trying to dress up Mercy—all by themselves, even though Mercy had insisted on the maids doing it—and Mercy standing awkwardly in the middle of the room.

"You must wear a beautiful dress for Lord Griffiths!" Olive declared as she picked up a maroon gown. "This is a big moment for you."

Alice nodded her head vehemently. She grabbed a powder from the vanity and began to roughly pat it on Mercy's cheeks.

Mercy kept her mouth shut.

Thirty minutes ago, Olive and Alice had hounded

Mercy with their excitement. It seemed to flood into Mercy without warning; the sisters' thrill was more like an ambush than a congratulatory gesture. Mercy had been sitting on the bed, trying not to think about the events of that night and what dinner with Lord Griffiths would mean when Olive and Alice had barged inside.

They ran toward the wardrobe, immediately seeking the most beautiful dress for Mercy. Mercy had outright refused their help. She was perfectly all right with wearing her most comfortable dress and leaving her hair as it was—which its few tangles here and there. But Olive and Alice had shaken their heads resolutely, both adamant on not allowing Mercy to take full reign over her attire.

"This is more than just a dinner, Mercy," Alice had shrieked. *"We will not allow you to lose this wonderful opportunity."*

Mercy tried not to feel offended. Sure, she didn't put much effort into her appearance, but she didn't think she dressed all that badly. The way Olive and Alice had taken over the wardrobe, however, made Mercy think otherwise.

Mercy repeatedly tried to stop Olive and Alice from dressing her up, but once the sisters got started on something, there was no stopping them. By the time Mercy was on her tenth *No*, Alice had apparently gotten annoyed, and so she asserted to Mercy, *"You have to try—for the sake of our family at least."*

Now, she was here, stuck in place as Alice patted her

face and pulled her hair into multiple different directions while Olive posed numerous dresses in front of Mercy to see which one suited her better. Mercy felt like a poor block of stone getting daubed with paint.

This entire ordeal made her feel uncomfortable and out of place. Everything would change from this moment onwards. She had relented to give Lord Griffiths a chance, but she did not expect it to happen so soon—on this exact night! When she heard from her father that he had sent a messenger to invite Lord Griffiths to dinner, Mercy gawked at her father with unabashed shock. No matter how much she wanted to argue about the rapidity with which her father had moved on, she could not. It was she who had acquiesced and agreed with her father. Besides, if this didn't happen now, there would be less of a chance that Mercy would agree to another opportunity to spend time with Lord Griffiths. She had to get this over with quickly and try her best to see what Lord Griffiths was worth.

"There, you're all done!" Olive said cheerfully.

Her sisters backed away and allowed Mercy to take a good look at her reflection. She was too caught up in her thoughts that she hadn't noticed that her sisters had finished dolling her up. In the mirror, Mercy saw a beautiful woman staring back at her. The dress was dark blue with a low and wide neckline, exposing a dazzling silver necklace that wrapped around her slender neck. The bodice was emblazoned with embroidered roses and vines and fitted perfectly to her chest and waist. The gown flourished down the length of her legs, and every time Mercy shifted, the skirt flayed out, back and forth. And instead of wrapping her hair up in a tight chignon, Olive had decided to let her long, brown hair down her back, with the upper half strung back with a little black bow. Though her hair was down, this tie allowed everyone to see Mercy's features fully.

"You look so beautiful," Olive muttered with a soft smile.

Alice met Mercy's eyes in the mirror, and she gave her a knowing look. "She's always been beautiful."

Mercy wasn't normally a shy person, but the suddenness of her new, clean appearance and her sisters' voices laced with awe made her feel a little bashful.

Before she could find the right words to explain how she felt, someone began knocking on the door.

A maid entered the room. She opened her mouth, but no words came out. It seemed as if she was frozen to the spot, her eyes slightly wide and her jaw slack. She was staring at Mercy in surprise, and Mercy wondered if she indeed looked that different. "Good evening, ladies," she finally managed to utter. "The baron has arrived for dinner and is seated in the drawing room with the duke."

Mercy's heart stuttered in her chest as she nodded. "We will be out momentarily."

The maid bowed before quickly leaving the bedchamber.

Olive and Alice gave each other excited looks, but Mercy felt anything but excited. Nerves ate her up from the inside out, and she clenched and unclenched her hands. Lord Griffiths was here already! He was inside her house, just down the stairs. It was only just this morning that she had rejected and yelled at him to leave her alone. Now, they were about to dine together.

She began to feel embarrassed about everything. Every time she had conversed with Lord Griffiths, she had somehow blown up on him. She had said some very rude things—she even called him a compulsive flirt! Now, here she was, accepting his flirtations and even going so far as to...return them, in a way.

Mercy shivered. How could one's life change so drastically?

It was as outlandish as her marrying Lord Pembroke just after she told him that she would rather die than dance with him. Completely spontaneous and without any sense.

But at least Lord Griffiths was younger and admittedly more attractive.

She emerged from her thoughts with a start as Olive and Alice pulled on her arms and dragged her out of the room. They led her down the stairs since Mercy couldn't trust herself to walk by herself without stumbling from nerves.

If she were to fall on her face in front of Lord Griffiths, she would never be able to live with herself!

When they entered the drawing room, Mercy first looked for her father. The duke was standing in front of the couch, his chin held high and his hair brushed back. His cheeks were round as she smiled at the girls. He splayed his hands out beside him, toward Lord Griffiths.

Mercy gulped as her eyes slid to Lord Griffiths, who was already watching her. His eyes were trained on her as she briefly observed his appearance. He wore a form-fitted suit that looked nicely tailored; Mercy didn't really care about the intricacies of a gentleman's formal attire. She only cared about men's casual attire and how comfortable it would be to lounge about in trousers without being conscious of the wary stares thrown her way.

She did not understand anything about formal attire, but she did understand that Lord Griffiths looked good in it. His black hair was well-combed; a stray strand curved over his eye, giving him a sort of aloof look to him.

It seemed that she had been staring for too long because her father cleared his throat, which disrupted Mercy and Lord Griffiths' eye contact.

"The Baron of Cornwall, Lord Griffiths," her father introduced.

Mercy and her sisters curtsied.

"We thank you dearly for joining us tonight, Lord Griffiths," Olive spoke first when Mercy didn't say anything.

Lord Griffiths smiled. "It was my pleasure." He turned toward the duke. "Thank you for inviting me."

"The ball at Cunthor Manor was very fun," Olive spoke again. "You are a splendid dancer. And I am not sure if you knew of this, but Mercy is a very good dancer as well."

"Really?" Lord Griffiths slid his eyes to meet Mercy's gaze.

"Yes! You must experience her dancing. It is truly magical."

"Well, then for the next ball, I hope to see it. Preferably, while I dance with you." He addressed the last part to Mercy, who stiffened in her spot.

Mercy raised her head and glared at him from across the room. "You couldn't keep up with me, I'm afraid."

The air in the room turned cold. She could feel the wide stares from her sisters and the scolding look from her father. But she did not care.

"You might be right," Lord Griffiths said as he cleared his throat. "But I will try my best."

"The last time I danced with a man, I squashed his toes so hard he couldn't walk out of the ball by himself."

"*Mercy*," Alice reprimanded.

"He must have been a poor dancer," Lord Griffiths said.

"Oh, he was," Mercy replied. "I think every man in the ton is a poor dancer."

Lord Griffiths unexpectedly laughed, and his eyes crinkled into two crescent moons. "I must be very lucky to be the only one who can dance, then."

Mercy clenched her jaw.

"Enough about dancing," her father said with a laugh, though Mercy could hear a hint of frustration in his voice. "Lord Griffiths, I would like to formally apologize for the incident this morning. Have you gotten better?"

Lord Griffiths quickly nodded his head. "I am much better, thank you. And no need to apologize again. It was only a mistake."

Mercy rolled her eyes. "You seem to be doing *too* well," she muttered to herself.

Apparently, Lord Griffiths seemed to have heard, as he lowered his eyes and smiled to himself. "It was because of your care and absolute concern over me that I have healed so quickly."

"I shouldn't have worried at all, then."

Her sisters gasped, and her father sighed deeply.

Mercy knew that what she was doing was not right. She was being rude, and she had told her father that she would at least *try*. But the moment she had seen Lord Griffiths' face, a feeling of irritation bloomed in her chest until it suffocated her entire being. She couldn't explain it, but she felt as if she had to say these things. The offensiveness was like second nature to her. She could not respond to Lord Griffiths' blatant flirtations with the expected response of complete submission and shyness that she hated seeing in all of those ladies of the ton, all of whom Lord Griffiths' had no doubt interacted with. She didn't want to be another lady for him to conquer.

Therefore, everything she had said to her father this afternoon—about her agreeing to give Lord Griffiths a chance—dissipated into thin air. The second she entered the dining room, she regretted it all.

Now, all she wanted to do was try to appear as unattractive and unattainable as possible, so that Lord Griffiths' would become absolutely repelled by her and stop his courtship. Then, she would be free from this uncomfortable feeling consuming her.

This feeling was so big, in fact, that it muddled all her thoughts. She could only think negatively, and she wanted to shout every rude thing she could think of. She was so absorbed in it that she couldn't even care about how her sisters, or her father would think of her. She wanted Lord Griffiths to see how awful of a person she was.

Just then, a maid walked into the drawing room and announced that the table was set.

They all moved out of the drawing room and headed for the dining room. Caleb held out his arm for Mercy to take, but she looked away and sped up to stand next to her father instead. With a quick glance over her shoulder, she saw Lord Griffiths beside Olive, appearing to be saying something.

They all seated themselves around the table. Her father sat at the head of the table, and

Mercy sat to the left of him; her sisters sat next to her; Lord Griffiths sat to the right of the duke, directly in front of Mercy. She couldn't even be upset about it because she was momentarily distracted by the deliciousness of the food. There were bowls of soft mashed potatoes dripping with a glob of butter that sunk in the middle and plates of sliced ham that were still warm from the fire. Trays of corn on the cob and cups of diced onions, loaves of glossed bread slathered with butter, and flutes of wine and cups of tea. A whole feast greeted Mercy.

Dinner ensued, and they all dug into the food. Mercy was just bringing a spoonful of mashed potatoes to her mouth when Lord Griffiths spoke to her.

"You look very beautiful tonight, as always."

Mercy stuck a fork in the ham and ferociously cut into it with the knife.

"I was thinking," he said again, "one day we could go horse riding together. I have a beautiful stallion named Johnny. My friend Ben named him that when we were little. I'm not sure why he wanted the name Johnny, though," he laughed.

Mercy felt Olive shift beside her at the mention of Ben, and so she turned and was utterly shocked to see two pink blotches on Olive's cheeks.

"Mercy's horse is named Apple," Alice answered in

Mercy's stead. "I'm sure you can guess why; she loves eating apples."

"Apple does make more sense than Johnny."

There was laughter around the table, but Mercy kept to herself. She bit into the corn and chewed and chewed. The clink of silverware rang in the room, along with a few short conversations relegated to Olive and Alice.

Sometimes, Mercy could feel a pair of eyes on the side of her face; no doubt Lord Griffiths was trying to catch her eye. But she would not relent, and she looked at either the wall or down at her plate of food. She pretended as if Lord Griffiths was invisible. And perhaps this had worked, because he did not try to talk to her again for the rest of the dinner.

When the plates were cleared, Lord Griffiths dabbed his mouth with a napkin and cleared his throat before turning to the duke. "Is it all right if Lady Mercy and I go out for a walk?"

Before her father could reply, Mercy shook her head and answered for him. "No, I hate walking. And I am very tired and must go to sleep."

Her father gave her a serious look before telling Lord Griffiths, "I have no problem with it if Mercy agrees. Olive can come along with you."

Lord Griffiths nodded and looked at Mercy. It was the first time since dinner had begun that they had looked at each other directly. Mercy wanted to look away, but before she could do so, Lord Griffiths brought out his hand for her to take. His lips tugged up into a warm smile as he asked again, "Will you go for a walk with me. Please?"

Mercy bit the inside of her cheek. Everyone was waiting for her answer. His outstretched hand was right in front of her, and his smile did not waver. She took a moment to truly observe his features, and she realized, startlingly, that he did not look arrogant at all. She knew that if she refused, he would probably give a pitiful smile and retract his hand. The night would end with her ignoring his existence.

Although it sounded nice, she knew she had to give his ambitiousness credit. So, to her utter disbelief, she slowly slid her own hand into his.

His fingers curled around hers, and she felt how unexpectedly warm his hands were. Her cold fingers instantly relaxed. Something tingled in her hand, and she reeled back slightly in shock. Her breath hitched. Mercy looked up to see if Lord Griffiths felt the same thing, but his expression was concealed, and Mercy could not figure out what he was thinking.

Despite that, Lord Griffiths gently escorted Mercy out of the dining room and out into the fresh air. The moon hung in the sky, and the moonlight lit the tops of the trees with a blue flush. The bugs buzzed and croaked in the darkness. For a few seconds, Mercy felt lighter.

They walked in the garden, and Lord Griffiths' arm was warm against Mercy's hands. Olive was walking behind them a distance away, allowing them to have a bit of privacy. The outside air was a little chilled, so she couldn't help but move closer to him. But she caught herself at the last second and stepped away.

Lord Griffiths apparently had noticed. "It's cold outside, isn't it? Come closer to me."

Mercy scoffed. "I would rather freeze and die."

"I heard from your sister that you like spending time outside," he said, ignoring what Mercy had said. "Do you like to walk in the gardens at night?"

"No," Mercy refuted. "Usually at this time, I'm in my room, relaxing and getting ready to sleep. Something I wish I was doing now."

A sigh came from beside her and before she knew it, Lord Griffiths stopped walking. He tugged her arm so that she turned and looked at him. She pulled her arm away from him, but she didn't walk away. Instead, she stayed and waited for whatever he had to say.

His brows were raised, and there was amusement in his eyes. "I know what you're trying to do."

Mercy crossed her arms. "And what am I doing?"

"You're trying to make me hate you, but it's not working."

She stiffened and opened her mouth to argue, but he interrupted her.

"The harder you try, the harder I'll try, too, because I truly love you, Mercy. I won't back down from this."

Her heart began to beat erratically. It seemed that no matter how many times he confessed, she would always be left speechless. She could never get used to it. And he had called her *Mercy*. Not Lady Mercy. Somehow that simple omission of her title made her shy. It was more intimate, as if he were talking to her as a close friend, not as a stranger speaking with formal pleasantries.

Seeing that she had nothing to say, Lord Griffiths said, "Let me take you back inside."

She could only nod.

When they entered the manor again, her father and Alice seemed to have been talking about them. Because as soon as they spotted her and Lord Griffiths, they fell silent and kept their mouths sealed.

"Thank you for giving me the pleasure of dining with you all," Lord Griffiths said with a bow. "The food was very delicious."

"Thank *you* for coming," her father said.

Lord Griffiths bid them farewell and a good night, and he opened the door to leave. He did not cast Mercy another glance, and she shamed herself for expecting it.

The door shut, and he was gone.

She didn't allow anyone to say anything to her because

she didn't want to hear it. She ran up into her bedchamber and closed the door. Her heart was beating so fast that she needed to take a second to breathe in the solace of her room.

Without thinking, she rushed to the window, but she couldn't see Lord Griffiths. There was no trace of him. It was as if he had never come.

But he did. Caleb Griffiths was here, and her hand had been in his. His warmth was unforgettable—and his confession had felt different in the darkness of the garden.

15

The next morning during breakfast, Mercy ate in silence.

Her sisters were engaged in a discussion about an upcoming ball, but it was obvious by the way their eyes flickered to Mercy every now and then that they were only delaying talk about Lord Griffiths. Mercy was thankful for this short reprieve. As she dug into her egg and sausages, she couldn't help but replay the events of last night over and over.

During dinner, she had a straightforward objective: To make Lord Griffiths take back his words and give up his courtship with Mercy. However, the goal seemed to have flown away as the night progressed. By the night's end, the result had been the complete opposite!

His confession in the garden should have resonated

with Mercy the same way it had in the stable room. But somehow it did not. Perhaps it was because of the slow acceptance she had given to her father just prior to the dinner that she had heard the confession in an entirely different light. Perhaps it was the darkness of the night that helped veil her flustered cheeks, which took away some of her discomfort. Perhaps it was just Lord Griffiths himself.

Mercy stabbed into a slice of sausage with force.

What a complicated predicament! She wanted to reject Lord Griffiths over and over again; she had no qualms about doing so, and she would never tire of it. But last night had changed things. All of a sudden, her throat had closed, and her tongue felt heavy in her mouth; she could not part her lips and spew hateful things to him, as she usually would to such foolish words. Mercy lay in bed for the rest of the night, as sleep did not come to her for some time, and thought about how she should have responded to him. She should have done *something* rather than stand there stupidly in front of him, mouth opening and closing like a fish.

*Or maybe...*Mercy thought with trepidation. He seemed to take up every inch of her mind; she could not stop thinking about him. Perhaps this was how it felt to fall in love with someone, and it made Mercy's heart stop dead in her chest. She *could not* fall for Lord Griffiths. Or maybe... maybe she could. If she allowed herself to let this pass through her and accept his charms, it would make everything easier. She had agreed that she would at least give Lord Griffiths a chance, and Olive and Alice needed Mercy to marry someone so that they could too. She knew all of this. Though it would be hard to accept the stuttering feeling in her chest as *love*, maybe she could withstand the trials of courtship by viewing the feeling as something beneficial for her. If she loved him, a marriage to him wouldn't be as painful for her to endure.

It wasn't entirely too hard to picture. When they had first held hands in the dining room, Mercy had felt a shock go through her. It started from the tips of her fingers, through the warmth of their touching palms, slithering down her arm into her chest, which reverberated with the thundering beat of her heart. She had never felt like that before. That feeling lasted for the rest of the night, and in bed, she clutched her heart under the covers, willing it to calm down, but it never did.

Mercy knew for certain that the feeling wasn't anger, and that revelation struck her mind with great surprise.

Everything was beginning to change. She had told herself that she would never fall for a man, but it seemed like her soul was saying otherwise.

Mercy was snapped out of her thoughts with a start when Olive touched her shoulder.

"Breakfast is over," she said. "Let's go to the drawing room."

Mercy looked around and saw that her father and

Alice's seats were now empty. It was just her and Olive. How long had she been sitting there, thinking?

They moved to the drawing room, and Alice had her head hung low, absorbed in another book. Olive walked over to her knitting kit and continued her previous craft. They were acting normally as if the events of last night were a simple event, nothing major. It should have made Mercy feel better, even relieved, but it didn't.

Did they know something she didn't?

Mercy remembered Lord Griffiths exchanging a few words with Olive last night, right after Mercy ignored his outstretched arm and ran to her father. Was it then? Did Lord Griffiths whisper something to Olive about Mercy? Paranoia consumed her, and she didn't know what overcame her. She wanted to ask Olive about it—her sister was right there in front of her—but it was a little embarrassing. If the first thing Mercy talked about was Lord Griffiths, then the girls would squeal with excitement and embark on a long speech about how the couple should get married soon.

It was too early in the morning for that.

Thankfully, a maid entered the room with a quick announcement, saving Mercy from any further humiliation.

"Lord Curzon has arrived and wishes to visit Lady Alice if she permits it."

Alice immediately put her book down on the space

beside her and jumped out, her face morphing into a look of complete excitement. She practically shrieked her approval, and soon after, Lord Curzon entered the drawing room.

Olive and Mercy curtsied, welcoming Lord Curzon to their home. He bowed in response.

With just one look, Mercy thought that he must be a likely candidate for one of the most handsome men in the ton. He had chestnut brown hair that was a little long, curling around the back of his neck; in the sunlight, his hair appeared slightly red. He had dark blue eyes that rivaled a stormy sky, but she could see how magnetizing they could be. So could Alice apparently, since she could not stop staring at him. He was tall with a lean build, and his posture was ramrod straight. He held himself like the respectable man some would deem him to be, and Mercy admitted that he didn't seem like a man undeserving of her lovely sister.

However, at the end of her observation, she didn't think he was the *most* handsome man in the ton. Someone else held that spot.

Lord Curzon did not waste any time before approaching Alice with a long stride. They stood close together but not touching; Olive and Mercy gave each other a quick knowing glance.

"Thank you for coming," Alice said; her voice was so soft that Mercy had to strain her ears to hear her words.

Thankfully, Lord Curzon was close enough to Alice that he could understand. "It is my absolute pleasure. It has been quite a while since we've last spoken. I wouldn't be surprised if it's been a decade."

Mercy quirked a brow. *Hasn't it been four days?*

Alice did not wince at the hyperbole, and she nodded her head rapidly, staring up into Lord Curzon's eyes in a way that appeared as if she would never see him again. "Too long! I have thought about you every day, every second. In order to feel as if you were with me, I read the books that you recommended. Sometimes, I feel like we're having conversations as I read the pages."

"I have been reading, too! If I really focus, sometimes it is like *you're* saying the words." A wide smile split across Lord Curzon's face, and he seemed to be absolutely glowing. He did not take his eyes away from Alice's. "Obviously that was not enough for me. I had to come see you again, and here you are. Your voice is better than in my imagination!"

Alice giggled; her cheeks turned pink.

Olive was knitting again, but her ears were perked. A smile would appear on her face every now and then, and she seemed to be very invested in the two's conversation. Mercy was watching the whole interaction with a nauseated look on her face. Before, she would have been annoyed by how dramatic Alice and Lord Curzon were being, but now, she looked sick because she could not help but think about Lord Griffiths.

Would they speak like this, too, one day?

Suddenly, the thought of Lord Griffiths' voice invaded her mind, and she had to shake her head to rid herself of the idea.

She looked back at her sister and Lord Curzon, and upon closer inspection, Mercy knew that her sister was different than her. Of course, she was. Alice was much more invested, she was kind, and she was shy in the best way possible. Whenever Lord Curzon said anything, Alice responded in a way that delighted him. Mercy could tell by his widening smile, the blush on his cheeks, his reddening ears, and his unflinching gaze that he was completely absorbed in Alice. She could tell just by his body language—always positioned before Alice, one hundred percent focused on her—that he was very invested in her.

They looked as if they were in love.

Just then, Mercy heard her name in the conversation, and she creased her face with confusion.

"Isn't that right, Mercy?" Alice asked.

"Huh? I mean—could you repeat that?"

"Don't you have a special someone, too?" Alice turned to Lord Curzon. "She might be betrothed very soon, which will make things easier for us on all accounts."

Lord Curzon's eyes widened slightly, and he gave Mercy a large smile. "Congratulations!"

Mercy was at a loss for words. She could only respond with a straining smile.

"Speaking of that, would you mind if I spoke to your father now?" He asked Alice. "I have no desire to wait any longer."

Alice nodded her head. "Go ahead!"

Alice called for a maid to bring her father into the room, then she bit her lip and suddenly seemed jittery. Lord Curzon wrung his hands together, and the two looked away from each other, suddenly embarrassed by what they were about to do. Based on the sudden change in the atmosphere, Mercy was aware of what was happening. Lord Curzon was about to ask their father for Alice's hand in marriage. The quickness with which all of this was happening startled Mercy. She knew it was bound to happen sooner or later. With the way Alice and Lord Curzon interacted, it was obvious they were smitten with each other and wanted to get married quickly.

And Mercy knew that Alice only allowed Lord Curzon to ask their father because Mercy was on the brink of getting married. Alice thought that everything would be all right because Lord Griffiths was so adamant about getting married to Mercy. This brought solace to Alice, and so she accepted Lord Curzon. Mercy felt nervous suddenly.

This was more of a reason for her to give Lord Griffiths a chance. Because if they didn't work out, then Alice and Lord Curzon's marriage would be put to a halt. But Mercy could not fathom that. Alice was currently pacing the room, biting her nails and twiddling with her hair. She had a faint blush on her cheeks, and her eyes were bright. Mercy saw that Alice was genuinely excited to be with Lord Curzon, so much so that she was nervous about their father's rejection—though that was difficult to fathom.

Mercy closed her eyes. A pressure, unlike anything she had ever experienced settled on her shoulders. She wanted Alice to be happy. And if that happiness was with Lord Curzon, then Mercy needed to try with Lord Griffiths.

Even though she knew that this was the only way, fear gnawed at her. All her life, she believed that she would live for herself, her sole responsibility being to protect her family. She never envisioned herself being shackled to a man through marriage. Now, her plans had morphed into something else. Lord Griffiths had come into her life, and even though his presence and his obsession with Mercy were foreign to her, she knew, deep down, that she couldn't lose him. And that scared her. Because if she did, her sisters would be heartbroken.

Her dampening mood was disrupted by the sudden presence of their father. He entered the drawing room with an expectant look. Once he saw that Lord Curzon there, he straightened his back and regarded him professionally. "Lord Curzon, to what do I owe the pleasure?"

Lord Curzon stepped forward and bowed. "Duke White. I am here..." He took a deep breath and steeled himself. "I am here to ask for permission for your daughter. I intend to marry her."

Mercy watched as her father quickly covered his shock with unabashed happiness. It was apparent that he was very ecstatic by the way his eyes shone brightly, clapping his hands, giddy at the news. Lord Curzon's shoulders sagged with relief, and tears brimmed in Alice's eyes.

"Of course!" Her father agreed immediately. "I wholeheartedly give my permission for you to marry my daughter, Alice. We will announce this great news at the ball tomorrow!"

Alice and Lord Curzon turned to each other, and they embraced with love in their eyes. Mercy could feel their affection from the other side of the room. She could not remember the last time she'd seen Alice look *that* happy. She was almost bawling. Turning her head, Mercy saw Olive suppressing her own tears. She was staring at Alice with joy, but Mercy did not fail to detect a hint of jealousy in her eyes.

Mercy's heart squeezed.

Her sisters' wishes were to get married to the man of their dreams. That was what they'd always wanted. Alice was close to achieving it, and happiness was practically radiating off her. This was what it was like to protect her sisters, Mercy knew. She wanted them to be happy and safe in the solace of their homes with a loving husband. Mercy wanted to give them that, and to do so, she had to give herself up. She would have to marry Lord Griffiths so that Alice and Olive could get married without any worries about the tarnishing of their reputations.

Mercy closed her eyes, something in her chest settling: Acceptance.

She loved her independence, but she loved her sisters more.

16

The following evening, Mercy and her sisters were getting ready for the ball. A couple of maids assisted them with their dresses—as it would be one of the most important events in the family. Alice's betrothal would be announced, initiating the first of the White sisters' marriages. It was a big step in their family, and they wanted it to go splendidly.

Mercy observed Alice from the other side of the room. There was a bright smile on her face, so much so that there was no need for any blush powder; her cheeks were already reddened from her being flustered about the whole ordeal. Ever since Lord Curzon had left, Alice could not stop smiling. Olive had immediately dived into a tight embrace, but Mercy hung back. Her heart was touched by the happiness radiating off Alice; it was just that she could not help but feel fear slowly consuming her. The fear of the possibility that someday, perhaps that happiness would be taken away from Alice.

"I am so excited for tonight; I cannot even stand still!" Alice squealed after one of the maids requested that she stop moving so much.

"We can take it from here," Mercy told the maids, and they all quickly fled the room. She approached Alice, who was currently fiddling her thumbs together. "Let's finish getting you dressed so we can go to the ballroom sooner." Though that was the last thing Mercy wanted to do, she knew that it was what Alice really wanted, so she let it go just this once.

Alice nodded ferociously before allowing Mercy and Olive to pamper her. Olive applied the cosmetics that gave Alice a very innocent, natural look. Mercy tried to style her hair, but after fumbling with the brush and clumsily slipping a few strands of hair from the chignon, she had to quit, and Olive took over. All Mercy could do was stare at her sister through the mirror: Alice stood, still fidgeting, with an aquamarine-blue dress on, a long silk skirt that flayed around her legs. Her brown hair was wrapped in a smooth chignon—thanks to Olive's help—and her lips were colored vermilion. Mercy thought that she looked like a fairy.

"I love Lord Curzon so much."

Mercy and Olive's eyes snapped to Alice, who seemed a

little shocked herself. Then the shock slowly dissolved into something so much more: understanding and acceptance. She nodded her head as if she was finally willing to acknowledge her feelings. "Yes, I love Lord Curzon. I love him so much. I could shout it from the rooftops and let the whole world know...I cannot imagine a life without him; I simply cannot!"

Her outburst made Olive shriek with excitement, and she dashed toward Alice for another hug, but upon seeing Alice's dress and hair, Olive stopped herself. They resorted to holding hands and squealing with one another. From the bed, Mercy smiled to herself. To see her little sister all grown up, betrothed to the man of her dreams, was a miracle in and of itself. Seeing Alice completely enamored with Lord Curzon made Mercy think of all the possibilities of love. For instance—could Mercy ever feel so intensely? Could she ever look at a man and want to shout her love from the rooftops for all the world to hear?

Immediately, her thoughts turned to Lord Griffiths. She imagined his face, the way his eyes would pierce into hers. She imagined him right in front of her. She imagined the puff of air between them as he spoke to her in the cold night, saying that he loved her and that nothing could ever stop that feeling. Was his love so intense, such that the feeling would utterly consume him inside and out? Mercy wondered if she could ever reciprocate his affections. One day, if a miracle truly happened and she accepted Lord

Griffiths' proposal, would she stand in front of the mirror, jittery with excitement over the prospect of marrying Lord Griffiths? The idea seemed outrageous, but if she thought about it deeply some more, perhaps such a conclusion wouldn't be so crazy.

Thinking so far ahead in the future always made Mercy antsy and uncomfortable. It was uncontrollable; she could try her best to prevent something from happening, but at the end of the day, fate would strike, and her future would come barreling toward her. So, for now, all Mercy could do was to at least try to get to know Lord Griffiths. His feelings for her were already out in the open; now it would be Mercy's turn to evaluate her own feelings. Slowly, she would try her best to understand Lord Griffiths and give him a chance. All for the sake of Olive and Alice.

Alice was giggling about something Olive had said, and Mercy wanted to trap the sound and hold it forever. If this was what was gifted to Mercy after marrying Lord Griffiths, then she would do everything she could to *try*.

She had made a promise to her mother that day. Mercy was completely responsible for her little sisters; she could not be selfish. If marrying Lord Griffiths was what it took, then Alice's happiness would be worth it.

As determination seized Mercy's heart, the memory of Lord Griffiths in the stable room suddenly came back. Mercy cringed inwardly. She remembered his unabashed confession. He did not sugarcoat his words, nor did he appear shy. *I have fallen in love with you,* he said, and the words were strong and enunciated. It seemed that Lord Griffiths was not afraid to express his emotions, and that type of love language made Mercy slightly uncomfortable.

If she were to spend more time with him, then she would have to accept that part about him. But she just could not fathom the idea of outwardly swooning for Lord Griffiths.

For a moment, she imagined it.

"Oh, Lord Griffiths, you've swayed my heart! Every day, you are all that I think of!"

"Is that so? What a lucky day for me! Every moment without you is a tragedy bestowed upon me."

"Hurry! Hold my hands so that I may remember you every time I flip the page of a book or hold the fork to bring a slice of ham to my lips. When I look down at my hands, I will remember you."

"Oh, Mercy!"

"Oh, Cale—"

"Mercy?"

Mercy was snapped out of her thoughts as Alice shook her shoulders. Mercy's cheeks instantly warmed, though that was silly since there was no way her sisters could hear her thoughts.

"Why do you look like you were going to throw up?" Olive asked.

"Oh, just a bit nervous is all," Mercy laughed. The

image of her and Lord Griffiths exchanging a few...pleasantries was enough to make her want to keel over and die. Could such soft words ever leave her mouth? *No!* But if that was her destiny, then she would have to bite her tongue and let it happen.

Perhaps she would just have to let Lord Griffiths do all the talking. She would be happy to sit back and relax, and let the marriage run its course.

"Stand up," Alice ordered Mercy. "Now it's your turn. Get out of the dress you're wearing; I have found a better one!"

Mercy begrudgingly allowed her sisters to put on a dark green gown that slid perfectly over her body. The sleeves were slightly puffed, giving her enough space to move freely. The neckline was low and wide, but the chest piece wasn't so tight that she could not breathe. Her skirt flowed down to her toes, and when she walked to the side, she found that the silk was so smooth she could stride without any restriction.

Just then, Mercy heard Olive sigh wistfully, "I know I see you every day, but I still get astounded by your beauty."

"Me too," Alice agreed. "It's no wonder Lord Griffiths is so smitten with you."

Before, Mercy would have rejected the entire notion, but now she found herself blushing fiercely. For a second, as she stared into her reflection, Mercy thought that maybe Olive had applied too much blush powder. But the more

Alice's words echoed in her head, the darker the blush on her cheeks became. She was flustered!

Mercy's heart started to beat wildly; she didn't know if it was because she was panicking or if she was nervous. Suddenly, her features were highlighted. The vibrant green of her eyes, an exact replica of her mother's. The smooth glide of her nose. Her plump lips. The dark brown waves of her hair. Her high cheekbones. Before she had never really cared about how she looked. But now…things had changed, it seemed.

When Lord Griffiths looks at me, what does he see?

Does his heart thunder in his chest? Does his mind go completely muddled until he is at a loss for words? She wanted to know just as much as she feared the answer. The feeling of someone being in love with her was too foreign. Everything about her became starker and more accentuated. It made her unnerved; she couldn't make much sense of the feeling. From now on, would she be able to do anything without considering Lord Griffiths' opinion of her?

Mercy shook her head to rid of these complicated thoughts. The only truth that could ground her was that she was doing all of this for her sisters' happiness. This marriage would allow her little sisters to get married, which was what they wanted most. Mercy squared her shoulders and ignored the blush on her cheeks. There was no time for these conflicted feelings. She needed to focus on the true goal of all of this: To secure the marriages of her two baby sisters.

They might be her weakness, but they were also her strength. Mercy was able to find the beauty of the world through her sisters. She would do anything for them.

When she finished getting ready, Mercy told Olive and Alice that she would wait for them in the drawing room. She needed to take a breath and calm down. In the room, she found herself pacing. She clenched and unclenched her hands and ground her molars.

She did not know why she was feeling so tense, just that she was. But she knew deep inside that she would find Lord Griffiths at the ball. Then what would happen? The last time they had talked, he had confessed to her once again, and then he had simply left. He had been so annoying during the dinner—trying to get her attention and inviting her into multiple conversations that she did not want to engage in. Lord Griffiths did everything Mercy abhorred, yet she could not stop thinking about him.

Mercy told herself that all of this was because he was so aggravating. His actions and words were so foolish that she could not help but replay them over and over, and that the rapid beating of her heart was because he angered her. Lord Griffiths was just another man. He was not anything special. Mercy would have to tolerate him for the sake of her sisters.

The door suddenly opened, and Mercy spun around to

see her father entering the room. A smile lit his face as he observed her daughter. But when he looked at her face, his brows drew together, and he asked, "What's the matter? Is everything all right?"

Before Mercy knew it, she had flung herself on her father, enveloping him in a tight hug. The words tumbled out without provocation. "I feel...I feel like my sisters' happiness is completely dependent on me."

"That is not true!" her father responded as he rubbed her back. "You shouldn't pressure yourself into marrying Lord Griffiths if you do not wish to."

"But..." Mercy felt tears brimming her eyes, so she looked up into the ceiling, trying to stop the tears from falling. *I shouldn't cry...I must be strong,* Mercy thought. But the past few days along with the onslaught of these foreign feelings overwhelmed her to the point where she could not contain the tears anymore.

She felt her father pull away and squeeze her shoulders tight. His eyes were soft as he wiped a stray tear from her cheek; she hadn't realized that she let one slip.

"When I met your mother," he began, "it was *not* love at first sight. In fact, I did not consider her at all. And she must have thought that I was some silly boy. But after a few months, we began conversing with one another. I learned what her favorite flower was, what food she liked, and which book she cried over. I told her everything about me, too, and none of it felt forced because your mother was one of the most truthful people I've ever met. And I could not only see, but I could feel her listening to me. Our love was slow, but it was there. Then we got married, and we loved each other every single second we were granted."

Mercy's chest ached at the wistful look in her father's eyes. Whenever he talked about her mother, he seemed to escape into a different world, one where they were still together. To the whole family, she was alive in their hearts.

Her father continued. "Every love is different, Mercy—that's the beauty of it. And it will come to you differently. It may come to you years after you meet; it may come to you in the next hour. Love at first sight is not the only type of love out there. So, I ask you for a favor: please get to know Lord Griffiths and see if he is the right person for you. And if he is not the one, then that is no problem; there are many other men in the world! You have nothing to worry about."

He was right. She shouldn't act as if Lord Griffiths was her only chance. Years from now, there could be someone else. Or perhaps another man might gallop into town in the next few minutes. Regardless, Mercy didn't have to worry. Men had always been repelled by her, but there would come a man who would learn to appreciate her for who she was. Instead of being offended by her, they would be amused by her. Love came in many different forms. Maybe, if she allowed, it would come in the shape of a tall, lean man with dark hair and even darker eyes. Maybe it would come bearing the name of Lord Griffiths.

Her sisters walked into the drawing room, dolled up and ready to go. Mercy's father gave her a fond look before leading all of them out into the carriage.

As they departed for the ball, Mercy looked out of the window and thought about love.

17

I cannot believe my luck, Caleb thought to himself as he stared into the mirror in his bedchamber, minutes before he had to depart for the ball.

Everything had fallen into line. The opportunity loomed before him like a beacon, calling to him. He knew that his proposal had not fallen on deaf ears. At the dinner, Caleb studied perceptively; he watched as Lady Mercy's sisters engaged in his conversation, how they tried to pull Lady Mercy's attention to him, and how the duke supported him throughout the whole evening. It all fell into place like puzzle pieces—especially when he had asked Lady Mercy to accompany him for a walk, and she had accepted his hand. At the time, he could feel his fingers spark and tingle for a breath of a single moment; he managed to conceal his surprise by telling himself that it was only an electrical shock.

When they walked in the garden, and when he confessed to her again, he could see something shift in her eyes. There it was—the golden opportunity. Before it could disappear, he escorted her back inside and left, knowing that the small bit of interest sparked within Lady Mercy would sit in her chest for the rest of the night.

He had finally caught her in his hold. Now, all he had to do was reel her in. Slowly, because he knew Lady Mercy to be a very stubborn, reluctant person. He would woo her until she had no choice but to marry him. This was enough to make him holler in victory.

It also helped that he knew what the situation was like in the White family.

Caleb knew that Lady Olive and Lady Alice desperately wanted to get married; it was apparent in the way they earnestly tried to appeal to Caleb throughout dinner.

"Lord Griffiths, not only is our dear sister the most beautiful girl in the ton, but she is also very intelligent. She has read almost every book in our library!" Lady Alice had praised her sister.

Lady Olive nodded in agreement. "She will not have trouble in keeping up with any conversation with you, her husband—oops, did I say husband? I meant to say friend."

The two sisters gave each other a quick glance, to which they then tried to hide their giggles behind their napkins. Lady Mercy was unresponsive; her head was lowered as she shoveled food into her mouth.

Caleb had to hide his amusement. The sisters were obviously calling attention to the proposal hanging over their heads. Unfortunately, Caleb could not bring the topic up for discussion, for Lady Mercy was completely ignoring him. Even if he did talk about the proposal, she would have shut down and fled the room. He needed to be patient.

But, although Lady Mercy might have been unwilling to talk throughout the whole dinner, Caleb knew that Lady Olive and Lady Alice were trying their best because they simply *needed* this marriage more than Lady Mercy did. Since she was the oldest sister in the family, she must be married first for it to be deemed appropriate for the younger sisters to marry. But Lady Mercy had been repelling men since the beginning of time, so she was unwed. Now that she had a courtship dangling before her, of course, her sisters would seize the chance and desire for her to get married.

Caleb knew that Lady Mercy loved her sisters dearly—more so than any other person in the world. More than herself. So, she would have to learn to ignore her own desires and sacrifice her independence for the fate of her baby sisters. Caleb knew this. And he wanted to view this as an advantage for him, but deep inside, he couldn't help but admire this quality about her.

Therefore, not only did he have the support of the duke

but also Lady Mercy's little sisters. Her entire family was on his side—all except for her. Caleb just needed Lady Mercy to catch up and understand what Caleb was bringing to the table. Not only would this benefit him, but it would benefit her. They could work together to achieve their legacy.

As Caleb adjusted the tie on his form-fitting suit, he scolded himself slightly. Although the plan seemed easy in his head, he knew it would be much harder in reality. He had gotten the entire family's approval—all except the most important member: Lady Mercy. There was a reason why she was the last person to approve of him; she was absolutely and irrevocably *difficult*.

He might have wooed her for a single moment in the garden the other night—he could remember the way her breath hitched and the way her cheeks had faintly blushed—but she was quick to change her temper. One moment she could be flustered and the next she would lash out and spew hateful words without any regard for how the recipient felt. Caleb needed to understand that before talking to her. He had to remain calm before gently approaching her. In order for him to succeed, he would have to be the perfect gentleman and charm her in a way that he had never done for any other girl because Lady Mercy was *not* like any other girl.

Emerging from his rampant thoughts, Caleb quickly smoothed down his suit—a fine-tailored dark blue coat over his cream-colored tunic. A fluffed cravat wrapped around his neck and gave him a more sophisticated look. As always, his dark hair was styled in a lackadaisical manner; not too formal, but also not too casual. For an extra measure, he styled a strand of hair to fall into his eyes, giving him a dreamy look that women couldn't help but fall for.

Once he was ready, he left the manor and boarded his carriage. The road was smooth, and the horses were fast as he told the driver to take him to Sielle Manor; he and Ben had planned to go to the ball together

Caleb could see the outline of his friend as the carriage approached the manor. Once they arrived, Caleb dropped down from the carriage and greeted his friend.

Immediately he could tell that Ben was very excited. His eyes were glowing, and his cheeks were round and red as he smiled. Caleb wondered what had happened to make his friend appear so exuberant. "What's got you so thrilled this evening? Excited for the ball?" he asked with a hint of amusement.

"I have heard great news," Ben said. "Apparently Lord Curzon has asked for Lady Alice's hand in marriage. Their betrothal will be announced later tonight at the ball."

Caleb's eyebrows rose. With this latest news and the way Ben's face was lit up, Caleb only thought of one thing. This was a great step forward for Ben. This marriage announcement brought up the possibility of the youngest sister receiving a proposal. Lady Alice was soon to be wed.

It was only right for Lady Olive to be engaged next. And Caleb knew that Ben had been wanting to court her for some time. It would not be foolish to presume that Lady Olive would accept his hand in marriage shortly after hearing about her sister getting engaged. She was sure to be a little envious by now. Why had she not been proposed to yet? When was her prince coming to whisk her away?

Caleb was staring at him. Ben was smiling from ear to ear. Without him even needing to

tell Caleb why he was so happy, Caleb gripped Ben's shoulder. "Congratulations, my friend. This is your chance."

Ben nodded. "Indeed. I must hurry and ask her before someone else comes in my stead."

"Does Lady Olive fancy you?"

"I'm sure she does…At the previous ball, I tried my best to dance with her, but she was

escorted by someone else." Ben gave Caleb a serious look, then he broke out into laughter. "By the end of the night, we had only talked for a brief second. It wasn't much but it was enough."

Caleb chuckled. "Lady Olive is a very kind and sweet woman. And don't worry—when we danced, I am very sure that she knew what I was trying to do. We only talked about Lady Mercy. And at dinner, she was persistent in pushing Lady Mercy and I's marriage. Don't worry, Ben—she is kind as much as she is smart; she would be foolish not to accept your hand. I have a good feeling about this match."

"Yes, yes. I was only joking. I guess I am just nervous about how little we have interacted. But I am absolutely sure that it is her I want to marry. As you said, she is the most amiable daughter in the family. I cannot help but be wooed by her." Ben had a dreamy look on his face; Caleb couldn't remember the last time he saw his friend so infatuated with a girl.

Filled with renewed vigor, Caleb leveled Ben with a stern gaze. "Your assuredness for Lady Olive has revived me with determination. I will also try my best to impress Lady Mercy tonight so that she will agree to marry me without any objections."

It was imperative that he made this work with Lady Mercy. The benefits that would come out of this marriage far outweighed the amount of effort it would take to court a woman like Lady Mercy. The image was perfect: Caleb and Lady Mercy getting married; him taking on the title of duke, fulfilling his lifelong wish; Ben slipping a ring on the finger of the woman he had fallen in love with. With wealth, status, and his best friend becoming his family, Caleb would be the happiest man alive. The fact that this could become a reality soon made him thrilled. He could not wait any longer.

Tonight's ball would be unlike any other ball. Caleb could not be distracted by anything. His main focus would be Lady Mercy and her alone. She was the ticket to Caleb's wildest dreams. He only needed to charm her, make her fall in love with him, and everything would come pouring into his hands.

He tried to imagine what his ten-year-old self would think if he knew that in the future, his wishes had the possibility of coming true. Born into the lowest tier of the British nobility, Caleb had always felt like he wasn't worth anything. He had watched all the dukes of the ton with their riches, their fancy suits, and their pompous airs, where they only received flattery and thrived on it. He had watched them from a distance for the entirety of his life, and the jealousy inside him festered until it utterly consumed him. Caleb wanted, more than anything, to become like them. The desire to hold the highest title of nobility had seized his heart; he no longer wanted anything else.

Just then, Caleb saw his past self's eyes glimmer with hope. It had seemed like fantasy then. But now it would become a reality. Lady Mercy would give him her hand, and he would grab onto it for dear life. He would marry her and receive her father's dukedom. It was so close; Caleb could practically already feel her hands in his.

Though it would take time—he would gladly spend the rest of his time working to get what he truly wanted.

Ben snapped him out of his thoughts by clapping him on the side of his arm. He gave Caleb an earnest look. "I am sure that you'll be successful," Ben said. "I might have been wary before, but that was because I was worried that you might have been thinking too rashly. Now I see your ambition. I have never seen you so adamant on winning the heart of a girl. One day, you might understand why that is… Lady Mercy will come around to it."

With this, they both left the manor thinking happy thoughts. They hopped into the carriage and began their trip to the ball. Ben was staring out of the window and looking up into the sky, no doubt—based on his delighted face—thinking about how he would ask Lady Olive for a dance. On the other side, Caleb sat with a faint smile and a straight back.

Though he might have appeared confident on the outside, deep inside, his heart thundered wildly. For the rest of the night, his heart persisted like this, and he could not figure out why he was so nervous. He told himself that it was because of the unpredictability of what the night might bring, perhaps a setback or a small failure. He made excuses for his wariness, but he couldn't help but feel like there was another reason for his rapidly beating heart.

18

*L*ike all the others, the ball was extravagant in every sense of the word. A large, glittering chandelier hung from the high-domed ceiling; mosaic tiles appeared in flashes as dresses swayed in movement; and sparks of light glinted from champagne flutes, the clinking of silverware penetrating the room. A plethora of people mingled around the expansive room, and Mercy was immediately overwhelmed.

Olive and Alice stuck to both of her sides, pulling her arm this way and that, from one group of people to another. Their father followed diligently behind them, allowing the girls to do as they pleased. They curtsied and exchanged pleasantries, and it was all a façade as Mercy tried to appear as if she wasn't about to keel over and spill the contents of her stomach on the pristine floor.

There were too many people, and the music was too loud. The quartet sat in the balcony looking over the dance floor, so the musical notes echoed throughout the entire room. Mercy swore her ears were ringing. To make things worse, she could practically hear everyone speaking around her. Obnoxious words from obnoxious people. There wasn't any substance in what they were saying; Mercy had no time for it.

Mercy looked at her two sisters and wondered what they found appealing about this. Olive looked vibrant as always; soft eyes and soft smiles were given to the people they greeted, who all seemed to adore her. Mercy could understand that. Olive White was the youngest and the sweetest, and she was the most approachable out of the three sisters. She knew how to talk to people, and everyone loved her.

Mercy wondered what it would be like to be like her little sister: Open to love.

On the other side, Mercy saw Alice look completely distracted. She seemed to be craning her neck trying to find someone. Her eyes flit back and forth, moving from one face to another. A man had come up to her, bowing and introducing himself. Alice had simply nodded her head curtly, then began looking around the room again. The men quickly realized that she was not interested in talking to them anymore and left.

Maybe I should act like I'm distracted and looking for

someone else...that'll get the men to stay away, Mercy pondered to herself with a nod.

"Lady Alice!"

It was as if she had absorbed all the light in the room. Alice grinned widely and took off in a random direction, leaving Mercy and Olive to stare in her wake. Lord Curzon was approaching them with a big smile of his own. He wore a black coat, with a long coattail behind his legs. A puffed white cravat circled his neck, a stark contrast to his auburn hair that was long enough to be tied in a low ponytail. His stunning features seemed to elevate significantly the longer he stared at Alice. Perhaps love could do that to someone.

He bowed in an exaggerating manner, which caused Alice to giggle.

Then they began whispering to one another, so Mercy could not hear what they were giggling about. They were glued together, though they were not outwardly touching. If eyes had bodies of their own, Lord Curzon and Alice would be embracing each other until the end of time. The longer Mercy observed them from afar, the more that feeling in her chest ached. Alice seemed to be rambling about something—a habit of hers whenever she was overcome with giddiness—and Lord Curzon admired her, all whilst listening intently.

At that moment, Mercy was incredibly happy for them.

That was when she remembered the announcement they would be giving tonight, and she marched toward the two. She felt a little bad about breaking up their moment, but she needed to ask.

"Lord Curzon," she greeted. "When will you be announcing the betrothal?"

He finally tore his eyes from Alice and bowed his head in greeting. "Lady Mercy, you look very pretty tonight. I will give the announcement soon, just after all the guests arrive."

Mercy nodded in understanding before her eyes practically bulged from their sockets. *There are going to be* more *guests coming?* It looked as if the whole town was at the ball! She tried to ignore the suffocating presence of all the people around her. Olive didn't appear aggrieved by this unfortunate news; in fact, she seemed delighted. More guests meant more time to talk and introduce herself to people. Mercy grimaced. How could two sisters be so different?

Just then, Mercy's chest squeezed tight, and it wasn't because of her claustrophobia.

Lord Griffiths entered the room, along with Lord Morris, who seemed to always be glued to his side. She remembered seeing both of them together in the past. At the time she hadn't given them another spare glance, but times had changed significantly. Right as they entered the ball, Mercy noticed a lot of different things.

First, Lord Griffiths looked more handsome, if that was even possible. His dark hair tumbled over his forehead, with a stray strand falling into his eyes, giving him a disheveled look that separated him from all the other distinguished men in the room. But it was not a bad thing. If anything, it made him more noticeable. He was also very tall, standing over most people. Mercy could move in any direction, and she would always be able to see him. It was a curse as much as it was a blessing. She was not so foolish to think he was anything but attractive.

Second, Lord Morris was handsome as well, though he was not any more handsome than Lord Griffiths. His blonde hair was slicked back, exposing his soft features. His blue eyes were so bright; they were apparent from his pale skin. He was just under an inch shorter than Lord Griffiths, but he was still tall, nonetheless. Mercy also noticed that he was staring in her direction.

She felt Olive shift beside her. Then, a startling revelation hit her.

Olive and Lord Morris?

Before Mercy could ask Olive anything, Lord Griffiths and Lord Morris were already heading toward them. She didn't have any time to panic before they appeared right in front of them. The two men bowed low to the duke, who had walked forward to stand beside Mercy.

The men exchanged their greetings, and Lord Griffiths introduced Lord Morris as his close friend.

Throughout the entire interaction, Lord Morris kept glancing, rather obviously, at Olive. He was standing so that he was close to her; his body positioned itself so that every time he talked, he could surreptitiously inch nearer to her. Mercy raised a brow as she watched his apparent interest in Olive. She was about to tell him to back away but was shocked to see that Olive was blushing profusely. She liked him! Her eyelashes fluttered against her cheeks as she glanced at the floor shyly. Her pink cheeks were round as a smile split across her face. After a few seconds, she was able to look up at Lord Morris.

When their eyes connected, electrifying energy hit the air; even Mercy could feel it!

Had Mercy been stuck in her head so much that she hadn't noticed their insurmountable interest in one another?

When had this happened?

Mercy suddenly felt awful for not paying close attention to her baby sister.

If they liked each other, then there was a possibility of there being another betrothal. What if Lord Morris was Olive's dream man? Alice had already found hers, and now it was obviously Olive's turn.

Mercy gnawed on her lip. Both of her sisters' dreams now hung in the balance of Mercy's decision. She would have to get married soon…

As soon as that thought hit her, she remembered Lord Griffiths' presence right next to her. Her stomach clenched, and she tried not to show the nervousness on her face.

"Good evening," she managed to say before curtsying. It was an awkward movement of limbs, where she almost stumbled in her shoes and fell forward into another lady's dress. Lord Griffiths' hand shot out as if to grab her, but Mercy instinctually backed away before she realized.

If Lord Griffiths noticed, he didn't show it. "Careful," he chuckled.

Mercy winced. She had dreaded this moment. In her head, it was easy to say that she would try with him and give him a chance. It was easy to assert her determination and to just think that there could be a possibility of them getting married in the near future. But the moment she saw him enter the room, Mercy knew how difficult that would be. His presence was intimidating. The energy between them had changed since the dinner. She didn't know what, just that there was something tense hanging in the air as he stared at her. She had no idea how to react to him.

Saving her from the torture of finding something else to say, Lord Griffiths gave her his arm and asked silently for her to walk with him.

Before, Mercy would have balked at the idea. She would have cursed at him or threatened him for thinking that he had the audacity to touch her. But that was before. Now, she found herself hesitating before tentatively wrapping her hand around the crook of his elbow. She had never allowed any man to escort her—except her father.

This was foreign to her, so she did not know why she had agreed to do it this time without arguing.

Still, Lord Griffiths gave her a look of pleasure before gently pulling her forward.

In the garden, they had walked just like this: Her hand on his arm and him leading the way. She remembered the warmth of his presence, and it felt the same way now. It seemed as if he was a walking torch, a beacon in a dark, suffocating tunnel. And as they continued to walk through the crowd, Mercy realized that she hadn't thought about the large number of people surrounding her since the moment Lord Griffiths had entered the room.

For a single moment, Mercy felt as if the whole room had cleared, and it was just him and her.

But that was a stupid thought, so Mercy waved it away.

They approached a group of people, to whom Lord Griffiths greeted politely. He introduced Mercy, then engaged in fruitless conversation. Mercy immediately tuned it all out. This proceeded for a couple more minutes, which seemed to drone on for hours. Each time, Lord Griffiths behaved with an air of politeness, neither arrogant nor pompous. Every time a man said something with a hint of rudeness in his tone, Lord Griffiths brushed it off easily. Mercy had gritted her teeth to stop herself from reprimanding the man, but Lord Griffiths had squeezed her hand in reassurance.

As they walked away from one group, Mercy felt an

onslaught of eyes piercing the back of her head. She cast a look over her shoulder and saw a couple of women giving her a nasty look. They didn't even try to hide the suspicious looks on their faces.

Mercy straightened her back, suddenly apprehensive. *Why were they looking at her like that?* In the past, all the women of the ton gave looks of pity or confusion. They couldn't understand why the duke's eldest daughter was so adamant about rejecting the men giving her any attention.

But the looks they were giving her now were completely different. They weren't pity or confusion.

"Why are all the ladies looking at me like that?" she whispered.

She heard Lord Griffiths laugh softly. "They are just jealous."

"*Jealous?*"

"Yes—because I am not giving them any attention."

Mercy couldn't help but scoff. "Why should they be upset because you don't openly flirt with them?"

Lord Griffiths ignored the stab at his compulsive flirting habits. He smiled instead, and his eyes creased as he leveled Mercy with a direct look. "I think I understand how they feel. To want someone's attention so badly."

The grimace on Mercy's face immediately fell as Lord Griffiths stared at her. He was only looking at her—no one else. She forgot about the scornful looks from the other women. A warm feeling flooded her chest; she had to look away to hide the blush on her cheeks. *Why is it suddenly so hot in this room?*

She didn't want to admit it, but she felt a little flattered. Mercy had called him a compulsive flirt the first time they had talked with each other, and she meant what she said. However, as they walked together through the room, she realized that he had not spared another woman a single glance tonight. He had greeted them respectfully, then dismissed himself.

Mercy was the only one whom he truly spoke to.

And that revelation was a heavy weight in her heart.

"Lady Mercy, if I may ask..." Lord Griffiths said, hesitating at first. If Mercy was foolish, she would think that he was shy! "What are your likes? Your dislikes?"

Mercy blinked. She had not expected him to ask that. Olive had told her the day after the previous ball that he had asked the same question to Olive when they danced. Perhaps he just wanted to hear the answer from Mercy herself. That made her feel a little appreciative.

"What do you like to do in your free time?" He asked.

Mercy paused to think before answering. "I like to read."

Lord Griffiths' face lit up. "Me too! Wordsworth has my heart, though Coleridge can be hard to beat."

Mercy's eyes widened slightly. She listened attentively as Lord Griffiths began to talk about all the literary scholars and poets he deemed to be the world's founding authors.

His face brightened the more he talked, and Mercy was startled to learn that he was well-versed in the literary world. As he continued to give his input, Mercy agreed with everything he said. She didn't know how to feel about that.

Significantly impressed, Mercy and Lord Griffiths engaged in a long conversation about books and who they thought would change the trajectory of literature indefinitely. They found themselves agreeing on almost everything, and every time they disagreed on a certain opinion, they listened to each other's opinions.

By the time Mercy's father hushed the crowd by clinking his glass, Mercy realized that they had been talking for a very long time. Shockingly, she was a little upset about the disruption.

"Ladies and gentlemen," her father's voice boomed across the room. Everyone's eyes turned on him, immediately quiet and attentive. "I have very big news that I would like to announce. As a duke, it is a wish for our legacies to pursue through generations. And as a father, it is a wish for our children to be happy. I am very glad to say that both of my wishes are beginning to come true. Ladies and gentlemen...please give jubilant applause for my daughter Alice White and Lord Curzon...on their betrothal!"

A couple of gasps flew around the room before a triumphant roar of applause vibrated the floor. Mercy watched as everyone flooded toward the couple, congratulating them with bright smiles and handshakes. Alice and

Lord Curzon appeared to be in paradise. Their faces were flushed, and Mercy thought for a second that Alice might be crying.

Everyone in the room was happy.

Just then, Lord Griffiths lowered his head and turned so that his lips were right by her ear. He murmured so that only she could hear. "This could be us, if only you agree to it. We could be just as happy as them—perhaps even more."

Mercy felt how close he was to her; they were practically touching. Her heart drummed in her chest wildly, and she couldn't calm it down. It seemed to have a mind of its own, and it was currently thinking that Lord Griffiths was very, *very* close to her. And as soon as his words registered in her head, her face heated up like the sun.

Before she could say anything in response, the floor cleared, and the quartet began a romantic piece. The maids snuffed out a few candles so that the room would have low, dim lighting, emitting an amorous aura for the dancing couples.

One by one, people walked onto the dance floor and positioned themselves appropriately. Lord Griffiths tugged on Mercy's arm and asked softly, "Dance with me?"

Mercy nodded without thinking, and he whisked her away before she could take it back. They floated toward the dance floor, followed by Lord Morris and Olive and Lord Curzon, who already had Alice in his arms.

As the dance began, all of the couples moved fluidly, all of them floating around the floor, the ladies' dresses flying around like spinning umbrellas, and the man leading them with assuredness and confidence.

Just as Mercy placed her hand in Lord Griffiths' to begin the dance, it was as if all the nerves bunched inside her loosened. This she understood. She was a fantastic dancer; her sisters did not lie about that. Knowing the foot patterns and when to spin and how to pull and be pulled by one's dance partner were skills that she could fathom.

So, before Lord Griffiths could get prepared, Mercy was already pulling him along, leading him without realizing it. She danced with such precision that it was hard for one to keep up with her. Before, when she had begrudgingly acquiesced to a man's request to dance—he had likely been bothering her for much too long, so she had to do something—she had moved quickly, her movements sharp and smooth. She was a professional. The man inevitably gave up halfway through, going out into the hallway to vomit in a nearby plant.

Mercy expected Lord Griffiths to react the same way— but she felt his hand tighten in hers. Her eyes widened as he tugged her to his chest. He gave her a wink before flinging her outwards and then back to his body. Her hair flew in her face from his speed. Then, he flicked his wrist, and she separated from him. Their arms snapped in place, and they twirled around the dance floor, their eyes never straying from one another.

They danced together perfectly; their movements were in sync and coordinated, such that it likely seemed that they had rehearsed this dance. But they hadn't. They just immediately fell into place, as if they were always meant to be partners.

Mercy then realized, when he tipped her backward, that the entire dance floor was empty. Everyone's eyes were on them—*only* them. They were the only couple dancing. She could hear a few people clapping and a scattering of cheers. She could also feel the penetrating glares from a couple of women standing on the outskirts of the dance floor.

Mercy was not used to this much attention; she almost stopped dancing.

Lord Griffiths must have noticed because he brought her closer to him with a speed that made her lose her breath. They were so close that their noses almost touched.

"Don't look at them," he said. "Look at me."

So Mercy did.

19

Mercy could feel her skin beginning to sweat. Suddenly, her hair stuck to the back of her neck and her forehead; she felt her clammy hands slip from Lord Griffiths' hold; the dress that fit so comfortably back at home seemed to tighten on her body. The dance droned on and on until all Mercy heard was the quartet's crescendo and her quick breathing.

This had all happened the moment she realized that the entire ballroom was focused on them. Before, she moved with the grace of a practiced performer, letting the melodic music guide her arms and feet. This was why she danced well. She did not have to think; she did not have to rely on her mind to know which foot stepped forward and which hand gripped her partners. It was instinctual.

However, when she saw everyone's eyes on her, everything had stopped. Reality dawned on her, and she remembered where she was and *who* she was dancing with.

Mercy had not danced with another man in a very long time, so it would come as no surprise to see the shocked and expectant look on the guests' faces. Judging by their rapt attention, Mercy assumed that she would be the talk of the ton for the next few weeks. And that thought alone made her sweat profusely.

Lord Griffiths' words tried to bring her back into the moment, to bring her back into the blissful moment where a blanket of calm had descended on her. *Look at me*, he had said. Focus on the dance partner, not the crowd. But Mercy couldn't.

She felt incredibly self-conscious, aware of every movement she made now and how she might look.

Lord Griffiths must have noticed because she felt his grip tighten on her hand and waist. It should have felt like a weight bringing her back down to earth and out of her head, but it didn't work. Mercy was always on the sidelines during these balls, standing by the wall with nothing but a drink in hand and an occasional pastry she managed to grab from a passing servant. This time, she stood in the center of the room, on the dance floor, with Lord Griffiths as her partner. And everyone was watching, no doubt thinking to themselves: *Who does she think she is? Mercy White—isn't she the daughter who has refused every other man? Perhaps she just wants to take the attention away from her younger sister.*

These troubling thoughts bombarded Mercy's head like a mantra. She knew that this was derived from the deepest part of her subconscious, that perhaps *she* was the one thinking this way. Based on the looks thrown her way, however, Mercy could argue that they shared the same sentiment as her.

Finally, after what seemed to last an eternity, the music came to an end. Mercy's ears were ringing by then, so she couldn't hear if anyone clapped or not. All she could focus on was the rapid rise and fall of her chest and a little fluff of a feather that had probably fallen from one of the guest's dresses. She homed in on those details before Lord Griffiths' gingerly placed his hand on the small of her back, guiding her off the dance floor.

Mercy kept her eyes lowered as Lord Griffiths' led her out of the stuffy room and onto the balcony. The fresh air was a welcome reprieve from the suffocating atmosphere inside. She took in a deep breath, and, before she knew it, she was at the very edge of the balcony, leaning over the railing. She looked up at the night sky and saw constellations of stars glittering in the darkness. They glittered and winked, and Mercy could not count how many there were because there were so many. And she wondered why that didn't matter to her. In the ballroom, the pressing bodies of the guests made her feel sick and uncomfortable as if she was being observed and judged. With the stars, there could be a million or a billion of them staring down at her, and she would feel *seen*.

Mercy took another deep breath and closed her eyes. Before she knew it, she was breathing normally, and her skin had cooled down.

She would have loved to stay out here forever, gazing up into the night and thinking about everything and nothing at all. There was no one here to judge her, no reminders of the responsibilities constantly weighing her down, and fake people with their fake smiles. She would love to live out here on the balcony.

Then she heard someone shift behind her, their shoes scuffing the floor, and Mercy remembered that Lord Griffiths' had accompanied her. The reminder of his presence suddenly made her blood roar, and she began to grow hot.

Anger, unlike anything she'd felt before, surged through her. She quickly spun around and gave Lord Griffiths a glare that she knew had once made Olive and Alice cry; it was the same look that she gave them when they repeatedly ignored her orders.

The only hint that Lord Griffiths had felt her penetrating glare was his throat bobbing up and down, gulping nervously. He then approached her freely and reached out to grab her hand, but she flinched away.

"Your sisters were right," he said, speaking softly in a

tentative way. "You are a terrific dancer, and you should be proud of yourself."

Mercy clenched her jaw. "Have you lost your mind?" Her voice was low-pitched, and her words were slow. This feeling, she realized, was more intense than when Olive and Alice had disobeyed her. This was *real* anger.

"This," she said, "is *all* your fault. Since the moment you entered my life, I have been ravaged by the most annoying headache. Every day, it seems, I cannot get a break from it."

Lord Griffiths opened his mouth to say something, but Mercy cut him off. "You shouldn't have entered my life in the first place. You shouldn't have danced with Olive and asked her those questions. You shouldn't have met me in those woods, and I shouldn't have gone hunting that day. Every time I talk with you, my head buzzes, and my chest hurts! I have never felt this...sick in my entire life!" Her voice was rising in volume, but she didn't care. She needed to somehow describe all these indescribable feelings that had been tormenting her these past few days. "Lord Griffiths, you are a liar. A *liar*. I know you do not love me at all —you are only playing games so that you may ridicule me in front of everyone!"

By now, a large crowd had formed around the entrance of the balcony. Multiple guests were almost spilling outside, looking aghast. Mercy was so loud that her voice rang in the air. The music had stopped. No one else talked; they were now listening. A few ladies hid behind their gloved hands, giving each other occasional shocked glances. They were all no doubt gossiping about Mercy's circumstances and ridiculing her for it.

But, for once, Mercy didn't focus on their stares and unbridled judgment. She just wanted to let it all out, and the frustration and anger in her body begged to be released. So, she continued her onslaught of accusations.

"You are fake, just like the rest of them! And I know, and I fear, that you will try to make me believe otherwise—by trying to talk to me, by smiling at me, by confessing to me over and over again, and by dancing with me. But, at the end of the day, it is all for naught. Because I *cannot* care!"

"Lady Mercy," Lord Griffiths managed to say as Mercy took a second to breathe. "Please, calm down. Let us go somewhere more private to talk."

"There is no privacy in this world! If I eat eggs in the morning, the ladies in the ton will know by the end of the day which chicken the eggs were harvested from and bet on how I might not fit into my dress the following day. If I trip down the stairs, the men will regard me as a clumsy woman, and make that the reason why I had rejected them every single time they approached me at a ball. Lord Griffiths, you should know that there is no privacy in a society like ours. You are a despicable man with despicable intentions, and I know you intend to show all my misfortunes to the world."

"Lady Mercy—"

"You must like the fact that everyone is watching us right at this very moment, don't you? You thrive on attention. And they will all see me as the villain, and you as the downtrodden hero. You will always triumph, and I will always fall. I am sick and tired of bearing such responsibilities!"

Lord Griffiths' eyes had widened significantly; his jaw had slackened. It was so quiet, it seemed that even the insects had stopped chirping and buzzing. Mercy could not stop the words from flooding out. She thought it would feel good as everything in her chest was exposed, but she only felt worse. The way Lord Griffiths was looking at her made her feel anything but satisfied. Her words were the truth, but she didn't know if she was telling the right person.

Just then, there was a loud commotion from the crowd. As Mercy spared them a glance, she saw a few guests step aside and a path opened for two girls to march through. Mercy was astonished to see Olive and Alice barreling toward her, their skirts bunched in their hands and their forehead scrunched with worry.

Olive was the first to make it to Mercy, and her hands immediately gripped Mercy's shoulder. Alice was next; she breathed heavily as she reached for Mercy's hand. Seeing her two baby sisters should have helped extinguish the flame of anger inside her, but it seemed to only fuel it.

"Mercy, what are you doing?" Olive asked. "What is all this ruckus about?"

Alice sighed. "Let's go. Don't make any more of a scene, okay?"

Mercy's lips wobbled and the vein in her forehead pulsed as she tore away from her sisters. A look of complete shock appeared on their faces, but Mercy didn't care. She stepped away from them and spoke to them in a manner that she had never done before. It was of complete heartbreak and a week's worth of contained frustration barreling out.

"You are the selfish ones," she said, and Olive and Alice both gasped, taken aback. "It

has been so troubling for me—to endure all of these responsibilities. I want...I just want to *want*. But all of my desires seem fruitless. I do not have time for myself anymore, and it was always about you and you. It is never about *me*. And I don't think you understand how draining that can be. Truly. You are both so happy, and I—I find myself thinking, in the deepest parts of the night when it is just myself alone, that I don't think I can ever be happy just for myself. And you are both selfish for making me feel that way."

Olive and Alice were stunned, so much so that they were paralyzed on the spot. The color had been drained from their face, and their eyes were perpetually widened. And for a horrible moment, Mercy was scared that she had ruined everything. She was scared about where all of these thoughts had come from and how *true* they were. She couldn't lie anymore, put a smile on her face, and do things that she hated. She wanted them to know everything and sometimes reality hurt.

"Nobody cares about what I want," Mercy muttered, her voice cracking. "Sometimes, I feel as if both of you are not my sisters but Lord Griffiths' accomplices. You never think about my happiness at all. That hurts me, because I love you both so much, the most in the whole world. But you don't love me at all."

Her voice had lowered in volume by the end, but her words still held a bite to them that made everyone flinch back. She felt irrevocably broken as if she had laid all the pieces of herself bare before them, and she didn't know if anyone would dare pick up the pieces to put her back together again.

Another person entered the balcony, and Mercy immediately burst into tears. She let the tears fall freely because, in the presence of her father, nothing really mattered. He rushed forward and enveloped her in an embrace. He didn't even have to say anything before pulling her inside, away from the balcony, away from everyone.

As they left, Mercy thought about how everything she said was true, and she had never felt more real than in that moment. She had said what she had to say, but perhaps she had said the truth in the worst way possible.

But Mercy only knew how to deal with anger, and that was the saddest truth of all.

20

The carriage door had only slightly opened when Mercy jumped out and rushed into the house. She stumbled up the stairs and dove into her bedchamber, her movements fast and messy, though she had no regard for how crazy she may have appeared.

She took great heaving gasps, but it didn't stop the tears from spilling. She covered her face with her arm, trying to stifle the sobs; when was the last time she had cried this hard? Not even when her mother had passed—that day, she had to appear strong, not wracked with sadness, for her sisters. During the funeral, not a single tear had dropped.

No, this type of physical reaction, where she couldn't breathe and could only cry, was due solely to the humiliation. Back at the ball, she had screamed at Lord Griffiths in such a way that no lady had ever behaved in public. An entire crowd had circled them, watching both of them out on the balcony. Every single one of her words was digested, picked apart, and judged.

You are fake, just like the rest of them!

Mercy buried her face in the covers. Suddenly everything she said echoed in her ear like a horrible herald. *This is the end of your life, Mercy,* she cursed herself. *Everything you said is the reason why you will be hated forever.*

The ball, the lights, the people, Lord Griffiths, her sister's engagement—they all jumbled together and prodded at Mercy until she cracked and exploded. It was so overwhelming that everyone had seen her outburst, ultimately seeing her true nature. At the time, Mercy knew that everything she said was true. She didn't think that she would feel better saying those things; she didn't think at all. Everything had just come out of her mouth, like they were venomous thoughts she had swallowed. Subconsciously, Mercy needed to get all the bitterness out of her in the hopes of feeling better. But this wasn't the way, and she should have known better.

The shock on Lord Griffiths' face and the horror on Olive and Alice's faces would haunt Mercy for the rest of her life.

She thought that she was telling the truth, but she said those things in a severely inappropriate way. In such a way that made everyone even more scared and warier of her. She should not have gone to such an extent. It was as if they were at the theater, and she was the number one act of the night. There was certainly an audience for it. In their eyes, she was the ruthless villain attacking innocent civilians.

And they will all see me as the villain, and you as the downtrodden hero.

She had said that with such vigor that Lord Griffiths had reeled backward, as if he had been hit squarely in the face. Those words were certainly correct, and, in retrospect, Mercy could see herself portrayed as such. An embarrassing villain acting in an embarrassing way. She was screaming so loud that the music had stopped. There was not a single sound to be heard, only Mercy's projected voice, echoing in the distance, her biting words ringing in the air.

Lord Griffiths had tried to calm her down, to speak in a more private setting. Thinking back on it now, Mercy realized in shame that he had been trying to protect her reputation. But instead, Mercy had screamed at him some more.

She had messed up.

And her sisters—Mercy had *hurt* them. She wondered what they were doing now—what they were thinking. They had to hate her now. They had only wanted to help, to calm Mercy down, but she had pushed them away and called them *selfish*.

The tears became a flood, and Mercy had to keep quiet because she had already been too loud tonight. So she stifled her tears, and they came out in choked sobs that wracked her whole body. But she couldn't stop crying. She had promised her mother that she would protect her sisters and ensure their happiness. Since that unforgettable day, Mercy had decided that she would be their protector, but tonight, she had broken that promise. She might as well have spat in her face with the way they looked at Mercy. Horror and shock and hurt pulled their faces. Mercy had *caused* those expressions. How could she ever apologize to them?

It was Alice's engagement announcement this evening, and of course, Mercy had to ruin the celebration with her offensiveness. Alice had looked so happy, with Lord Curzon embracing her and the cheers from the crowd goading them on. It was her moment. And Mercy had snatched that spotlight away from her.

At that moment, Mercy hated herself.

How could she be so selfish?

Why couldn't she keep all those tormenting thoughts to herself? Mercy had no idea what had come over her to say all those things. Usually, Mercy was skilled enough to keep it inside, but tonight something had caved in, cracked a little chip in her stone-cold façade, and a flood of emotions had come barreling out, hurting everyone near her.

How many people did she have to hurt in the hopes of feeling good about herself?

Suddenly there was a knock on the door, and, before Mercy could open her mouth to

deny anyone entry, her father had already walked into the bedchamber.

His face was that of complete solemnity. His brows were pulled down; he seemed to have more wrinkles, and even his usually brown hair was beginning to gray. The Duke of Norfolk seemed to have aged ten years in the span of one night.

And Mercy did not doubt—not one single bit—that it was all her fault.

Her father sat down next to her with a grunt. He gave Mercy a look with pity written all over his face. Normally, Mercy hated being pitied. But it must have been because of the long night and what she had done because she fell forward and gave her father a huge embrace.

She squished her face into his neck; her shoulders shaking were the only telltale signs that she had begun to cry again. Her father rubbed circles on her back, and they sat like that for an indefinite amount of time. But neither of them complained.

After what seemed like an eternity, Mercy finally pulled away. She tried to wipe the tears away so that he wouldn't see her in such a horrid state, but it was too late. Her father's face softened, and he reached forward to palm her face.

"Do you want to tell me what happened back there?"

His voice was so soft that Mercy almost started sobbing again, but she held it back. "Why did you create such a scene?"

Mercy was already shaking her head before he could finish the sentence. "*I don't know,*" she said, and her voice cracked. "Everything happened so fast, and everyone was looking at me. I couldn't breathe. Then I said...those terrible things. I am so, so sorry."

"I shouldn't be the one receiving the apology," he sighed. "Caleb and your sisters deserve it."

"I cannot believe I called them fake and selfish. How could I..."

"Do not put yourself down like that. Honestly, it must have been hard for you; your sisters had unknowingly placed so much responsibility on your shoulders.," he said, his tone soft and gentle "You are not the monster here..."

"Of course I know that," Mercy said, exasperated. Her sisters were her sole priority in this world; there was no one who could ever take that away from her. Mercy loved them so much that she wanted to shrink them and hold them in her hands, so then perhaps they'd be spared from any harm. And she knew that what she felt was love because at the end of the day, she wanted them to be happy. And how could they be happy if they were imprisoned in Mercy's hands? Olive and Alice always came first.

But tonight, Mercy had put herself first, and that selfish act had cost all of them.

"I was not in my right senses when I called them selfish," Mercy confessed. *She* was the selfish one. "Never in my life have I acted in such a disgraceful manner; I am so embarrassed and upset, you cannot even imagine. I promise you, Father, I will make it up to Olive and Alice. Whatever it takes."

Her father sighed, and he looked so tired at that moment. Something panged in Mercy's chest, and she closed her eyes to quell the pain. Her actions had ruined almost everything; she had to make things right.

Whatever it takes.

First thing in the morning, Mercy entered the dining room, preparing to face her sisters and apologize to them directly. However, the moment she stepped inside, Olive and Alice stood from their chairs, causing them to screech against the tile flooring; Mercy flinched. They didn't even spare her a single glance before leaving.

Mercy's heart squeezed. They could not even *look* at her.

She should have known that what she did last night had hurt them deeply, but it still pained her to see them act as if Mercy didn't even exist.

The sisters had gotten into many fights, but they were always over trivial things. Once, Olive had worn Mercy's clothing without telling her, almost ripping them. They had argued for a couple of hours, but by the end of the day, the two sisters were glued to each other, talking joyously, as if their fight had never happened. Another time, Alice had gotten profusely angry over Mercy's countless rejections to dance at the balls. They didn't sit near each other at the dinner table, but after Alice asked quietly if Mercy thought the food tasted good, their relationship had smoothed over once again.

But never—in all their years—had her sisters ignored her outright. And it was made worse by the fact that their behavior was warranted. Mercy had humiliated them in public. What was supposed to be a fun, eventful night had taken a turn for the worse.

Still, Mercy would have much preferred for them to scream at her, rather than this cold shoulder.

There was no one more important to Mercy than her baby sisters. Without them, she wouldn't be able to find beauty in the world. Nothing could trump their happiness and their simple existence. To see them so affected by Mercy's horrible words made her irrevocably heartbroken.

She knew she had to fix what seemed to be unmendable pain.

So she left the dining room—she wasn't hungry anyway—and followed her sisters into the drawing room.

Olive and Alice were both reading on the couches, their eyes glued to the pages. They did not even flinch when

Mercy barged through the doors. They went about their routines as if nothing had happened.

Mercy couldn't handle it any longer. "*Please*—Please look at me! Olive, Alice, I'm sorry. I'm so, so sorry about last night. None of what I said was true. I don't even know why I said that…"

Alice sighed, appearing as if Mercy's apology hadn't fazed her, not one bit. "Olive, did you hear something?"

"Stop. Please," Mercy expressed. "Just look at me. Stop acting like I'm not right in front of you, apologizing."

A couple of seconds passed, and Mercy thought they were the longest seconds recorded in history. But then, miraculously, Olive and Alice both lifted their heads. Nothing changed in their blank reflections, which stung Mercy. But they were looking at her. And that was all that mattered.

"Well, Mercy," Olive began, "if you deem us so selfish, why don't you stay away from us and live your own life? Isn't that what you really want? To be rid of the burden of our presence?"

"That's not true, and you know it."

"That's what I *thought* was true," Alice said, and a ripple of anger overcame her face. It was the first hint of emotion since last night. "But apparently not, because you seemed very impassioned on the balcony. You shoved us away."

Mercy fisted her skirt so they wouldn't see her hands shaking. "I was not in my right senses, therefore none of what I said was meaningful. I didn't even know what I was saying. Believe me."

Olive shook her head, and Alice went back to reading her book.

"Please!"

"No!" Olive practically screamed.

Mercy reeled back in shock. Olive never screamed—not to anyone. There was a reason why she was deemed the kindest and sweetest sister of the three. No matter how angry she was, she would never resort to yelling or violence. Soft as a pillow, Olive White would never hurt a fly.

But at that moment, when Olive had screamed in anger for the first time, Mercy was scared.

"No," Olive repeated, but her voice was shaking. "I—*we*—refuse to believe your lies. Not anymore. So do us a favor and stop talking to us. My head hurts from trying to figure out which of your words are truths and which are lies. Frankly, I don't have time to decipher the difference."

Alice nodded, her eyes still on the book. "You don't even deserve someone as sweet and kind as Lord Griffiths. Because at the end of the day, *you* are the selfish one, Mercy." Her eyes snapped up to meet Mercy. "Not me, not Olive, it has always been *you*. You only care about yourself."

Mercy would later look back on this heart-wrenching moment and know that Alice's last words were what caused her to completely break apart. *You only care about yourself.*

Perhaps that was true, and everything Mercy had ever done was selfishness veiled as a selfless act. For her entire life, she may have acted in a way that she thought was for Olive and Alice, but instead, it was for herself. Hearing her sisters speak so foully about her made Mercy cave in.

She fell to her knees, and she broke down.

A flood of tears streamed down her face. There was so many that she choked on the tears, and she couldn't breathe. Broken gasps made her body convulse, and her face was heating up. She had never felt so horrible than in that second.

A second.

Yes, it only took a single second for Mercy to tear in two for the first time in what seemed like her entire life.

Through her blurry vision, Mercy could see two figures tumbling towards her, arms outstretched. After another blink, she could see more clearly the distraught faces of her two sisters. Shock marred their features. Their eyes were blown wide open, their lips were moving; perhaps they were speaking, or they were shouting something at her.

They were worried.

And seeing this familiar emotion was such a relief that Mercy almost smiled. She pulled their arms and dragged them into her embrace. She felt them stiffen for a second, and Mercy almost pulled back. *They hate you,* she reprimanded herself. *Why would you hug them?*

But before she could apologize, Olive and Alice held her tight, and she felt tears drip on her own shoulders.

They were crying.

And they were not silent about it either. They wailed and wailed and wailed, and all three sisters cried until there were no more tears left.

"I didn't mean what I said!" Olive moaned.

"I don't even know why I said that!" Alice echoed.

"Me too," Mercy replied. "*Me too.*"

They had all said such terrible things to one another—all of them false—that it felt like such a relief to say something true for once.

21

*L*unch went better than breakfast.

Olive and Alice were back to normal as if nothing had happened between the three of them. Olive rambled about how much she wished for the next ball to come sooner, and Alice spoke with stars in her eyes about Lord Curzon. As they both took their turns talking, Mercy listened to them with complete focus, soaking in everything they said like she couldn't live without it.

She must have been focusing too much, though, because shortly after lunch, Mercy felt her head pounding. A headache was coming on. She tried to go to the drawing room with her sisters to read, but after a couple of minutes of staring at the book, stuck on the same sentence, she knew that she had to get out of the house.

Mercy was thankful that she was able to reconcile with

her sisters, but her other problems concerning Lord Griffiths were still hanging in the air, looming over her as a reminder of what she had done last night.

Pressing the heel of her hands to her eyes, Mercy slowly stood up from the couch.

"Are you all right?" Olive asked, worry piercing her eyes.

"Yes—well, no. I need to get some fresh air." And with that, Mercy trudged out the door, leaving behind two concerned sisters. Before she knew it, she was leaving the back door and walking toward the stables. Apple whinnied when Mercy patted her back. Once she was saddled, Mercy threw herself onto Apple and urged her to go forward, into the woods.

As they walked, Mercy took a deep breath. The pine scent and chill in the air was a welcome reprieve from the suffocating heat inside the manor. The past few days, she had been stuck inside the house or at the ball, surrounded by walls that seemed to close in on her. Being outside and feeling the wind caress her cheeks made Mercy feel less trapped, and for once, she could be free.

It seemed that the horrifying memory of last night had slowly eased further into her mind, and Mercy could concentrate on something else. The twitter of a bird or the flutter of its wings. The leaves rustling as a rabbit hops from one log to another. A frog's croak. A small river streaming down the bank somewhere in the far distance. Apple's breathing. Mercy's breathing.

They all coalesced together to form a symphony that calmed Mercy's heartbeat.

This was her home, a safe place for her to just simply exist without the burden of messing up and ruining her family's entire reputation.

Then suddenly, Apple stopped walking.

"What's wrong, girl?" Mercy asked as she was pulled out of her daze.

Apple bent down to chew on the grass; Mercy was about to scold her horse when her eyes caught on something dark between the trees.

Then she heard another pair of hoofbeats.

"Who's there?" She called out.

In response, a familiar white stallion walked through the trees, along with a familiar man wearing dark outdoor clothes.

When she saw Lord Griffiths, she swore her heart stopped beating.

His timing was impeccable as always. She was out in the woods for the sole reason of not being able to apologize to him, and here he was: Right in front of her. Mercy had wanted to practice her apology speech before meeting Lord Griffiths; she wanted to rehearse her words so that she would be able to express her emotions clearly. And since she had hurt him the most last night, she wanted her apology to be perfect.

But now, he was here.

It was too late. She needed to talk to him, and her apology would have to be completely made up on the spot. Mercy's heart started to beat rapidly again. What should she say? What was the appropriate response? She couldn't run away now; he had already seen her. She needed to toughen up and pay for the repercussions of her own mistakes. She was done running away.

It was as if Lord Griffiths had seen all these emotions overcome her face because he let out a soft laugh and gently eased down from his horse. *Johnny*, Mercy remembered. *That was his horse's name.* His eyes weren't filled with vengeance and resentment; he stared at her the same way he had every other time: With affection and endearment. Mercy would admit that she was shocked. She had expected him to hold a grudge against her, just like her sisters. She expected him to curse at her and never speak to her again. She expected him to act as if he had never had any feelings for her.

Perhaps that was why she had such a pounding migraine earlier.

Just the thought of Lord Griffiths behaving as if Mercy never even existed made her body almost shut down.

She didn't want to think about *why* this might be.

Realizing that she was still on top of Apple, she deftly

swung down and landed with an *oomph*. She was always clumsy when she was nervous.

They walked toward each other—Lord Griffiths moving smoothly and Mercy stumbling forward—until they both stood directly in front of one another. Mercy realized then that they were alone again, just the two of them in the wide expanse of the trees stretching for miles and miles. And it seemed, they were the only two people to exist at that moment. It was exactly like the first time they had spoken to each other without her father and her sisters.

Mercy cringed thinking about it. That time, she had exploded and shouted obscene things at him as well.

This time, the air between them was not taut with tension. This time, there was a more nervous energy. Mercy could feel her face warming up, and she couldn't find her voice. *Was she shy?* Mercy's eyes widened slightly. She couldn't be shy at a time like this! She needed to apologize to him and get it over with, make sure he knew that what she said wasn't true. She needed to act appropriately.

But he was so close to her, and his eyes were trained on hers, never once looking away.

An eternity seemed to pass before Mercy parted her lips and spoke, her tone soft. "Lord Griffiths, I want to apologize—about everything that happened last night. Everything I said. I should not have embarrassed you like that, especially in front of everyone." Mercy wrung her hands together, feeling her palms perspire with each passing second. She wanted to say more, but she couldn't find the words. *This is why I needed to rehearse*, Mercy thought to herself. *I need him to understand.*

Lord Griffiths did not answer immediately, which made Mercy droop down with shame. Of course, he wouldn't accept the apology. The first time she had apologized to Olive and Alice, they had ignored her outright, acting as if she wasn't in the room talking to them. It wasn't shocking for Lord Griffiths to do the same.

But, for some reason, it still hurt. And Mercy was about to apologize again for apologizing, for thinking that she had the audacity to speak to him after belittling him in front of the entire ton.

However, she was interrupted by his abrupt question. "Can I hold your hands?"

The question was so sudden, so *different*, that Mercy was entirely speechless for a couple of seconds. His brows were lifted, his eyes gentle, and a smile curved his lips. Mercy thought, in that second, that she would let him do anything.

So she nodded and allowed him to intertwine his fingers with hers. She felt something flutter in her stomach, and she had a difficult time meeting his eyes. His hands were warm. Everything about him was warm. It was so warm, in fact, that Mercy swore the temperature had elevated somehow, and she was sweating.

If Lord Griffiths noticed her sweaty palms, he didn't

show it. He simply held her tighter. "I am not upset at all," he said suddenly, and Mercy's eyes snapped to his again, widening. "I can understand why you did that, saying all those things."

Confused, Mercy tilted her head. He responded by lowering them both down to the grass, sitting side by side. Their legs almost touched, but Mercy moved away. They were already breaking rules by interacting in solitude. She wouldn't touch him—well, except for his hands of course. That was required; Mercy came up with that rule.

They tilted their heads up to the sky and observed the ocean blue sky, seen between the slivers of the canopy of trees. A bird soared over them, squawking. It was such a simple moment, Mercy almost forgot that something serious was passing between her and Lord Griffiths. "I knew you were very tense and self-conscious last night," he began. "I would have been a fool to not see it. Everyone watching us dance together did not make things any better. And I gave you a lot of attention, and I didn't think about how overwhelming that would have been for you." His head hung down, and true regret dulled his eyes. "I should be the one apologizing for forcing you into the spotlight. Anyone would have been troubled in such a position; it is not your fault."

When he finished speaking, he looked her directly in the eyes, and Mercy didn't turn away. She didn't know that those words were the ones she desperately wanted to hear until he said them. *It is not your fault at all.* All Mercy did was blame herself. If she kept pushing this man away, she would be the reason why Olive and Alice would miss out on marrying the loves of their lives. *She* was the reason why everything had been ruined. *She* was the sole person responsible for their family's destiny.

Shouldering all these responsibilities had weighed her down more than she had noticed. It was when she finally heard those words—*not your fault*—that Mercy felt her shoulders lighten, and she could breathe.

And it was Lord Griffiths who had said them. The air between them changed, and it seemed as if everything had morphed from something small to something grand, grander than the two of them. Mercy looked at Lord Griffiths for the first time. And her heart thudded in her chest. The words that she had unknowingly been seeking were gifted to her from Lord Griffiths himself. Not from her sisters and not from her father.

For some reason, the fact that the words were from Lord Griffiths didn't bother her.

She finally felt seen for once.

And Lord Griffiths was certainly looking at her.

"I will be honest with you," Mercy said, and she was surprised to hear the

sincerity in her words. "I was very upset and embarrassed about what I did. I shouldn't have hurt you or my sisters like that. I love my sisters so much, truly. And I never imagined that I could be so mean to them."

"Have your sisters forgiven you?"

A soft smile appeared on her lips. "They have. And I am forever grateful for that; I wouldn't know what I would have done without their forgiveness. They are the sweetest creatures in the world, and I learned today how much they love me. They also understand that I love them, too, and that I would never hurt them on purpose—*ever*."

"You are lucky to have such a nice, loving family," Lord Griffiths replied, a warm look on his face. "You deserve all the love in the world."

Mercy tried not to dwell too much on his last sentence. If she did, her heart would truly stop. So instead, she expressed her gratitude. "Thank you for listening to me; I know it's not the most entertaining activity to do on such a lovely day," she laughed. "I never thought I would ever say this but...Lord Griffiths, you are a very kind person. I misjudged you. And again, I apologize for last night."

"I hold nothing against you," he assured. Then the smile fell from his lips, and he suddenly looked very serious. "I still love you very much. And I will wait for you—until you are ready to have me in your life. No matter how long it may take. Perhaps a decade, perhaps a century. I am a very patient man."

Mercy's face heated up instantly, and she tried to say something, but nothing came out. Ultimately, she decided on keeping quiet, hiding her blush behind the curtain of her long brown hair. *How could someone say such things with a straight face?* The sentiment was still foreign to her.

Seeing that she would not respond anytime soon, Lord Griffiths lived up to his patient nature and stood. He stretched out a hand, and she accepted it naturally, as if they had always held hands before. He pulled Apple's reins closer and helped Mercy onto her horse.

He gave her a simple nod and parted with a single glance—a glance that held a thousand words. One that voiced all his affection for her. Mercy didn't respond, as usual, and led Apple away, back toward Norfolk Manor.

And as they trotted home, Lord Griffiths' words rang in Mercy's head, over and over

again:

You deserve all the love in the world.

22

Caleb found himself watching Lady Mercy retreat to where she came from, disappearing through the slivers between the trees. Her long brown hair was loose, swaying behind her back as she trotted away. Something in his heart tugged.

Realizing that he had been staring for an awfully long time now, he shook his head and hopped onto his horse, Johnny. They, too, trotted back home, but it was not a quiet ride. His head was bombarded with a flurry of new thoughts. Images of Lady Mercy flashed in his mind: The relaxed look on her face; the sincerity in her eyes, a forest-green hue more beautiful than the wildlife around them; the smile on her lips that he wanted to hold still forever in a painting. Then it was her words. Caleb had received apologies from many different types of people, and they usually meant nothing at all. They were apologies meant to move on from a problem, not for the true reason of feeling sorry.

With Lady Mercy, however, Caleb could feel her palpable feelings. She had apologized, and he could see the truth not just in her quivering voice, but in the way she carried herself. She was usually the confident one, with her shoulders pushed back, chin high in the air so that she could look at someone by lowering her eyes, appearing above them. But when she had apologized a few minutes ago, she seemed to cave in on herself. She looked smaller. And there was nothing embarrassing about it. She was basically encumbered by the weight of her mistakes, and her apology held so much remorse that Caleb could not fathom anyone ever refusing to forgive her.

He would have fallen to his knees and accepted all of her if he could.

Instead, he had opted to pull her down on the grass to talk. And it was a decision that Caleb would never regret. Their conversation was so deep and exemplary that Caleb knew that he was done for. He would continue to think about their words for the rest of his life. He would look back on this day, on their first real conversation together, and treasure it closely. It was a rare moment of truth they shared together, and Caleb did not remember ever experiencing such a tight bond with anyone in a long time.

I will be honest with you. Her soft yet resolute words

echoed in his head, and he sighed a deep sigh, knowing that she would be his reckoning.

It seemed as if a bubble had formed around them, barring them from the outside world where people talked about responsibilities and boasted about their wealth and status. Time had seized and it was just the two of them, alone, speaking with their hearts and not their heads. Caleb was astonished to realize, in retrospect, that a lot of the things he said were *real.*

It might have been the trees swaying in the breeze as innocent bystanders, or the birds chirping in the trees—or perhaps it was Lady Mercy and her soft eyes and soft smiles—that made Caleb's chest warm. There was a feeling of comfort blanketing over them, and Caleb desired to feel that again. He *wanted* to experience that again.

Because, for a moment, he felt as if he was home.

Caleb's eyes widened. The revelation was so intense that he almost stumbled off of Johnny, who whinnied in response.

Once he stabled himself, the thoughts came back in full force.

Lady Mercy held the reputation of having a bad mouth and an offensive nature. In the beginning, Caleb had believed all the rumors. She had yelled at him the first time they truly interacted in the woods. She rejected his confessions. And she was nothing but rude to him during the dinner at Norfolk Manor. Not to mention the whole incident at the ball when she had blown up at him in front of the entire ton.

To be fair, he had been flushed with embarrassment. It was the first time in his life that he had been called out so unabashedly, without any regard for the people around them. Lady Mercy said exactly what was on her mind, and at first, he had distrusted her for it. For a moment, he disliked her for it. However, he could begin to see the pain evident on her face, not so much the anger. She was hurt, and he could see it plain as day. That shocked him so much that he didn't even care that everyone was watching his humiliation; he cared for the fact that they might see Lady Mercy as a terrible human being rather than a pained woman who had been pushed too far.

Caleb wanted to move them to a private setting so that the ton could not judge her for her emotions, but she had steadfastly refused. She marched on, hurtling painful things that still hurt him, but he had endured it, because, for some reason, he knew that saying those things hurt her more.

Now that she had apologized to him sincerely, his feeling of protectiveness over her increased. She invaded every crevice of his mind. Now that he knew there was a softness, something very earnest and human, inside of her, Caleb felt lucky to have been the one to spot the vulnerabilities inside her hard exterior.

Once Caleb arrived back home, he saw Ben waiting on the front lawn.

By way of greeting, Ben immediately asked, "Where were you?"

Caleb hopped down from Johnny before allowing the stableboy to lead his horse away. "I was riding in the woods." A small smile formed on his lips. "I met Lady Mercy…of course."

"Is that so? Why do you look so happy? Especially after everything she said to you."

"She apologized, Ben," Caleb said. "She *apologized* to me. It didn't seem fake either. She looked so earnest and sad that I knew she was haunted by what she had done last night. I can understand it, too."

Ben slowly nodded before clapping Caleb on the shoulder. "Well, I'm glad she felt truly sorry and realized her mistake."

"She is the perfect balance between strength and sensitivity." Caleb began walking inside the house while Ben trailed after him, hanging onto his every word. "She isn't afraid to speak her mind, but she also understands when things go too far. For example, last night, I know that some of the things she said were true. It must have been all the pent-up emotions she had bottled inside. Of course, the words were true; they were from her heart. But she spoke with such venom that it hurt the people around her, and she realized her mistake. She humbled herself to apologize to *me*, whom she had no qualms about hating before. She showed her vulnerable side, and I—oh, Ben. She is the most perfect woman in the world."

Caleb felt a hard tug on his sleeve, forcing him to stop. He turned and saw Ben's wide eyes, a small smile playing on his lips. There was a slight tilt to his head before he asked, slowly, "Caleb...are you falling in love with Lady Mercy?"

He was about to answer, but then Caleb closed his mouth. *Was* he falling in love with her? Is this what love felt like? He was entirely unsure. Caleb Griffiths had never fallen in love before. The feeling was foreign to him, so he didn't understand if this rapid, startling feeling inside of his chest meant *love*.

All he was certain about was that the desire to marry Lady Mercy had heightened, so much so that he was willing to marry her that night.

Caleb ended up changing the subject, much to Ben's dismay; he allowed the conversation to steer in a different direction, but that didn't stop Caleb from giving Ben wary glances. Ben even wore a meaningful smirk the rest of the evening, until eventually, Caleb left the manor.

Now that Caleb was alone, Lady Mercy became his every thought once more. When he was in his office. When he tried reading a book it seemed that every sentence only said *Lady Mercy, Lady Mercy, Lady Mercy*. And finally, when he was eating dinner, he couldn't help but remember the time that he ate with Lady Mercy and her family. Would things be different if he visited now? Would she act as if he didn't exist at all, or would she watch him the whole night, just as enamored with him as he was with her?

The idea was so stunning that he was overwhelmed with the idea of seeing her again.

So, he quickly finished dinner and ran out of the house. Grabbing Johnny and saddling him—with the speed and efficiency of a professional horse rider—Caleb zoomed into the night.

If anyone saw him from a distance, they would think that this flying shadow of a man riding his horse was a soldier speeding into war.

But he was only just a man seized with the need to see a lady.

Before he knew it, he was on the grounds of Norfolk Manor, the big building suddenly intimidating. Perhaps in another world, it was a high tower, caging a beautiful princess inside, blocking her beauty from the entire world. And Caleb was a prince, wanting to see her beauty, no matter how selfish that desire might be.

He left Johnny by a tree that was far away from the manor so that no one would see it. With quiet efficiency, Caleb stealthily hopped over the fence, hoping to not alert anyone. There were a plethora of windows—as to be expected of a mansion—so Caleb decided to check the main wing of the house, on the right side, and looked at the windows that peeked into the bedchambers. Luckily there was a large tree standing before the windows, so he deftly climbed the branches, making sure that he didn't make too much noise.

To his complete and utter luck, the first window he approached showed a wide, expansive room with a large single bed. There was a wooden wardrobe and an empty vanity. There were more books than dresses, it seemed. And sitting on the edge of the bed was Lady Mercy herself.

She was facing the other direction, so Caleb opted to knock on the window.

Three rapt knocks caused Lady Mercy to jump slightly. She turned with wide eyes, which widened further when she saw Caleb through the window. She quickly rushed toward him, opened the glass window, and said breathlessly, "What are you doing here?"

Caleb couldn't help the large smile that overtook his entire face. It was a pearly-white-teeth kind of smile, the one with dimples, and it kind of hurt, but Caleb could not care less. He held her stare as he replied, "I wanted to see you."

She laughed, and it was the sort of sound that poets created sonnets for. "If anyone finds you, we'll both be dead."

"If you don't help me in, I might fall—then I'll be dead before they find us."

Lady Mercy rolled her eyes, but it wasn't with the usual air of annoyance. There was amusement in her eyes.

She pulled him so that he could sit comfortably on the window ledge, and, he noticed, she left her hand on his arm for a second too long. A faint blush appeared on her cheeks, and she asked, "Well, what do you suppose—"

"I want to sing a song for you."

The words tumbled out before he could stop them. But he didn't take them back. Before, he would've balked at the idea of singing to a woman, but once he thought about it now, it didn't seem so foolish. Especially if the woman was Lady Mercy, who now appeared entirely shocked. He loved getting these sorts of reactions out of her. It was like an accomplishment. Slowly, he was unlocking all her different faces.

"Can you sing?" she asked, slightly wary.

Caleb stabbed his heart with an invisible sword, pinching his face with exaggerated pain. "You wound me! Of course, I can sing. Please refrain from spoiling my ego with such questions."

Lady Mercy nodded, and Caleb was amused at the way she refused to meet his eyes. "Go on, then. Show me what you got."

Clearing his throat and straightening himself against the window frame, Caleb opened his mouth and sang an old tune, one that he heard years ago.

"Do you hear me now or do you hear me tomorrow?

Oh, don't you worry, darling,
Since the words never seem to change.
My heart still rings true to the eyes of a lover
As long as it's still beating,
My words will never change."

It was a song about a man begging for love. He would wait a million years for her, and he would assure her every time they met that his feelings never changed. It was an intense sort of romance, one that Caleb never cared for. When he heard it for the first time, he only liked the melody of the song, not so much the words.

Suddenly, Lady Mercy joined him in the song. Caleb was slightly taken aback, but he continued to sing. They sang the repeated verse again, and he found her voice to be angelical, so soft and beautiful, like a siren's voice. Caleb's eyes crinkled as he smiled at her and sang. She, too, was grinning from ear to ear, but it didn't stunt the way she sang.

After they finished the song, Lady Mercy started another song, and then another. Caleb surprisingly knew all of them, and it was probably because Ben had forced him to listen to this type of music. He thanked the world for giving him such a hopelessly romantic friend.

The night had deepened when they finished their final song. Lady Mercy's eyes grew tired, and so Caleb told her that he should leave soon.

She seemed reluctant at first, but then she nodded when a huge yawn overtook her body.

Carefully, he moved onto the tree branch, and Lady Mercy helped ease him down without falling. She called down to him, "Good night, Lord Griffiths..." and it was the sort of whisper that held secrets.

As he landed on the grass, he gave her a huge wave, then ran toward the tree in the distance that held Johnny's reins. He rushed home with newfound strength, finding himself not tired at all. He was far from it. There was an overwhelming sensation coursing through him, a feeling that he had never felt before. It was startling as much as it was frightening. He didn't understand what was becoming of him.

What he did understand, though, was that he longed to see Lady Mercy again.

In the quiet bedchamber of Norfolk Manor, Lady Mercy found herself unable to sleep.

She was tired, but, somehow, she was restless and could not fall into slumber. She was staring up at the ceiling as Lord Griffiths consumed her thoughts. *Amazing,* she thought. *I was thinking about him when he appeared at my window!* The world was revealing itself to be very witty. To think that he actually came to see her! It made her heart flutter, and that was when she knew that she would not be able to sleep for the rest of the night.

Their relationship had taken a sudden turn, and there was an air of comfort now instead of tension. She no longer looked at him and felt angered by his presence. Now, she longed for it. Perhaps she shouldn't reject the idea any longer and accept him fully.

The night droned on and on, and all Mercy could think about was how lucky she was to be courted by the only man she was finally interested in.

23

The following morning, Ben arrived at Cornwall Mansion with a small pep in his step. Caleb had come to expect his best friend's frequent visits now; they didn't bother Caleb because Ben was like family. He invited himself over with a gleeful expression. With rosy cheeks and an ear-to-ear grin smothering his face, Caleb could only raise a single brow in question.

"Good morning, Ben," he greeted as his friend entered his bedchamber.

Ben twirled before tumbling onto one of the chaise lounges. "Morning!"

Caleb was about to ask why Ben had decided to come over when he was interrupted by a huge yawn. His eyes were so tired that he had to rub them to get the sleep out. If he was allowed, he would jump right back into bed and sleep for another few hours. His body was begging for reprieve.

It seemed that Ben had noticed this, and he asked, "Are you all right there, Caleb? You look as if you hadn't slept in days."

"I didn't get to sleep much last night." A small hint of a smile showed on his face. Memories from last night emerged, and he couldn't help but feel giddy. Flashes of Lady Mercy's joyful expression—her smile, her bright eyes. The way she sang, and the way they sang together. The brush of their hands when he went back down the tree. It must have been a dream! But alas, it was real. His subconscious was not so smart as to create a dream where he and Lady Mercy had sung together. It had truly happened. "I was with Lady Mercy for most of last night. Just talking. And singing."

Ben looked very impressed; his grin grew wider. "Singing? That's amazing! Lady Mercy must be smitten with you!"

The idea of Lady Mercy being *smitten* with him was too much, but Caleb hoped that it was true. What was happening to him? Before, he would never have entertained the idea of desiring a woman to be smitten with him. A woman's affections were only the means of getting what he wanted. He didn't care if a lady, much less a dozen ladies, was in love with him. If anything, their love was a burden for him. All through multiple events, he would have to smile through the countless conversations with these ladies, and it would be painfully obvious how much they were wooed by him. It didn't bother him much because he was charming them for a reason: To gain an advantage and to grow his network so that he could achieve favors from them. But with Lady Mercy, he craved her attention in a different way. It was self-serving, but it also wasn't selfish. His chest felt lighter and every stress in the world disappeared from his mind.

Pulling away from his thoughts, Caleb shook his head and turned to Ben. "May I ask why you're here so early this morning?"

"I asked Lady Olive to go on a picnic today," Ben expressed with an excited wiggle of his shoulders.

Caleb laughed and clapped his shoulder. "That's great." Then an idea popped into his head. While talking with Ben, he slowly began to realize how much of a romantic Ben was. Which meant that Ben knew his way around women and the ways two people developed true feelings for one another. Prior to Caleb's plans, Ben had expressed the importance of prioritizing true love rather than an agenda to gain more status. An innocent person like Ben would know how to give good advice pertaining to winning a woman's heart. Caleb wondered why he never asked Ben for help sooner.

"Ben," he began. "Would you do me a favor? Help me with Lady Mercy. How do I effectively court her and make her fall in love with me? I feel like I might be almost there. I just need an extra push."

"I have good news, my friend," Ben said. "That is exactly why I am here this lovely morning. Lady Mercy will be joining Lady Olive and I's picnic to chaperone. So, I hurried on over here to invite you as well, so that you may have more time to spend with her."

Caleb suddenly stood up, his body reacting before his mind could. How lucky he was to have such a good friend! He enveloped Ben in a warm—quick—hug and ran to dress up for the day. Ben was pushed out of the room so that Caleb could have some privacy to change, as well as to think.

He shoved on a pair of white breeches, boots, and a white shirt that rose to a puffed cravat. Then he pulled on a waistcoat that was slim fit, hugging his body closely. While he was buttoning the last button, he realized that he had finished changing in record time. How fast he had put everything on! There was only one reason why—and her name was Lady Mercy.

It was obvious that he was excited to see her once more, though they had only just been with each other a few hours prior. But he found that time was unfair: It seemed to go egregiously slow in her absence, and it sped up when he was with her. There was not enough time with her, and so Caleb wanted to spend all his time in her presence.

This sudden revelation frightened Caleb.

He was starting to develop true feelings for Lady Mercy.

It almost took his breath away, and he wanted to strip away his clothing and dive

back into bed. But he knew, no matter how shocked he was about his newfound feelings, he would still go see her at the picnic. The desire to see her again trumped his fear of this fickle emotion called love.

Still, this was never supposed to happen.

He was supposed to charm *her*. He was the one who controlled everything, and she was merely the pawn in his game. The whole objective of his plan was to trick her into marrying him so that he would gain her father's dukedom. That was it. But somewhere along the way, *Caleb* had been the one to be charmed.

Somehow, he had fallen into his own trap.

Now, here he was—speedily dressing so that he could go chaperone his best friend's picnic, knowing that Lady Mercy would be there, too, and that Caleb desperately wanted to be in her presence again.

Caleb smacked his head in consternation. *No.* He needed to focus. *Focus. Remember the plan.* Getting the title of duke was his dream all along, not to fall for a woman. The little boy he once was would be so disappointed. Because at the end of the day, Caleb was doing this for *himself*. Lady Mercy was simply the vessel standing between him and that dream. There was no time to idle.

He needed to woo Lady Mercy for the money and

title, not for love. Because as far as he knew, love was a frail thing, completely fragile. If he loved, surely he'd become weak. All the duke's power would be for naught.

With that, he fled downstairs, meeting Ben along the way, and they both departed for Norfolk Manor.

When they arrived at the familiar estate, Caleb's eyes immediately strayed to the tall girl with cascading brown hair and a pair of electrifying green eyes, which grew larger as she, too, spotted Caleb in the distance.

Ben sped toward Lady Olive and greeted her with a bow. Caleb followed his friend's lead and bowed down, his eyes never leaving Lady Mercy's. The ladies curtsied as well. And once the pleasantries were over, Ben beckoned Lady Olive to take his arm so that he could lead her into the carriage.

Caleb followed suit and reached his arm out for Lady Mercy, who did not hesitate to curve her hand around the crook of his elbow.

As they entered the carriage, Caleb observed Lady Mercy with watchful eyes. He saw how pink her face was, a ripe fruit beneath the glowing sun. A small smile was on her lips, which were exposed by the swaying curtain of her hair. She peeked at him from under her lashes, and his heart lodged in his throat, and he found that he couldn't breathe.

It was clear on her face that she was happy to see him. If anything, she might have been as excited for this picnic as he had been earlier.

Perhaps...she had developed feelings for him too.

When they arrived at the park, all four of them helped set up the picnic. The sisters had brought a basket of pastries—warm croissants and buttered brioches. Shiny grapes and strawberries glinted under the rays of the sun. They lounged under the heat and ate to their heart's content. Their conversation was pleasant and modest. They asked one another about their plans for the upcoming season, as many events took place in winter. Caleb indulged in an innocent conversation with Lady Olive, who seemed to take pleasure in speaking with him. Her eyes would sometimes flit to her sister, watching her reaction every time Caleb spoke. It was amusing because of how obvious she was.

Then finally, when the plates and bowls were empty, Ben stood up from the ground and reached out a hand for Lady Olive. "Let's stretch out our legs, shall we? Just around this area so your sister can still see you."

And so they both began walking. Ben kept a respectable amount of space between them, though their arms were glued together. True to his words, he never left the boundaries of the park or strayed into the forest. Not only was he respecting Lady Olive's safety but also Lady Mercy's. Caleb had to hand it to him; Ben knew what he was doing.

Finding himself alone with Lady Mercy, Caleb couldn't help but smile freely. His posture relaxed, and he leaned backward, assuming a more comfortable position. Lady Mercy did the same thing; she leaned back and tilted her chin to the sky. Her eyes were closed as if she was soaking up the sun's rays.

In that moment, he allowed himself to appreciate her beauty. She was truly the most beautiful woman in the ton. There was no one else who could rival her appearance, and the more Caleb spent time with her, he was beginning to realize that there was no one else who could rival her personality either. All in all, Lady Mercy was the perfect woman. And he deemed himself to be lucky—to be granted the privilege of splaying out in the grass right next to her, free to observe all her glory without remorse.

Lady Mercy peeked open an eye and glanced at Caleb; he must not have been sly about his observations. He quickly looked away, his face growing warm. Caleb didn't understand why he was so shy. But something about Lady Mercy warranted a level of humiliation in him. She was perfect. And by that account, Caleb felt grateful just to be there.

"Did you sleep well last night?" Caleb suddenly asked.

It was a second before Lady Mercy started laughing in response. And so did Caleb.

Well, that was confirmation enough for Caleb. Last night had actually happened. And it seemed that Lady Mercy hadn't had enough sleep either. Perhaps she had stayed awake the rest of the night as well, clutching her heart, suddenly noticing how enormous it felt in her small chest. Perhaps the feeling expanded within her, and it was called *Love*.

Caleb understood because he had done this himself.

As her laughter died down, Caleb found himself wanting to make her laugh again. He wanted to make her happier. Maybe the happiest woman in the ton—or the world, if he was feeling ambitious.

This desire suddenly consumed him, and it was a feeling unlike anything he had ever felt before. Being in her presence did such foreign things to him. And although he reprimanded himself for becoming a victim of this tyrannical emotion, Caleb couldn't help but submit to it. It felt *good* being with Lady Mercy. He wanted to always be with her.

She was so *real*. She wasn't fake like the other women of the ton, who giggled with a hidden ulterior motive. They would look at him as if he was some kind of snack to be mauled, and they wanted him even though they didn't know him.

Lady Mercy was different.

She saw him as a human being, and when they spent time together, it felt like there wasn't any societal pressure to talk in a certain manner, behave in a proper way, or engage in fruitless conversations.

Simply sitting next to her would have sufficed.

"The sun is high in the sky today," Lady Mercy commented wistfully.

Caleb shielded his eyes from the sun and replied, "It is. Hopefully Ben and Lady Olive do not spend too much of their time walking, or else we'll burn ourselves by the end of the picnic."

"I agree. Though...it wouldn't be *too* bad if they continued to walk by themselves for a few more minutes."

Caleb turned and saw her cheeks tinged slightly pink. His heart started beating rapidly. "Now that I think about it, I think I'll be all right spending another few hours or so in the sun."

"Hours!"

"Days, even?"

Lady Mercy bumped her shoulder against his, and they both laughed once more.

A day had not passed, not even a single hour before Ben and Lady Olive returned to them. They cleaned up the picnic before departing for the carriage. It was a comfortable ride home, one where they did not have to speak to eliminate any awkward silences.

They arrived at Norfolk Manor, and Caleb watched as Ben begrudgingly bade farewell to Lady Olive. Then he turned to stare at Lady Mercy, who was also looking his way. She gave him a tentative smile and a small wave, which seemed so casual—as if they had always waved to each other—and the simpleness of the gesture made him smile.

Caleb waved to her, too.

When Ben hopped back inside the carriage, and the door closed, Caleb felt the emptiness in his chest.

He wished the carriage driver had been slower, he wished they hadn't cleaned the picnic materials so fast, and he wished Ben and Lady Olive had talked for a few more hours—no matter how hot the sun would have been. He did not want to say goodbye to Lady Mercy, and he found himself pondering the next time they would be able to meet again.

Caleb groaned internally and leaned his head back against the wall of the carriage.

This was not good for his heart.

He was not supposed to fall for her, but it was already too late.

24

Mercy awoke the next morning with a light-hearted feeling fluttering in her chest. She trailed down the stairs and entered the dining room for breakfast, where she dined with Olive and Alice. Warm, crusted croissants and sunny-side-up eggs. The sunlight streamed through the curtains. Mercy asked a maid to open the windows so she could hear the birds singing their early morning chorus, to which the maid gave her a very confused look, but Mercy ignored it

All was well, and when Mercy dabbed her lips with the napkin and finished her food, she asked her sisters, "What colors would suit my skin tone?"

Olive and Alice had mirroring expressions; their eyebrows rose high to their hairline, and their eyes widened significantly.

"Why?" Alice questioned.

"Yes, why?" Olive echoed. "Since when did you ever care about such *'trivial'* things, as you said?"

Mercy cleared her throat. "I would just like to know. Is that a crime?"

Olive and Alice both gave each other a furtive glance before nodding their heads in

silent agreement. "Well, since you have fair skin," Olive replied, "you would suit all of the colors! Red, blue, yellow, purple—they would look splendid on you!"

"We weren't lying when we said that you were the prettiest lady in the ton," Alice added. "There's only one way to find out which suits me more, then." Mercy stood from her chair. Her sisters watched as she started to leave the dining room. "Are you coming or not?" Mercy asked them from over her shoulder.

Olive and Alice looked very confused, but nonetheless, they followed.

They were all inside Mercy's bedchamber. The wardrobe had been completely ransacked. Every item of clothing was strewn across the floor. A light blue gown. A purple silk dress that she wore once to a wedding. A tight green dress that had a little tear in the seam because she had been so uncomfortable during the ball. And a plethora of other dresses among the mix.

Mercy didn't remember owning most of these dresses. Truthfully, all her life she had merely given them a passing glance—and only when the maids were filling her wardrobe after her sisters had ordered from a well-known modiste. Mercy had always been dragged along those shopping sprees. She would have rather stayed home or gone horse riding or even gone hunting with her father. But the world liked to make her suffer sometimes, so she had to oblige her sisters' adamant pleas.

There was a time when they had gone to *Mademoiselle Mittens*, owned by a young lady who did, in fact, wear mittens. She fashioned many different dresses, all of which Olive and Alice wore. Since she was a woman who owned a business, the store suffered a lot of setbacks. But with the help of Olive and Alice, the mademoiselle was able to continue her career.

The only one who really suffered from this was, of course, Mercy.

The streets were busy that day; civilians roamed the grounds, most of the families. There was a giant fountain in the town center, and even a few entertainers held performances for the passersby.

Olive and Alice were dragging a begrudging Mercy through the town center, forcing her to accompany them to the modiste.

"Must I come?" Mercy groaned. She could have been reading.

Or in the woods. Anything but this. The sun was high in the sky, the clouds were gone, and it was just a plain blue sky. It was the perfect weather to spend time outside—alone.

"Yes!" Olive and Alice both yelled simultaneously.

They finally arrived at Mademoiselle Mittens, *and it was a rather quaint building with red bricks, a yellow and white striped roof cover, and a wooden door with a sign hanging over the glass window: A drawing of a pair of mittens holding knitting needles.*

Through the window, Mercy could see all the dresses on display. And based on the excited expressions of both Olive and Alice, Mercy knew it would be a long day.

"I want this—Oh, and this!" Olive practically screeched.

"This would look lovely on me! How about this for you?" Alice *held up a dress that Mercy would eventually forget the design, and even color, of.*

As Mercy watched her sisters rummage the store with their quick hands and even quicker eyes, she saw how thrilled they were to wear these dresses. When Mercy asked them what the appeal was, Olive had said: "Because we look even more lovely in them! And men might agree as well." *She blushed at the last part.*

Mercy shook her head. She did not understand.

The dresses all looked incredibly uncomfortable, and her skin started to itch just by looking at them. How does a lady run in a tight dress like that? What good was a ball gown if one could not wear them when riding a horse? Was this sacrifice worth it—for a man? It all didn't make sense to her.

Until this moment.

All the suffering, she felt, was now worth it—if it meant that she could have all these dresses to pick from so that she may appear a little more feminine for once.

Mercy hovered a long red dress over her body. She tilted her head as she observed her reflection. Her brown hair was out of her ponytail; it cascaded down her slim shoulders and the line of her back. Since she wasn't actually wearing the dress, she didn't know if it looked good on her. But she had seen Olive and Alice do this multiple times: placing the dress right before their bodies, not actually wearing them. They told her that it was a more quick and efficient way to measure which dress might look better on them—but Mercy was currently having trouble.

She had never done this before! How was she supposed to know the ins and outs of being a traditional girl?

"Do you think Mercy is sick?" Mercy heard Olive whisper to Alice.

"I don't know...Her face *was* red this morning," Alice answered. "Perhaps she has a fever."

"Perhaps. Because there is no other possible reason as to why Mercy is acting like this."

Alice hummed. "Maybe she was abducted, and they sent back someone else, someone that just *looks* like Mercy."

Mercy sighed and swiveled around. Olive and Alice were both peering around the doorframe, huddled close together as they whispered to one another. When they heard Mercy sigh, their eyes snapped to hers, and they looked alarmed as if they had been caught red-handed. "I'm fine," Mercy said. "Will you stop creeping in the background and help me?"

One after the other, the two girls trailed inside the room. Olive slowly approached Mercy, asking tentatively, "Why *are* you acting like this?"

Mercy shrugged. "I just…feel more feminine today."

Olive hummed. "Are you in love with Lord Griffiths and trying to look pretty for him?"

The question was so sudden—and so true—that Mercy almost choked on her breath. She tried to hide the shock on her face by turning away from the mirror and bending down to retrieve another dress on the floor.

She felt her face heating up. Hearing *Lord Griffiths* and *love* in the same sentence did things to her heart.

It had taken her the entirety of the last night to come to terms with this new revelation: That Mercy was in love with Lord Griffiths.

It had taken her too long to realize that this whole time, she had been secretly in love with him without knowing. Perhaps since the beginning, when they had run into each other in the woods, there had been a string tugging them closer together. He gave off a magnetizing effect, and even though she wanted to make a thousand excuses as to why Lord Griffiths might be the worst human in the world, at the end of the day, she always thought about him, nonetheless.

And all her arguments had come crashing down last night, when he had visited her near midnight, sneaking onto her windowsill. She was surprised, of course, but it soon transformed into an unbridled glee, a warm feeling melting in her heart. Admittedly, she was happy to see him.

Then he had sung.

That was the moment that had turned the tide of the warring feelings in her mind. She was teetering on the edge of whether she was in love with him or if she was annoyed with him. But after he had sung for her, a song about lovers, no less, Mercy had fallen into the side of love.

She could not sleep, not until much later, and still, she could hear him singing in her dreams, along with the thunderous beating of her heart.

It seemed that ever since Lord Griffiths had barged into her life, she had not stopped thinking about him.

And now, Mercy had accepted her love of him.

But she could never, at least not now, confess this out loud.

Not to her father and not to her sisters.

She had the reputation for being a man-repeller. The majority of the men in the ton either feared her or were frustrated with her. With all the talk surrounding Mercy's rather obtuse threats toward these men, it was not shocking. Even Olive and Alice knew Mercy to be scornful toward men.

So how could she—realistically—tell her sisters that she had finally caved and fallen in love. With the most handsome man in the ton—someone who she had denied held such a highly esteemed title!

It was as humiliating as it was frightening.

She could not voice this feeling to the world. If she did, then it would become tangible, *real*. It would not only be within the solace of her own mind, where no one could look inside. Everyone would know the second Mercy told them about her feelings for Lord Griffiths. And that reality was so scary Mercy would rather keep it locked inside, for now.

She was not ready to say it out loud.

Seeing that Mercy was not going to respond to Olive's blatant question, Olive and Alice quietly began sifting through the dresses, thankfully letting the matter drop, which Mercy was eternally grateful for.

Alice picked up the red dress that Mercy had hung before her body earlier. "This dress is pretty, and it would suit you just fine. But I think there is a better dress out there, one that is *perfect* for you."

"I agree," Olive said. "Let's keep digging."

And so they all began shuffling through multiple different dresses. Olive gave Mercy advice. Most of them were about the significance of textures and how each might be more appropriate for a specific type of event. More light colors would suit ball events. Darker tones would be nice for important dinners or an outing with a suitor. When meeting important people, long and white silken gloves were divine.

Alice placed herself behind Mercy and pulled back her hair, exposing every plane of her face. "You must style your hair up, either in a chignon or a half-up, half-down style. Either way, style it up. That way, whoever you are talking to will be able to see you clearly, and you will appear much more confident. They will also be able to see your makeup!"

With that, Alice traded places with Olive, who began applying a light blush to her cheeks and feathering light puffs of something white and powdery all over her face.

Mercy sneezed ferociously.

"Stop moving!" Olive and Alice both reprimanded her.

Finally, when they were done with the makeup and Olive had found a beautiful dark green dress that flowed all the way down to Mercy's ankles, Mercy stood with a wobbly sort of a smile, her hands to her hips.

"The last step to appearing more feminine is to *behave* with femininity," Alice said.

"Huh?"

"Instead of 'huh' you have to say, 'Pardon?'"

Olive nodded. "Maybe add a little flutter of your eyelashes."

Mercy grimaced.

"And *don't* make that face!" Olive scolded. "Smile."

Mercy smiled widely.

"Too scary!"

Mercy closed her lips but maintained her smile.

"Don't widen your eyes," Alice added. "You look more angry than happy."

Mercy squinted her eyes.

On and on and on, their advice bounced back and forth until Mercy was left standing with an arched back, her hands clasped before her stomach, with a strained smile and a twitching eye.

"Stop! Stop!" Olive scrambled toward Mercy and pushed her down into a nearby chair. "Let's not focus on the facial features and postures for today—that'll be another day, another time. Today, let's just relax. Look in the mirror."

Mercy looked in the mirror.

And for the first time, she allowed herself to really look at herself. Alice had wrapped her hair in a high chignon but allowed a few strands to fall down the sides of her face. She had applied a light blush to Mercy's fair cheeks. The dark green dress that Olive had picked out fit perfectly to her body; the length was just right, and the bodice had an intricate floral design woven in, with patterns of vines trailing all down the length of her skirt.

"You look like Mother Nature herself," Alice whispered.

Mercy could not disagree.

She was surprised to see the transformation. Before, she had never really taken an eager glance at her reflection. It didn't matter much. Back then, the dresses were only a burden, an attire was that required for the balls that she was forced to attend.

But now, everything mattered.

For him.

Olive and Alice pull Mercy to her feet, and they lead her out of the bedchamber and down the stairs, all the way to their father's office.

When he lifted his head from his work, his eyes widened, looking pleasantly surprised. He stood from his chair, rounded his desk, and approached Mercy with a joyful, albeit confused, expression. "You look beautiful, my darling! Now, I must ask: What is the special occasion?"

Mercy laughed. "Nothing at all, Father."

"Oh?"

"Yes, I just...wanted to try on this wonderful dress." Mercy then cleared her throat and looked at the giant painting of a residential park that had always been hung on her father's wall. She tried to appear casual. "Father...since I am already dressed up and prepared...perhaps we could have a special dinner tonight…perhaps we may invite Lord Griffiths?"

Her father's eyebrows rose so high Mercy thought they would fly away.

She heard Olive and Alice giggling behind her back.

Mercy ignored them. "I am now feeling positive about this match, and I want to get to know him better."

Her father clapped his hands with an ecstatic expression, laughing and cheering. "Why, of course! What a brilliant plan! This is a special occasion; we will arrange only the best dishes and drinks. Let us invite both Lord Griffiths and his dear friend Lord Morris. That will suffice, I think. Plenty!"

Olive squealed. And Alice cheered.

Mercy tried to contain her excitement, but it must have been evident on her face because Olive and Alice pulled her into their little huddle, squealing altogether with the energy of three little girls on Christmas morning.

But Mercy couldn't help it. Lord Griffiths was coming, and she would be seeing him again. It was a gift better than Christmas.

25

Caleb and Ben both arrived at Norfolk Manor donned in their best suits with their styled hair and flashy smiles. Duke White greeted them at the front entrance, accompanied by his three daughters, who were all dressed head in tone in finery and silks, an ensemble fit for the most beautiful women in the ton.

Of course, Caleb's eyes flew to Lady Mercy; he could not help it. She looked magnificent, with her hair wrapped back, revealing her stunning and fair features. Her dress was regal, a dark green color that made her green eyes sharper. Caleb swore that if he hadn't known her, he would have thought she was a princess.

When Caleb walked toward Lady Mercy, bowing down in greeting, he saw her blush. He knew it wasn't the makeup's doing, for she had not looked this red when they arrived.

Although she may have seemed shy, she never once looked away from his eyes. There was a palpable feeling in the air between them, a secret shared of the night they had sung together. Caleb pretended like it wasn't there, but for some reason, he couldn't stop staring at her. He decided that he would indulge in Lady Mercy's presence without wondering about her behavior too much.

Before everyone could make their way to the dining room, Caleb took the moment to step forth and ask the duke's permission to go on a walk with Lady Mercy.

"Why, of course!" Duke White exclaimed, a joyous expression on his face. "Why don't you take Alice to chaperone you both. Lord Morris and Olive will stay behind and keep me company."

And with that, Caleb beckoned Lady Mercy to grab his arm so he could lead her outside and into the garden. Alice kept herself at a distance, trailing slowly along while sometimes getting distracted by a flower blooming or a bug on the ground. It was obvious to Caleb that she was merely trying to give them a moment of privacy—and for that, he was grateful.

The last time he and Lady Mercy had walked in this garden was when he had felt something shift between them. Prior to that night, there was animosity on Lady Mercy's end. He had confessed to her in that stable room, and Lady Mercy had rejected him outright. But when he confessed to her once more in this exact garden, she had hesitated.

Hesitated!

No offensive words shouted, no threats. Lady Mercy seemed almost *shy*, and Caleb knew that her feelings had somehow changed, even if she wouldn't admit it.

It was a good memory, the beginning of her affections perhaps.

The sun was lowering. Its brightness could be seen hovering in the sky, ready to light the darkness. There was a warm purple glow to everything. It was a time between day and night, an intimate moment of the day.

Perfect.

Caleb turned to look at Lady Mercy, and her eyes were lowered. A stray strand of hair fell and curtained her eyes, and Caleb had the instinctive urge to reach out and tuck it behind her ears.

Somehow, she looked more beautiful than usual. He couldn't stop staring. Once, at a ball, he had heard that although Lady Mercy might have been the most offensive lady in the ton, she was by far the most beautiful. Caleb had scoffed at that, wondering if a woman with a sharp tongue could ever be considered beautiful. But as he continued to stare at Lady Mercy, in the middle of the darkening garden, he couldn't help but think that she was more than just the most beautiful girl in the ton. Words couldn't describe her beauty.

He did not know how to voice this, but he tried his best. "Lady Mercy, you are the most divine woman I've ever laid eyes on. I cannot put it into simple words how beautiful you are, just that you are glorious. But glorious isn't enough either…"

Lady Mercy's eyes widened significantly before she looked the other way, obviously trying to hide the growing blush on her cheeks.

An immediate smile overcame his face. He was delighted to know that he could affect Lady Mercy this way. She couldn't even respond; she only tugged him forward silently, urging him to continue their walk.

Caleb had never seen Lady Mercy dressed like this before. At the ball, she had always looked like she was in great pain. There was no doubt that the dresses were uncomfortable on her, and unlike the other ladies, she wasn't afraid to show her disdain. When riding horses, she would wear men's riding clothes; Caleb was shocked to find that he liked how it looked on her. When he had attended the first dinner, she had worn a regular gown, nothing spectacular; she wasn't even wearing any cosmetics.

She still looked beautiful, but today it seemed as if she had transformed entirely. Not only was she wearing the most dazzling dress in the world, but she looked as if she was comfortable in it. Since Caleb had stepped foot inside the Norfolk estate, he had not spotted a single frown on her face. Lady Mercy was undeniably glowing; her aura had changed completely. She was stunning, in every sense of the word.

Caleb couldn't help but think that she had done all of this for him. It was no coincidence that the duke had decided to invite him after their night together singing and the picnic where they had shared a nice conversation. She had affection for him, Caleb knew that. But the knowledge still sent his heart beating like crazy. And knowing that she had dressed so beautifully—for him, no less—was the best gift he could ever ask for.

It wasn't for any other suitor in the ton; it was for Caleb Griffiths only.

After their walk around in the garden, they went back inside and joined the rest of the family in the dining room.

The duke sat at the head of the table, along with Ben on the left side, and an empty spot for Caleb. On the duke's right were Lady Olive and Lady Alice, with an empty seat reserved for Lady Mercy.

They assumed their spots and waited as the maids each came out, neatly and efficiently, with trays and trays of warm food balanced on their arms. A full roasted chicken, gleaming with butter and oil; boiled salmon cut with thyme; smoked hickory bacon wrapped around potato cubes; and more plates filled with all sorts of cooked vegetables, wafting with a delectable aroma.

Soon after all the food was set down on the table, they all began eating. The duke patted his belly and asked Caleb and Ben if they were enjoying the meal.

"Before we leave, I must ask to speak with your chef," Ben declared. "This is absolutely delightful!"

"I would like to speak with him as well," Caleb agreed.

The duke laughed, making his round cheeks even rounder. Lady Olive giggled, too, as she covered her mouth with a napkin.

Helping his friend out, Caleb said, "Lady Olive, did you know that Ben likes to bake sometimes? His mother taught him many different recipes, and Lady Morris made the best plum cakes."

"Is that so?" Lady Olive looked so intrigued that Ben started stuttering.

"Well, Caleb gives me too much credit. I—I am still learning some of my mother's recipes."

"You must make me something one day! I would be very grateful for it."

"Of course!"

Ben and Lady Olive looked very happy with this outcome; Caleb gave himself an imaginary pat on the back.

"Can you cook, Lord Griffiths?" Lady Mercy suddenly asked.

It seemed as if all the noise in the room had ceased. The clinking of the silverware stopped, even the last remnants of the conversation between Alice and the duke.

Everyone was too busy staring at Lady Mercy, shock on their faces.

Caleb couldn't help feeling shocked, too. He knew that Lady Mercy felt affectionate toward him, but she had never initiated a conversation before, especially in front of her family. It was always Caleb pursuing her. But she had engaged him first, and that made him feel giddy, like a schoolboy who was finally noticed by the prettiest girl in school.

"I...I can make a honey cake," Caleb stuttered. "If you would like, I can bake some for you."

Lady Mercy nodded nonchalantly. "I don't hate honey cakes..."

A smile tugged at Caleb's lips, and it stayed there for the rest of the night. Conversation ensued, and pleasantries over the amazing dinner were shared. Laughter resounded through the manor, and it was a bright moment for all of them.

Once dinner was over and the last maid had cleaned up the plates, Ben shifted in his seat, and Caleb knew what was coming.

Ben was readjusting his suit, readying himself for the big question. He turned in his seat, facing the duke directly. A hush fell over the room, and all the sisters were looking at Ben with wide eyes. Lady Olive immediately covered her mouth. *Smart girl*, Caleb thought. Lady Mercy looked a little confused as to what the fuss was about, but she continued to stare at Ben. Lady Alice raised her brows in wonderment.

"Duke White," Ben began, his voice unflinching and sure. "For the past few weeks, I have been very interested in your beautiful daughter, Lady Olive. I've talked with her, spent time with her, and by the end of it all, I have found, without surprise, how sweet and kind she is. She is truly one of a kind, and I cannot imagine another man holding her hand in marriage, stealing all her gentle words and sweet laughter. So, I ask of you, Duke White: May I have Lady Olive's hand in marriage?"

Gasps flew around the room, but the duke did not seem at all surprised. He only seemed elated. A huge grin took over half of his face. His face reddened, probably from all the joy that tonight had brought. He immediately rose to his feet and clapped wildly. "Yes, Yes!" he yelled uproariously. "I could not have asked for a better man for my darling girl!"

The dining room was soon filled with cheer. Lady Mercy and Lady Alice embraced their sister. Lady Alice seemed to be crying, and Lady Mercy had a fond look in her eyes, a softness that Caleb selfishly wanted to be thrown his way. As for Lady Olive, she looked shocked at first, especially from the sudden turn of this seemingly innocent dinner, but then tears burst from her eyes, and her cheeks bloomed with red. She shouted in excitement, and Lady Alice followed suit.

Caleb clapped Ben's shoulder in support, proud of his friend for taking the next step in adulthood. As he stared at Lady Olive, Caleb knew that Ben was truly happy. He had always been yapping on about true love and marriages. The day had finally come, and Ben found the sweetest girl in the ton to wed.

Caleb knew that Ben and Lady Olive's love was a happily-ever-after sort of story. It would last for an eternity, filled with a soft fondness and gentleness that could never be poisoned. Their love was special, and Caleb was happy for his best friend.

When the short celebration ended, they all huddled in the drawing room, where they began talking again.

However, before Caleb could sit down near Lady Mercy, Ben grabbed his arm. "Will you help me with something?" There was a glint in his eye, and Caleb knew that he wanted to speak with him.

"Yes, of course," Caleb replied then looked at the duke. "I must go help Ben with something momentarily, if that is all right with you."."

"Take your time!" The duke shouted gleefully. It seemed that he was drunk on happiness.

Ben pulled him out of the drawing room and down the hallway before pushing him into a nearby empty room. He turned Caleb toward him, a sudden look of absolute seriousness dawning on his face. "Caleb."

"Ben. What's wrong?"

"Have you developed *true* feelings for Lady Mercy?"

Caleb fell silent, his chest suddenly squeezing tight. The question was so sudden and invasive, that he couldn't think. "What?"

"Have you actually fallen in love with her?" Ben asked with stern eyes, deeply set brows, and a clenched jaw. Caleb knew that Ben was being genuine.

"Why are you suddenly so concerned with Lady Mercy and me? You are finally betrothed to the girl of your dreams—"

"Do not change the subject." Ben looked so serious that Caleb suddenly grew nervous. "I see the way you look at her, so answer the question."

"I…" Caleb lost his breath for a second. He couldn't voice how he felt; there was no possible way. Everything had become too difficult. But at the end of the day, no matter how he might feel for her, Caleb wanted that title of duke more than anything else. That was how he had always felt. He had promised himself this goal, so he could not allow himself to get distracted by anything—or anyone—else. This was true, but…Caleb still wondered about the way his heart ached whenever he thought of Lady Mercy. A tiny, fluttering feeling would be set loose inside his chest, almost suffocating him. It was all so foreign to him; he couldn't put a name to it.

But the only thing he was certain of was that there was a plan.

It had always been about the plan.

"I have not," Caleb finally replied. "This is all just part of the plan, Ben; you know this."

"But," Ben interjected, "I see something completely different. You look at Lady Mercy as if you are already married. Trust me, Caleb, I know the difference between charming a girl and *loving* a girl."

Caleb shook his head, refusing to admit it. He would never say this out loud, but he was scared. He was frightened of this feeling called *love*, and how new it was to him. In his entire life, he had never fallen in love with a woman. It had always been meaningless. That was how it was supposed to be with Lady Mercy: Meaningless love with a free ticket to a dukedom. But life had always made things tricky for Caleb. Of course, he had to develop true feelings for Lady Mercy.

He was supposed to stick to the plan. It was supposed to be easy. But of course, he had diverged from the plan completely. He had fallen for her.

However, Caleb was not a hopeless romantic. He didn't know the right way to say these things. So he acted the only way he knew how: He lied.

"Well, Ben," he said. "I guess you don't really know the difference, then. I'm only doing this to become a duke. Besides, I would never fall in love with someone like Lady Mercy."

As Mercy sat waiting in the drawing room, she realized how long Lord Griffiths and Lord Morris were taking. It was only a matter of time before impatience got the better of her, and she rose from the couch. "Let me go check on them. Perhaps something has happened." Then she quickly left the room without a look back.

She walked down the hallway until she heard two deep voices talking.

Mercy recognized them to be Lord Griffiths and Lord Morris. She was about to open the door and show herself when she heard something.

"This is all just part of the plan, Ben; you know this."

Her brows knit together in confusion. *What plan?*

Curiosity took over her body, and she kneeled closer to the door, pressing her ear against the frame. She wanted to know what plan Lord Griffiths was talking about.

She could tell by the slightly lighter voice that it was Ben speaking. "But I see something completely different. You look at Lady Mercy as if you are already married." Mercy's heart began beating ferociously. *Me?!* "Trust me, Caleb, I know the difference between charming a girl and *loving* a girl."

She couldn't believe this. Mercy was always so focused on the way she reacted to Lord Griffiths' every advance, or even just his simple presence. Did he truly look at her like that? Mercy would have to pay attention next time.

Mercy was about to leave them be when Lord Griffiths started talking. And that was when everything went quiet, and her heart plummeted to the pit of her stomach.

"...I guess you really don't know the difference, then. I'm only doing this to become a duke. Besides, I would never fall in love with someone like Lady Mercy."

Everything stopped.

Mercy couldn't breathe. She felt as if her legs would give out on her. *Is the world tilting?* Mercy fell to her knees and felt her chest tighten with each breath.

Is this true?

Did Lord Griffiths just want to become a duke this whole time?

Mercy was the eldest daughter of the Duke of Norfolk. She wasn't married. And there were no sons to inherit the title. The only way for her father's title to pass on would be if she married a man to take on the dukedom.

It all made sense...

So this is why...

Before she could think twice, she pushed open the door with a *bang!* Lord Griffiths spun around in shock, and Lord Morris said something, but Mercy couldn't hear. She didn't care to hear. Everything around them became a blur; all she could see was Lord Griffiths and his haunted expression. He knew he had messed up, but Mercy did not care.

All she could feel was the shattering of her heart.

It was all fake. Everything between them had been fake. The *one* time Mercy had felt something that might have been beautiful and sweet toward a man—it had all been fake.

"How could you?" Mercy wanted to sound angry and strong; she wanted to scare Lord Griffiths. But she only sounded broken. She sounded pathetic. "How could you do this to me?"

He reached toward her. "Mercy—"

"*No!* It is *Lady White*—or better yet, don't *ever* refer to me again! I hate you! I hate you so much...the way I felt for you at the beginning was nothing compared to how I feel about you now."

"*Please.* I beg of you, let me explain—"

"I cannot believe that you were only courting me for money and my father's title. That was your *plan*, right? From the beginning?" Her voice broke at the end, and she had to take a breath. She felt as if she was breaking everywhere, and the pain was so severe that she had to close her eyes, causing a tear to slide down her cheek. "Don't lie to me and tell me that you truly cared for me at all."

"It...it was true at the beginning. The title was all I wanted. But not anymore. I have been lying to myself this whole time, even just now." He was panicking. There was sweat coating his skin. His eyes were wide open, and his hands were shaking. "I am in love with you. That is the truth. If you don't believe anything else I say, believe *this*. I love you. I *love* you."

Mercy shook her head adamantly, tears streaming down her cheeks. She heard a commotion behind her and knew that her father and sisters had come up behind her. The humiliation was so overwhelming she didn't know if she could ever recover from this.

"I—"

Before Lord Griffiths could utter another word, she marched forward and slapped him straight across the face.

She didn't wait for the silence that would dawn over the entire room, both from Lord Griffiths, Lord Morris, and her entire family. She didn't care what they thought or how she might appear. She hated him, truly. She wanted him to feel a sliver of the pain she felt at that moment.

But a slap would never be enough.

The worst part was that she was in love with him. She would scream at the top of her lungs that she hated Lord Griffiths. But it wouldn't be true. Still, embarrassingly, she loved him. Since the beginning, he had not left her mind, and she feared that he never would. She had thought that he would be different. Different from all the other pathetic men in the world. However, he ended up being like all the others. This shouldn't have been surprising. Mercy was an unfortunate girl. So of course, the world would give her a beautiful man to fall in love with.

And made him a liar.

26

When Caleb returned home from the dinner at Norfolk Manor, he locked himself in his office. He stuffed his head in his hands, crouched over in the chair, completely in shambles. The room was dark; only a single lit candle flickered on the ebony desk, casting a small, eerie glow over Caleb, which matched the lack of warmth in his now-empty chest.

It's over, he kept repeating to himself. There was no going back to the way things were before. He had finally warmed Lady Mercy's cold heart, had finally broken down the walls that surrounded her. And he had to ruin it all because he was *scared*.

He was too scared of revealing the truth: That he was completely in love with her. He had been for a while but acknowledging it out loud was close to impossible.

Besides, the whole time, Caleb was adamant about succeeding in his plan. The plan to secure a marriage with a duke's eldest daughter so he could take over the title of the duke. That was supposed to be his main goal, nothing else. For his whole life, that was all he wanted. He wanted to be powerful and of the highest-tiered nobility.

But then he met Lady Mercy.

Before he knew it, he was falling for her. Under all of that hard exterior, Caleb found an earnest, loving, strong woman who made him feel like he couldn't breathe when he was without her. But even still, he couldn't breathe when he was with her. It didn't help that she was the most beautiful woman in the ton. He could stare at her all day and never be bored.

Lady Mercy was his vulnerability, and that was what scared him. He didn't want to announce to the ton, much less his friend, that he was in love with her because it would show that he was weak. For so long, he had been the charmer. He had charmed countless women, all of them swooning for him by the end of the night. Caleb didn't even remember their faces, just that they were there, and they were utterly infatuated with him. It was not anything special, and it was only for fun. But to be in *love* with someone was something entirely different.

He didn't want to be wrapped around someone's finger. He didn't want to submit himself to a woman and be emotionally dependent on her every word. His one true need was to become the duke, not a husband.

Yet somehow, everything had turned itself inside out.

He was in love with Lady Mercy, and the thought of becoming a duke wasn't so important anymore, just that he wanted to be with her, forever.

All of that was ruined now.

The look on her face when she crashed into the room would haunt Caleb for the rest of his life. He never thought that Lady Mercy, a force of nature who had the sharp wit to repel every man in the ton, could look so heartbroken.

It was still engraved in his mind now as he sat in the dark room.

He had hurt her, and it was killing him.

Perhaps this would be his life now: Forever tortured by the fact that he had broken Lady Mercy because of a foolish lie. They would be two separate people now, just like before when they didn't acknowledge each other's presence.

Caleb almost vomited.

He couldn't do it. He couldn't imagine such a world again. There was no one else out there for him; he was convinced that he would always choose Lady Mercy, over and over again. And that didn't scare him one bit.

He needed her back; he would do anything to be with her again. It would be difficult to convince her of the truth, especially after she had overheard his terrible conversation with Ben. She would never believe anything he said again.

Lady Mercy now saw him as a liar—a liar pretending as if he was in love with her the whole time, just to earn the title of duke.

And she was right. He *was* a liar. But he lied about pretending that he *wasn't* in love with her.

Caleb needed to tell her this. There was no other option.

He scooted back his chair and stood up. The candle flickered and cast long shadows on the wall. A wax melted and simmered on the wooden surface.

"I need to speak with her," he said in the empty room. "I need to fix this."

Caleb was at the front entrance of Norfolk Manor, speaking with one of the maids. She looked pale and uncomfortable, constantly fidgeting under Caleb's watchful stare. He was growing more irritated by the second because the maid kept saying the same thing.

"I'm sorry, Lord Griffiths, but Lady Mercy is unable to see anyone right now."

Of course, he knew that by *anyone*, she meant Caleb.

"Please, just let me talk with her," he pleaded. "This is very urgent."

"I'm sorry—"

Another voice came. "Lord Griffiths?"

The maid hastily turned away, and Caleb saw Lady Olive marching toward the doors, followed by Lady Alice. They both looked angered to see him, if their pinched red faces were a clear sign.

"What are you doing here?" Lady Olive asked, her voice hard and rough.

Caleb gulped. "I am here to see your sister. About yesterday—"

"Mercy is not going to see you...*ever* again," Lady Alice said. "She won't even speak

to us."

Lady Olive nodded. "Because of *you,* she won't come out of her bedchamber. You wronged our sister, so please—go away. None of us want to see your face."

With that, Caleb had no choice but to leave. But he couldn't let that stop him from trying. So, for the next few days, he began writing letters to Lady Mercy. He pushed aside all his other work and set to writing about how he felt in a dozen or so notes, working in his office for hours on end. He put his entire heart into the letters, explaining everything from beginning to end. Caleb had never been so truthful until then. And the more he wrote, the more he fell in love with Lady Mercy.

He even sent her flowers. Bouquets of roses, carnations, and orchids. They would be delivered to the front door of Norfolk Manor with a handwritten note by him saying that he loved her and that he wanted to speak to her.

However, after long, grueling days of doing all of this, there was still no response back.

The silence was absolutely killing him.

There was only one last thing to do.

He rode to Sielle Manor one day and hopped off his horse to see his friend waiting for him.

"Are you all right?" Ben asked.

Caleb slowly shook his head. The simple question almost made him break again, his knees growing weak. He lowered his eyes, unable to look Ben in the face.

Ben was the one who had preached true love from the beginning. He had warned Caleb about the risk in all this. The one true way to marry is to marry for love, not greed. And Caleb had ignored him, and he had ruined his one chance at happiness.

He was selfish for thinking that Ben would help him, even after ignoring his advice countless times.

But then he felt a firm hand on his shoulder, and he raised his eyes to see that Ben was looking at him with understanding. "Don't worry, Caleb. I'll help you."

Caleb's chest warmed. He didn't even have to say anything. His friend knew the distress clear on Caleb's face. He wanted to hug him right then and there.

"I am about to meet Lady Olive; she wishes to hear

what I have to say about you, but I think…you should be the one to tell her. Come with me."

Caleb's eyes widened. "You would let me?"

"Of course, Caleb. You're my dear friend, why wouldn't I?"

He couldn't help it. Caleb embraced Ben with everything he had. He put his gratitude in it, showing him how thankful he was for Ben's constant support.

Ben laughed until the sound finally died, and his voice sounded serious. "I knew you were lying. This whole time, I knew. Your voice said you didn't love her, but your eyes said otherwise."

They rode to Norfolk Manor and entered together. They waited in the drawing room, tense and silent. Caleb could hear his heart beating loudly; he was nervous that everyone in the household would all hear its thunderous noise. Then, Lady Olive walked into the room, and when her eyes landed on Caleb's, she swiftly turned around to leave.

"Wait!" Ben said and rose to his feet. "I brought him with me because you need to listen to him."

"Why should I?" Lady Olive murmured.

"Because he is my good friend, and I know him. Listen to him, please. For me."

It seemed that an eternity passed before Lady Olive finally took a deep sigh and turned around. She sat down rigidly on the opposite chaise and regarded Caleb with a disinterested look. She nodded for him to speak, and Caleb tried not to tremble.

He explained everything.

From start to finish, he told Lady Olive what his true intentions were at first, which almost made her stand up and leave again, but he pushed through. He explained that yes, although he had initially wanted to marry Lady Mercy for the title of a duke, everything changed as time passed. He actually got to know Lady Mercy and everything that she was, and he fell for her. He didn't know when just that it happened very early on in their meetings. He told Lady Olive of his fears of commitment and love and that he had never experienced something like this before, which was why he had said what he said after dinner. In the end, he was only lying to himself.

When he finished, Lady Olive was quiet, gnawing on her lip and thinking deeply.

Caleb started sweating the longer the silence continued. But he had told her everything, all the truths unveiled. If she denied his reasoning, then his life was over.

But then, she slowly nodded her head. "I will take you to speak with my father."

Caleb let out a breath. "Thank you. Thank you so much."

Lady Olive took Caleb to the office room where the duke sat behind his large desk, his chin resting on his clasped hands. The Duke of Norfolk had always appeared as an unthreatening man, who, instead of reeking with ominous power, was filled with joy and love. But in that instant, he was the scariest man Caleb had ever seen. His hands trembled, and he swore his heart was lodged in his throat.

But Caleb was sick and tired of being scared.

"Duke White." Caleb bowed deeply.

"Lord Griffiths. You have a lot of nerve showing your face here again."

Caleb stood high and spoke with complete earnestness. "I am here to apologize for everything. For my terrible intentions, for hurting your daughter, and for lying to everyone, including myself."

The duke raised a brow.

"I was so full of greed that I failed to see that my heart had changed its mind. I no longer cared for the title and the power that comes with it, all I thought about was Lady Mercy. For the first time in my life, I fell in love, and I ruined it all. I've learned my lesson, and the punishment of experiencing Lady Mercy's absence from my life has injured me more than I ever thought capable. I want...I need her in my life, Duke White. You would know, more than anyone, how much of a gem Lady Mercy is, so please understand me. I cannot live without her."

The duke was unflinching in his glare. "Are you telling the truth or lying once again?"

This time, Caleb's voice rose unintentionally, but he

needed the duke to hear him clearly. "This is the truth. I am tired of hurting others and myself with my lies."

Everything fell to a standstill, and Caleb could only wait. The clock ticked on, but he would have waited there forever if it meant that he was granted the support of the love of his life's father. He would wait, and wait, and wait.

Especially when it ended with this result: The duke rising to his feet and saying, "I accept."

Caleb's chest loosened with great relief, but the duke rose his hand. "But it will all come down to whether or not Mercy accepts your apology. At the end of the day, it is her decision."

Caleb agreed. He needed to tell her everything; he couldn't wait any longer. But not now. He had just gotten the support of her sister and father. Next time, he would tell her. So, as Caleb left the manor, he did so with a new lightness in his heart. But he still felt burdened with pain, as if half of him was still aching with heartbreak, broken and bruised by their separation.

As he left, he looked back at the manor, and he could see her bedchamber window, the one where he had sat and sung with her.

She was right there, but still, she felt so far away.

27

Seven days. One whole week.

Mercy stayed in her bedchamber with swollen eyes and a tired heart. She barely left the room, only to use the restroom or to eat food. The humiliation from that night still lingered, and she couldn't bear to see anyone, much less talk to them. But staying inside, locked in the confines of her own room, alone with her thoughts, did not make for a better alternative. In fact, she felt as if she was still drowning. One of the maids had brought up a batch of letters, all addressed to "Lady Mercy," along with bouquets of flowers. She knew before opening them that they were from Lord Griffiths, but that didn't stop her from tearing them open.

Perhaps she wanted to hurt more. Or perhaps she just really, really wanted to know what he had to say.

The first few letters were filled with apologies. He confessed to his true intentions, and those, Mercy crumbled up, ripped them to shreds, and threw them away; she would later want to burn them. The last two letters were different; she knew immediately. Once opening them, she saw that they were longer, less messy, and more articulate. He wrote about all the things that he loved about her: her wit; her feisty disposition; her unabashed courage, even when they defied all societal traditions; and her love for her sisters. The list went on and on, and he went through excruciatingly minute details: how she would tilt her head downwards to hide her face behind a curtain of her hair; how didn't like holding eye contact, as it made her more nervous—that was why when they had danced, she kept looking away.

The more Mercy read, the more she found little things about her that she had never really thought anyone else had noticed.

It felt so intimate that she couldn't read the letters in one sitting. She would read a bit in the morning, a little in the afternoon, and then read it all over again at night, repeatedly. Mercy knew she shouldn't have given him the time of day, but she couldn't help it. It was an indulgence that she was guilty of, but her broken heart needed a little mending.

The last letter began with an apology, and then a confession all over again. It began with *"Dear Lady Mercy, who deserves so much more,"* and ended with *"Love, Lord Griffiths, who wishes to be more."* She couldn't stop crying by the end of it.

Even as she read all the letters, there was the fear of the whole thing being a lie. How much of what he wrote was true? What if he was tricking her again? These thoughts gnawed at her mind, making her shatter all over again. She just couldn't believe him again. And that hurt more than the letters themselves.

On the eighth day, she heard a knock at the door. Mercy assumed that it was the maid bringing another letter for her, but when she opened her door, she found her father standing there, a look of complete worry in his eyes as he observed her.

She knew she looked a mess, but frankly, she didn't have the energy to care.

Seeing her father made the mask of indifference crack, and she fell forward, collapsing into her father's arms. Tears streamed down her cheeks, soaking his shirt, but he didn't care; he only wrapped his arms around her, and she choked on a sob.

He rubbed her back for a long time, and as she calmed down, he kissed her forehead and backed away a step. "My darling Mercy, you have been cooped up in this bedchamber for far too long. You must see the sun."

Mercy wiped away her cheeks and was suddenly conscious of the open letters scattered on the floor. It was too late to hide them, and based on her father's gaze lingering on her floor, she could guess that he knew who they were from.

He sighed. "There is a hunting event today. Remember we used to always go to them? Accompany me, please. I want you to go outside."

It had been a while since she had gone outside and breathed in the fresh air. She didn't even have the energy to go out on horseback with Apple—that was how exhausted she felt. Mercy knew if she continued to lock herself inside the house, she would never get better. Her father and sisters were worried about her; she couldn't be selfish any longer.

So, reluctantly, she nodded her head and told her father that she would need to get ready.

The maids helped her clean and change, and she was soon outside in the stables. Her father had already saddled their horses. They trotted to the hunting event, where a plethora of nobles milled about, some with their horses, others with fans and petite umbrellas, resting under the blazing heat of the sun. Mercy and her father hopped off their horses and walked around a bit, greeting a few lords and ladies. None of them brought up her outburst at the last ball, which she was eternally thankful for. A few passersby gave her a furtive glance, but nothing more. She tried not to pay attention to them.

Instead, Mercy breathed in the air, and, although it was

very hot, she found herself enjoying the nice temperature and the occasional wind that gave them a reprieve. She was grateful that her father had asked her to go out today; she knew that, otherwise, she would have been cooped up inside, reading those letters again.

Just then, there was a hush. The crowd suddenly parted, and Mercy craned her neck to see what the fuss was about. Someone was walking through, but she couldn't see who it was. However, slowly, everyone's heads turned to her, and that was when she knew something big was about to happen.

Time seemed to slow down as Lord Griffiths appeared before her eyes. There were bags under his eyes and his skin was paler than usual, but still, to Mercy's great disdain, he managed to look beautiful. He was only looking at her, no one else, and Mercy found herself unable to look away. Her heart was about to burst; she couldn't breathe. Everyone else blurred into the background, and it was just the two of them.

She wanted to run away, but she was paralyzed to the spot.

Then everything took a turn when he stopped, bent down on his knees, and seated himself in a position that made it seem as if he was bowing down and submitting himself to her. It was a humbling position, especially for a baron toward a lady. She didn't know how to react; she could only gape at him.

Then he began speaking, and he was addressing everyone. "I'm here, in the eyes of the public, to address my mistakes. I want everyone to know that I was a selfish man who sought Lady Mercy out for the sole reason of attaining her father's dukedom."

Everyone gasped. Mercy could hear her heart pounding in her ears.

"I convinced myself of following through with this plan because I am a horrible man. But as I tried to charm Lady Mercy, it was *I* who ended up being charmed. I fell in love with her, and I do not regret this. I hurt her because she found out my initial intentions in the worst way possible. And I lost her—she is still apart from me now. So, I am here today to announce that still, I am selfish. I am selfish because I want you in my life, just you, nothing and no one else. Lady Mercy, please forgive me. I promise to never lie to you again, and that I will cherish you and every moment we spend together, and think only of you when we are apart—though, I can guarantee you that I do this even now."

Mercy didn't know what to say. It was as if all his letters had led up to this exact moment. All the apologies, all the heartfelt words. They all could have been lies, though, which gave Mercy pause. What if he was still scheming, tricking her again?

Before she could answer, Lord Griffiths turned to her father. "Duke White, I want no land, money, or title. I do not want to be a duke any longer. All I want is Lady Mercy." His eyes then trailed back to Mercy, and his dark eyes shone; she was astonished to think that he might have been crying. "Lady Mercy, will you please be my wife?"

Everyone turned their full attention to Mercy, and it seemed as if the whole world was waiting for her answer. But still, she was frozen. She couldn't say anything. She couldn't even think properly. The hot air was becoming more suffocating than fresh, and Mercy desperately wanted to leave.

So she did.

Slowly, as if her body was moving on its own, Mercy turned to find her horse, hopped onto Apple's back, tugged on the reins, and left, determined to go to the one spot that she had always found solace in.

A place where she could breathe.

Caleb watched her retreating form with an empty feeling in his chest. He was still on his knees, frozen and in shock. He had laid out his entire heart for her to see, and yet it did not work. He had irreversibly hurt her. It was all his own fault.

There was only silence; the crowd seemed to be in shock too. Caleb would have happily stayed there for the rest of his life. He was as embarrassed as he was sad.

But then a thick hand came into his vision, and he looked up to see Duke White reaching out a hand for him to take. Reluctantly, Caleb grabbed it and allowed himself to be pulled up, standing once again.

"Don't give up," the duke said and handed Caleb the reins to his own horse. "If you love her, you must try harder. Chase after her."

Caleb immediately snapped out of his surprise and swung himself into the horse's saddle. He didn't even look back as he yanked on the reins, causing them to go at a full-speed gallop. It was as if his body had reacted by itself, pulling Caleb's mind out of its frozen state, alerting him that he needed to run after Lady Mercy or it would be too late.

As he galloped further and further away from the hunting event, Caleb knew, somehow, where he was going. The only place that Lady Mercy would retreat to in order to rest and think would be the woods by Norfolk Manor. She had once mentioned that she always rode on the path in those woods, so it was easy to surmise that she would escape there; Lady Olive had even said that she would often go outside when she was stressed. With the clues connected, Caleb rode toward the woods.

Finally, once he reached the familiar woods, he slowed the horse and began trotting between the trees. He moved further and further inside, and he was about to call out for her when he heard a faint sobbing.

He moved the branches out of his face and saw, in the middle of a small open field in the forest, Lady Mercy, seated on the ground with her face buried in her arms. She was trembling and every so often, a cry would sound from her bent form.

Caleb jumped down from the horse and approached Lady Mercy. He leaned down and, without hesitating, slowly enveloped her in his arms. He tucked his chin on top of her head and placed his palm behind her neck, gently pulling her into his chest. She didn't even flinch; she only melted into him, and Caleb was grateful that she didn't pull away.

They stayed in that position for a long time, him holding her while she cried.

Then finally, as her tears subsided, Caleb murmured into the air, "I am sorry for hurting you. I shouldn't have ever done it—but I do not regret meeting you." His voice broke, but he didn't care how weak he sounded. "You may punish me, shout crude words to me, and even smack me a thousand times, if you like. Just be mine as you do it."

She slowly pulled herself away from him, but she didn't leave his embrace. Her head tilted back so that he could see every feature on her face—the tear-stained cheeks and her swollen green eyes. Her lip trembled slightly as she observed him.

"Marry me, Mercy," Caleb whispered. "Let me be your husband."

The wind blew, and the trees swayed. The leaves rustled, and a frog croaked nearby. The birds danced in a little circle in the sky.

Then a fist raised in the air and came down on Caleb's chest.

It wasn't a hard hit, but he was so surprised that he fell backward. Lady Mercy smacked him again. "This is for wanting to take my father's dukedom."

Another hit. "This is for bringing my sisters into this."

Another. "This is for lying and hurting me."

And another, which hurt more than all the other ones. "And this is for making me love you, despite everything."

Caleb's eyes widened.

"Of course I will marry you, Caleb Griffiths," she cried. "Although I am still upset with you, I cannot stop loving you. I don't think I ever stopped." She sniffled. "Promise me that you won't ever hurt me like that again."

Caleb felt a stray tear fall down his cheek, and he smiled. "Don't worry. I would be too scared."

As he expected, Lady Mercy raised a fist once again to no doubt smack him straight in the chest, but he grabbed her wrist before she could, pulled her closer, and planted his lips on hers.

He thought that she would yank away and punch him across the face this time, but she only relaxed her fingers and tugged on his shirt collar so that she could bring him closer. And at that moment, he wished that they could stay there forever.

28

The ride back to Norfolk Manor was a long one, mostly because Mercy could feel Caleb's eyes on her every few moments. She wanted to remember this moment forever. The trees formed a canopy of leaves over their heads, but the small cracks allowed the sunlight to shimmer through, casting bright rays throughout the woods. She could see the dust motes flying and the bugs buzzing by; the slight wind brought everything to life with the trees trembling and the leaves rustling. And at the center of it all, Caleb sat with a smile on his face, and she took note of the dimple protruding on his cheek.

He always looked handsome, but right now, to her, he looked beautiful.

She had to focus and lead Apple all the way home,

though she had memorized the route by now, all her attention was on catching small glimpses of the love of her life.

Love.

The word still felt awkward in her head, and it would take time for her to speak the words into existence. Because wasn't that what couples said to each other, "I love you"? Mercy didn't know if she could say it without turning into a bright tomato, but she would always know it, even without having to say it.

She would show it in the ways she looked at him. Like in this exact moment, she couldn't stop staring at him. If they could, she would have hopped off Apple and laid on the ground with Caleb by her side. She would show her love by lightly touching his shoulder with hers and by blushing when he didn't move away.

Everything was new, and they would treat their love as such. It would be quiet and subtle, but Mercy didn't care.

Soon they arrived home, and the smile on Caleb's face vanished. Mercy watched him gulp as he slid off his horse and the way his hands trembled slightly.

Mercy quickly went to his side and held his hand. Caleb's eyes flew to hers, and a faint blush appeared on his cheeks. Mercy bit her lip to contain the wide smile that almost overtook her entire face. "Don't be nervous," she whispered. "I'm here right beside you."

His smile returned, and he tightened his hand around

hers. "Thank you, but I have to be honest, I will always be a little bit nervous when you are beside me."

Mercy laughed, gently shoving him back in response. They then both walked inside the house, where it was completely silent. Noticing that the doors to the drawing room were slightly ajar, Mercy pulled Caleb inside.

To her surprise, she saw that Lord Morris and Lord Curzon were inside, sitting beside Olive and Alice. Her father stood by the windows. They all wore wary expressions, and none of them said a word. It looked as if they wanted to ask all sorts of questions, especially when Mercy and Caleb walked in holding hands.

Mercy broke the silence first. "I am going to marry Lord Griffiths."

The first one to move was Olive, who sprung up from the couch, her hands covering her mouth. Lord Morris only smiled, casting a proud look in Caleb's direction; he seemed the least surprised. It took a while before what Mercy said registered in Alice's mind, and she later gasped so loud that Mercy laughed in embarrassment; Lord Curzon smiled warmly.

Then, when Mercy looked at her father, she was surprised to see that he wasn't jumping up and down, cheering to the high heavens. She was shocked that he hadn't blown up the roof of the house by now with his yells and praise. Instead, there were tears in his eyes. And the smile on his face was brighter than the sun. He sped across the room and into Mercy's arms, hugging her so tight that she couldn't breathe.

"Do you truly love him?" he asked quietly into her hair.

Mercy's heart warmed. "With everything I have," she answered.

Soon after, her father let go of her, and her sisters dove into her arms next. They were both crying and laughing; Mercy couldn't calm them down.

"I'm so glad it worked out," Olive cried. "You deserve this."

"You both are perfect for each other," Alice appraised.

Mercy didn't know how long they all stood there. Lord Curzon and Lord Morris were congratulating Caleb. Lord Morris looked especially happy, giving Caleb an extra-long embrace.

The room was filled with so much love that Mercy almost started crying too. She had never felt happier than in that moment with her whole family there. She would remember this moment forever.

"Mercy," Olive called, pulling her out of her happy daze.

"Yes?"

"We should all get married on the same day, together. You, me, and Alice."

Alice's face lit up, and Mercy immediately smiled. They all took one look at each other and knew that it was the best idea ever. Mercy was already a little frightened and nervous about having a wedding, where everyone would be celebrating her and Caleb's love; she was still uncomfortable being the center of attention. But spending what would be the best day of her life with her two little sisters would make everything better and more manageable.

Mercy and Alice nodded their heads in agreement.

It seemed that their father had heard as well because he dove into the conversation with a loud cheer. "What a brilliant idea! A wedding day for all three of my beautiful daughters. It will be three times as exciting! We must begin planning soon!"

Mercy looked at her sisters with a raised brow, and they all erupted into laughter.

"We mustn't forget about the grooms now," Olive giggled. "Do all three of you lovely husbands-to-be agree with this arrangement?"

Lord Morris' smile widened. "Of course."

Lord Curzon nodded his head vehemently. "It is fine with me."

"As long as I can marry Lady Mercy, I agree to anything," Caleb replied.

With that, the entire family spent the rest of their day together, laughing and conversing joyously. They had a feast for dinner, where they all sat around the table, the sisters next to their fiancés, with their father at the head of the table, silently admiring the expansion of his lovely family.

It might have been the longest dinner they've ever had, purely because none of them wanted to end the blissfulness of this night. But sooner or later, it had to end, and as everyone began filing out of the dining room, Caleb pulled Mercy aside and asked if she would like to take a walk with him.

Mercy experienced a sense of déjà vu. Earlier, Caleb had asked to take a walk with her after dinner, back when she thought that she hated him. Now, she gladly took his hand with a large smile on her face.

They walked through the garden, and the moon was as bright as ever. There was a cool blue glow to everything. Caleb was still warm, and she clung to him the way she would stay by a warm fireplace.

She would have gladly walked with him in silence for the rest of the night, if only he was there next to her. But then he spoke, and his voice was serious. "Mercy, I want to apologize again, for everything I did—and *didn't* do." He stopped walking and faced her directly; Mercy's heartbeat sped up. "I should have loved you from the start, without my terrible intentions. From the moment I thought of this foolish plan, I was doomed. With you, of course, I was. I've truly fallen in love with you, Mercy. I tried to act as if I was not infatuated with you every second we spent together and say that it was all pretend. In truth, I was lying to myself. And I will forever hate myself and love you for forgiving me."

Mercy didn't realize she was crying until she felt the tears drip from her chin. She gripped his hand tightly and shivered when she answered. "We were both lying this whole time." They shared a broken laugh. "But I'm forever grateful that we persevered, thanks to our friends and family as well as our own bravery. So, thank you for running after me into the woods today. Thank you."

Caleb answered her with a kiss on the lips, and Mercy felt a flutter in her chest. Then, when he pulled away, he slid down to the ground. Her eyes widened as she saw him bend on one knee.

"Mercy." He was staring at her with stars in his eyes, and it wasn't the reflection of the night sky. It was her. It was always her. "I have and will always love you. Marry me, be mine and let me be yours."

How could she ever say no? Mercy choked on her tears as she crouched down so that she was eye level with him. She nodded silently and slid into his arms, and he wrapped around her perfectly, two broken pieces finally fitting together.

They stayed in that position for a very long time, just holding each other. They didn't have to say anything. Their love was too loud for mere words to interrupt.

The next morning, Mercy found her father reading the papers at the table. There was a proud look on his face, so she couldn't help but lean over to steal a glimpse at the news he was reading.

She shouldn't have been surprised to see that it was the announcement of her and her sisters' wedding, written all in bold.

There was a long article beneath the headline, no doubt droning on about how the duke's family would expand and the speculations about who the next duke would be. Mercy knew that the whole ton would be talking about it for the next few weeks, gossip spreading about everything and anything.

Their talk would likely all be lies, but none of it mattered anyway.

Because Mercy and Caleb would always know the truth.

EPILOGUE

One month later...

"Hold still!" Alice brushed a few strands of hair away from Mercy's face so that she could apply a few puffs of powder to her cheeks. On the other end of the room was Olive, who was being fitted into a beautiful yellow dress; her curly brown hair fell in tumbles, curling over her slim shoulders, with half of it tied back with a bow. She looked like a princess.

They all did.

The three sisters had decided to assist each other before the wedding ceremony, only with the help of a few maids. It was reminiscent of how they had all helped each other prepare for balls in the past.

One of the maids pulled Alice away from Mercy so that she could adjust her dress.

A large blue ribbon hung on the lower back of her light blue gown. Her brown hair was wrapped in a low chignon; an iris flower was tucked into her hair. Lord Curzon had picked the flower from his own garden a few days before and given it to Alice. It was only right that she would wear it on her wedding day.

And Mercy—although she might have dreaded the whole dressing-up fiasco—didn't really mind all the attention she was getting. Normally, she would have hated sliding on a dress and sitting down for hours while her hair got yanked back and forth. But today, the weather was bright, and the birds were chirping. She felt light, and nothing really bothered her much.

So, she *tried* to hold still for the entire duration.

And when they were all done, Olive and Alice both stared at her with their jaws slack. She stood in front of the mirror, amazed at herself. A long white gown hung on her figure, and her hair was pulled up in a chignon, Mercy managed to convince Alice that she didn't need to wear any cosmetics, mostly because she didn't want to sit still for another minute. But as she looked into the mirror now, she realized that she looked divine.

A blush came to her cheeks when she tried to imagine how Caleb would react.

Olive and Alice walked forward and held Mercy's

hands. They all looked into the mirror, and the maids hung by the walls, adoration plain on their faces. None of them said a word, but the message was clear: They looked absolutely and stunningly beautiful.

It was only when the maids had all left the bedchamber that the three sisters engulfed each other in a warm embrace, clinging on to each other as if they wouldn't ever see each other again.

The idea was frightening at first. Mercy broke out into a cold shiver, suddenly overcome with an unbridled fear, realizing that she would be separated from her baby sisters. And who would protect them in her absence? Then she remembered Lord Morris and Lord Curzon. They would take her spot and guide the girls and keep them safe. It wasn't Mercy's job anymore. That would take a bit of getting used to, but she had Caleb, and she wasn't alone.

They were all taking the next step in their lives.

Just then, the door opened, and their father walked in.

He only needed to glance at them once before erupting into a fit of tears. "My beautiful babies, growing up into beautiful wives! I have dreamed of this moment for so long." He tried to wrap his arms around all of them. "I love you all so very much, you cannot even imagine."

Mercy felt a tear slip down her cheek, and soon enough she was crying along with her father. Olive and Alice both sniffled, obviously trying to stem their tears and not mess up their ensembles. Their wedding ceremony was soon!

But Mercy didn't care. She clung to all of them, so happy that she couldn't breathe.

And as they all held each other, Mercy swore that she felt another warm presence among them, wrapping her arms around all of them, looking down on her beloved family.

Afterward, when they walked down the stairs and out the doors with nervous steps, they entered a beautiful ceremony that was already in motion. They had only invited their close friends and family, deciding to keep the wedding relatively small. Lord Curzon's family and friends as well as Lord Morris' family attended the event. Her father's close friends were also seen commenting on the food and wine. There was much to observe. A large fountain hung in the center of the garden, and a long, intricate floral arrangement sat every two inches along a stone-paved pathway. A white arch stood at the end of it, beautiful but domineering.

Mercy gulped nervously.

Caleb, Lord Curzon, and Lord Morris stood under the arch, and they were all looking at them. A hush fell over the crowd once they noticed the three girls. A quartet—which Mercy hadn't noticed before—began playing a faint tune, and the ceremony began.

Her father walked all three of them down the aisle. The guests wore stunned expressions as they took in Mercy and her sisters.

The grooms also looked speechless.

Mercy didn't notice how Lord Morris and Lord Curzon reacted because she was only looking at Caleb. He looked so handsome, she couldn't concentrate on her steps and almost slipped on the stones. A black wool-trimmed tailcoat fit tightly over his pearly white cuffs and buttoned shirt underneath; he wore black trousers that accentuated his long legs. His usually disheveled black hair was styled this time, exposing the entirety of his sharp face.

Mercy almost fainted.

When they all finally reached the end of the aisle, their father looked at them once before nodding to the grooms. He stepped away, and Mercy was surprised that he hadn't cried once since stepping outside.

Olive and Alice exchanged their vows first. A loud sniffle rang in the crowd, and Mercy didn't have to turn to know it was her father in tears.

Then, so suddenly that she wanted to run away, it was Mercy and Caleb's turn.

Caleb turned directly toward her, his dark eyes level with hers. There was an electrifying moment of silence. It seemed that an eternity had passed with just their eyes connecting; Mercy would have been happy to stay that way, but alas, the ceremony had to go on. "Lady Mercy," he began, addressing her formally. "I will be honest and say that I never imagined standing under the altar, filled with so much love and adoration for the woman holding my hand. I never dreamed of it. But now, as I stand here with you, I cannot help but wish that I could turn back the clock and dream only of you from the very beginning. I feel as if I have wasted so much time."

Mercy saw his eyes begin to shimmer, and she realized that he was beginning to cry.

"However, as we finish these vows and promise ourselves to each other, I will soak up every second we have with each other from henceforth, and selfishly take forever to learn everything about you. Though, it is unfortunate that forever is not long enough." He smiled as a tear slipped down his face.

Mercy was shaking, but it was her turn, and she needed to talk. Everyone's eyes were on hers, and she began to struggle with breathing. But then Caleb tightened his hold on her hand. Mercy looked into his eyes and saw how soft they were.

She wasn't alone.

From this day onwards, she never would be.

"Lord Griffiths," she said, but faltered and whispered "Caleb" instead. "I hated you very much at first. Whenever I saw you, I was suddenly filled with such anger and rage as I had never experienced before in my life. You irritated me, truly. And when you confessed to me—all those countless times—I was speechless, purely because there were no words capable of describing how I felt." Caleb quirked a brow, growing nervous as Mercy's vow dragged on; the crowd also seemed confused. Mercy tried not to laugh. "Then I woke up. I realized that what I felt was never hate, but it was interest. You were all I ever thought about, day in and day out. I pretended as if it was hate, because that was all I had ever felt toward a man. But you barged into my life without remorse, different than all the rest. So beware, if we ever argue in the future and I say, in a fit of stupid rage, that I hate you, know that it means: I love you. Until death, and even afterward."

There was a stunned silence over the crowd. Mercy was surprised that she was even able to say all of this in front of everyone. Then the frozen daze snapped, and everyone clapped. For all three of them. The music sprung back to life, and their father beckoned them all to dance with him.

Before that could happen though, Caleb pulled Mercy closer and kissed her full on the lips, holding her tight. Mercy blushed furiously but she didn't push away.

Cheers broke out, and their happiness echoed across the entire ton.

The next morning, everyone ate breakfast at Norfolk Manor. The maids were all busy pushing out plates on the tables, and Caleb helped, handing out slices of honey cake that he had made. Lord Morris also gave everyone a piece of his plum cake.

The celebration never seemed to end, and the smiles never dropped. Mercy wished that she could freeze time and stay forever in this blissful moment with her family. If only they had enough time.

But she and Caleb had to leave for their honeymoon soon, and sure enough, their carriage was in front of the house, ready for them to go.

Caleb carried all the bags to the carrier, and Mercy hung back at the entrance, hugging Olive and Alice.

"Have fun on your honeymoon," Olive cried; her tears were soaking Mercy's gown. "Bring back something for me."

"If you can make time," Alice laughed. "Traveling the world may take up the majority of your schedule."

Mercy smiled, and her heart felt warm. "Of course; I will always make time for my baby sisters."

With that, they parted, and her father came forth to give her a big hug, much like the one

He gave her as a little girl. She melted into his warm embrace, and for a second, she felt like a child again. "Your mother would be so proud of you, Mercy darling. Remember that."

Mercy held onto him tighter.

Unfortunately, they didn't have all the time in the world. Mercy pulled herself away from her family and toward Caleb, who had just ended his tearful conversation with Lord Morris. They entered their carriage together and waved farewell to everyone. They peeked out of the small window in the back of the carriage, looking out at Norfolk Manor and thinking of how much things had changed. A month ago Mercy never would have imagined that she would be here, sitting next to the most handsome man in the ton, her husband.

But here she was. From Norfolk Manor to the rest of the world, Lady and Lord Griffiths would begin their forever journey, hands held together and hearts converged into one.

THE END

Did you enjoy *The Duke's Rebellious Daughter*? Check out the story of *Nelly* and *Oliver* in *The Duke's Juliet* here.

If you want a Bonus Scene of this book visit the link below (or just click it): https://abbyayles.com/aa-059-exep/

THE DUKE'S JULIET

Preview

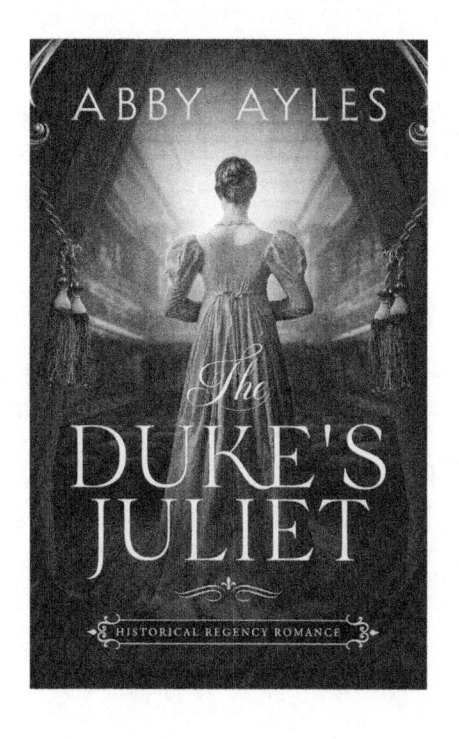

Read it now!
http://abbyayles.com/AmB060

His heart is a stage and she is his Leading Lady!

Oliver Northbury, the Duke of Grafton, dressed as a commoner, blends with the crowd that watches a street performance. A troupe of actors is playing in the inn's yard. And there she is. On stage. Nelly Woodcliff is in her first role! She is the most talented actress he has ever seen! And Oliver has seen many, as he grew up in his late father's theatre building -his own theatre building- the famous "Parastasi"! Oliver is the sponsor of the theatre company that plays in his theatre and wants Nelly to become his next leading Lady!

But Nelly is proud and her family is most valuable to her! Getting to know her better, Oliver discovers that she is defensive towards the high society. Her art belongs to the crowds. Oliver is afraid to tell her he is the Duke... so he cannot admit he is the sponsor of the theatre company she is proposed to join...

. . .

Nelly will find true love but she will also face Oliver's lies, her family's objections, the previous leading lady's jealousy, and the ton's scandal sheets.

Her fate has more twists and turns than any play she has read and any role she has brought to life!

If you like engaging characters, heart-wrenching twists and turns, and lots of romance, then you'll love "The Duke's Juliet"!

Buy "The Duke's Juliet" and unlock the exciting story of Oliver and Nelly today!

Also available with Kindle Unlimited!

Read it now!
http://abbyayles.com/AmB060

1

*N*elly Woodcliff was standing by the window in a small room overlooking the common area in a village inn. The acting company had been to the Plough Inn before, in the village of Lockley. But still, she was terrified of the scene below her. With a dry throat, she swallowed hard, creating an audible gulp. All she could do was pray that her nerves would hold. The crowds gathered inside the inn, were there to be entertained at the outdoor stage in the courtyard, once the play started. For a tiny moment, she teetered on the edge of pulling out.

Surrounding her, in the same room, was the chatter of cousins, along with other close family members who were to perform in the play. They all awaited their turn to take the stage. But Nelly had cut out their babbling noise, that was something she was good at, drifting deep into her thoughts. It was a skill she had learned over the years, as part of her training.

A good actor must shut out the ambient noise around them and concentrate solely on their role. I will overcome my stage fright so I can perform on the stage, and in front of my audience.

What if they laugh at me, instead of with me?

Her dark mop of curls sat atop her head, fixed in place with faux pearl hair pins to give her a look of wealth. All part of her role in the popular play, which was titled *Forced Marriage*.

What if they can tell this is my first performance?

She inhaled deeply again; another method of training that should help her relax. Nelly was ready for the performance. White-powder makeup had been dapped all over her already porcelain completion. Heavy makeup gave the actors a dramatic pale appearance. The dull white gown she wore, was to be her wedding dress in one of the scenes.

What if—

"I can see that you are agonizing over everything that could go wrong," her mother's voice came to her as she lay her arm over her daughter's shoulder. "With your skill and acting ability, nothing will be amiss."

"Oh, Mother, how do you know?" Nelly's dark red lips formed the question as her voice quivered. Her lips felt sticky, and her skin prickled with a cold sensation, sending rippling tingles through her body. The stage makeup felt constricting as if it was clogging her skin and depriving her of air.

"Because I know how talented my daughter is," her mother replied with a confident smile. "These last-minute nerves are good for you; did you know that?"

"I don't see how being a withering wreck could enhance my performance?" Nelly questioned, not convinced her mother spoke the truth.

"It means, my dear, that you are a true performer," her mother insisted. "Those who worry are the ones who care, which will push you on to perform at your very best."

"But is my best good enough?" Nelly asked, still unsure if she was ready for her first main role in the play. She had performed supporting roles aplenty, but none had placed her in the limelight. "Let's be honest, Mother, none of us know how I will perform. I may fall to pieces with the first word I utter."

"Acting is in your blood, child, and don't you forget that." Her mother refused to support her daughter's dreary thoughts. "You are as skilled as your mother ever was, and her mother before her too."

"You think so?" Nelly looked at her mother with a wide-eyed stare. "You will take some beating, Mother. If I recall, Delilah Woodcliff was the best around for years and years."

"Might I remind you that you have been acting since before you could even talk?" her mother smiled, wanting to remind her daughter that this was not new to her.

"I know, but that was for fun, this...this is for real," Nelly shook her head, raising her arm to indicate the audience below.

"You, my dear, are the ultimate professional and you know all the tricks in the book. If you forget your lines you improvise. No one will know, not if you do it with a natural flare. I don't need to tell you this though, do I?" her mother assured her. "You were born to take a leading role, and it is time to take up that mantle. The role in this play was written for you, that's how perfect you are."

"But...but look at them," she said, still with a tremor in her voice as she returned to peer through the glass of the small window. "They look like savages, Mother, untamed even. They will shred me to pieces if they suspect I am flawed."

"Look at yourself first, daughter. You are not only beautiful, but you are talented too. The women will envy you, and the men will all want to hold you."

"But will they appreciate my acting? Will they clap me off the stage instead of wanting me to stay on it?"

"The people you see before you in the crowd, they are watching you because they seek to be entertained. These people pay their hard-earned coin to see us telling them a tale. They truly want to be there my dear." Her mother tried to explain as she came to join her daughter at the small window. "It is true, some of them are a little rough around the edges."

"Yes, Mother, they have a look of wildness about them. And let's not forget that the mead might encourage them to be loud."

"If you capture their eyes, you will find no malice. They are here to escape their hard lives. You are right to worry that they do not appreciate those who are worthless, for they do not have the time to waste. What they long for is to be taken into a world of fantasy. That's why they are going to adore a talented young actor such as yourself. They are your future followers, my dear. What's more, they are going to fall in love with you."

"I wish I had your confidence, Mother," Nelly said, her eyes going to the floor as she felt her shame.

"By the end of the night, the mead will lull them into a peaceful daze. But to begin with, it heightens their senses. That means that they appreciate the time in which they can find an escape from the drudgery of their lives." Her mother continued to explain how her daughter should perceive her audience.

"I would imagine that an actor is more appreciated in theatre buildings than by the drunkards of an inn."

"No, that is far from the truth," her mother snapped back. "Whenever you perform to your own kind of people — the commoners, the farmers and factory workers, miners, beggars and even women of the street, you act from your heart because you will feel their appreciation. Theirs is a genuine love of a play, it is their only escape, as much as it is yours. Those who perform for the wealthier audience in the big theatre houses, like the nobility, they do so for financial gain only, and not for art. I am convinced of this."

"Hmmm...at least a wealthy audience will not look as rough and ready as that lot below," Nelly argued. "They petrify me, Mother. The disadvantaged will have no misgivings about throwing fists at me, should they decide I am not worthy of their time."

"You misjudge your people, my dear. Although I suppose there is some truth that they will be quick to judge. If they enjoy your performance, which they will, they will throw adoration your way. And that is priceless."

"Nelly! Nelly! Come over here and join us. We are rehearsing before we go on," Daisy, her cousin, shouted over

"Go on" her mother encouraged. "You know what it is I say all the time, practice makes perfect."

"Thank you, Mother," Nelly said, taking her mother's hand in hers. "I hope every daughter has a mother such as you. You make me feel so confident with your words of encouragement.

"What else is a mother to do?" her mother smiled at her daughter in fondness, "Besides, it's easy for me, I have every faith in your abilities."

"Do I look the part?"

"My darling, you *are* the part, now off you go and get some rehearsing done," her mother pushed. But before

Nelly moved away, she added, "You know we have performed this play multiple times for the people of the streets. And every time it has been a huge success. But never have we had such a beautifully talented *Dorimene* among our cast. You are the perfect, delicate butterfly to play this role."

Nelly's face flushed at such a wonderful compliment from her mother.

"Look in the mirror and see how you blush with innocence. My dear daughter, that is what is going to win over the hearts of your audience," her mother encouraged. "See how your bright red lips clash with your white powdered face? How you carry your elaborate hair style that sits upon your head with props aplenty. And beneath all of that, I can still see the softness in your eyes that will carry your expressions to your audience."

"I look like you, Mother, with all this stage makeup on," Nelly pointed out. "But I like looking like you. Knowing that will lend me some confidence.

"You do, my love. Now off you go, they're waiting for you."

Nelly hugged her mother and dashed over to the cast who would be out there on the stage with her any time soon. Some of them were family members and others were close friends, but they all loved her, and her heart filled with love for them too.

Straight away she was able to jump into the leading

role, not even needing to ask which part they were rehearsing. To add to the charm of the play, the main male role was being played by a female actor. The play had comedic scenes, but it built up to the grand finale of a tragic ending. Because that was what the audience loved, and they would be well and truly entertained.

Nelly's mother was the principal owner of the acting company, as her family had been since it began generations ago. The group of actors who toured with the company, whether family members or not, they were all like one big family. And so, Nelly knew them all, and each of them would support her developing role. Most of them had been with the touring company for many years. They had watched Nelly grow into the leading role she was about to perform for the first time. And all of them shared her mother's opinion, that Nelly was born to act.

"Are you to tell me that my new husband has taken on a mistress?" Nelly repeated her lines, getting into the drama without even realizing that she had done so, such was her talent. "But ours was a marriage born from a business agreement, and not out of love. What care I for such indiscretions?"

This scene dictated that she plays a cheated wife, and that she did not care, for hers was an arranged marriage, as the title implied. Later in the play, she would cheat on her husband, and by the end of it, he would murder her for her indiscretion. It was a play that brought about laughter and tears, written for a specific audience so that the poor could poke fun at the rich.

Nelly had seen the play re-enacted many times over the years, even with her parents in the leading roles. But now, it was her turn, and her cousin, Daisy, played her husband. It was also Daisy's debut and when rehearsals were done, they huddled together in a show of support for one another.

"I have the easier role, Daisy, at least I am playing the fairer sex," Nelly said. "You have the added awkwardness of playing a man!"

"Yes, but you have to die in the last scene, I wouldn't have a clue how to play such a part," Daisy said.

"Hah! So, you're comfortable with murdering me then?" Nelly asked, laughing.

"Oh, I hope we do the scene justice," Daisy added, burrowing her brows into a deep frown with worry.

"Every rehearsal has gone well, so why shouldn't the real thing?" Nelly encouraged, knowing her cousin needed as much support as she did.

"You are right, cousin, and playing alongside you is a real honour," Daisy told her, and she meant it. "You are by far the best actor in the group, Nelly, and don't you forget it."

"That's a lot for me to live up to," Nelly said, fretting over the thought. "With words like that, how can I dare make a mistake?"

"You have proven that you are good at covering over any mistakes, so you have nothing to worry over," Daisy assured her. "Besides, your mother would not have put you in the leading role if she thought for one moment you were not ready."

"There are others in the group who could play the part better, but Mother is pushing me to do it. She says it is time for me to consider taking over the company, but I don't know... I don't feel ready for it."

"You have me by your side, always, don't you ever forget that," Daisy said cheerfully.

"You are like a sister to me, Daisy—"

"Role call!" her mother shouted out, reeling off the names of the actors for the next scene, one of which was her daughter.

"Here we go." Nelly had a nervous quiver on her lips. She was anxious because a leading role was far more stressful than a supporting one. But her mother had been right, if she forgot her lines, she knew exactly how to flow with her dialogue. Now it was time to pray that her hands would stop shaking and that her voice would carry to the audience and not sound so fretful.

"Break a leg!" Daisy called after her.

"You too, Daisy. I'll see you out there soon."

She had changed into a plain cream day dress for the coming scene, for she was to look the part of a bride. The stage was set for her wedding day, and Daisy would be wearing a man's tailored jacket with tight pants and knee boots. As soon as she got to the last creaky, wooden step of the inn, she danced through the back door of the inn and into the yard. There, she climbed onto the wooden stage that she had acted upon so many times before, but never in such an important capacity. Nelly began her lines.

"Must I marry him, Father?" she began. *"My heart is with another, and well you know it."*

As she pointed her face upwards for the part, she spotted her mother peeking through the same window she had been looking through earlier. It eased her mind to know her mother was not far away.

The crowd in front of the stage watched her closely and in an eery silence. They saw it as their role to cheer of jeer, depending on their mood.

Read it now!
http://abbyayles.com/AmB060

2

The theatre appeared dark and lifeless inside. It was a typical dreary atmosphere when all the house lights were out. Even the huge high-ceiling room was filled with black and grey shadows lurking in the unseen crevices. The smoky, tallow candled, and oil-fed elaborate chandeliers would not be lit until the evening show. And then, the entire building would come to life with laughter and chatter, and the thunderous sound of applause.

Faint voices could be heard echoing from the stage, as a few actors rehearsed for the evening performance. From the edges of the stage, candle lamps illuminated it, giving it a warm and welcoming glow. The golden light fought hard to cut through the lonely darkness. But in the darkened shadows that blanketed the rows of seats, a man observed the actors. This was not just any gentleman, it was the owner of the theatre, Lord Oliver Northbury, the Duke of Grafton.

He was not an actor by any means, but his family had owned the theatre for many generations. Being involved in his father's business dealings as he grew up, he knew all the intricacies of a good performance. Yet what he was witnessing at the rehearsal was not at all good. One could say it was professional, and no doubt the critics would pen positive reviews. Yet the performers lacked a vibrancy in their craft. It was a vibrancy he had not seen in any performance for many years. Many of the older actors had retired from the theatre, and the upcoming ones didn't have the same level of pride in their craft. So, his search continued as he combed the area to find new talent.

He waited patiently for the rehearsal to conclude. As the actors stopped, he moved with silent footsteps. As he walked upon the carpeted floor, he took a few wooden steps to enter the back of the stage. There, he met his leading lady, Miss Margaret Lockhart. He knew her to be sensitive to criticism, so he would first start by complimenting her. That would lead on to telling her how he felt her performance was lifeless. Actors, he knew, were fickle creatures, and he would tread with the greatest of care when it came to doling out critique.

"Margaret, my stunning star of the show, let us talk if you have a spare moment for me?" Oliver said in a half-jolly tone as he approached his leading lady, though he bore the look of stressful worry. Being the owner of the theatre house and not an actor, he wasn't sure how if Margaret would take his criticism. He had learned to always start any conversation with an actor, with a compliment. Never so was this more necessary, given Margaret's temperament.

"If you're giving out such wonderful compliments, darling, I will talk with you anytime," Margaret replied. Oliver knew that she relished being the centre of attention, most especially from the wealthy theatre owner. From what he'd been told, she'd had a crush on him for years, but he paid no heed to idle gossip.

"I can only put it down to an off day, but where is the passion in your performance today?" Oliver asked, treading as lightly as he dared, without actually insulting her skills.

"Oh, my darling," Margaret called out in an exaggerated, husky voice, for she wanted all to see that the Oliver was paying her attention. "You know me, I'm saving my best performance for the real thing. You will see your *stunning star* of the show tonight."

Oliver watched Margaret wave her arms around as she spoke. This was a woman who played out her life as one big melodrama, and it reflected in her character

"I sincerely hope so. I want to see the terror in your eyes at the shock you have witnessed. I want to feel the heat in your heart emanate from the stage as your lover dies in your arms. What I don't want to see is this cold, stale-looking character that you have portrayed in rehearsals today."

"What?" Margaret looked horrified at the words that passed through Oliver's lips. "Stale-looking indeed! What do you know of acting?" she called out in her deep, husky tone, that often became hoarse if she shouted too loud. "The fault, Oliver, lays with you, my dear. Your expectations are far too great. Why should an actor need to shine in rehearsals? Tonight, you will see me in my full glory, as you always do in a show. I trust you will be there to witness my stunning performance, and then give me your sincere apologies?"

"Ah, alas no," Oliver told her, unperturbed by her outburst. "I have another engagement on this occasion. Nonetheless, do give your performance a little more care."

"Your role should be to attend every performance, darling, and not be drifting away from your responsibilities," Margaret tutted. He could see that she was readying for a sparring session that he did not care for.

"I bid you farewell, for now, Margaret. Please heed my words," he warned before turning to head straight to his office. Margaret did not have the opportunity to retort, though she looked enraged. He knew it would leave her frustrated with him, though he had little care.

As he opened the door to the office, Oliver was fuming under his collar. "That woman needs to improve, and soon, or I will be sending her packing," he mumbled to Charles, the company leader.

"I gather you've been upsetting our leading lady once again?" Charles asked as he looked upon the sour face of his employer.

The office was a windowless little room, and the air was stifling with the swirling smoke from lighted candles. It caused Oliver to cough as he started to take off his top clothes.

"Are you going out again? Surely, you're not going to miss the show?" Charles asked, his dark brown eyes going wide with surprise.

"Tuck in your ever-growing belly, Charles, and expand your mind a little. Both would do you some good," Oliver remarked, taking off his pants. "You know, Margaret is no longer a girl, and we would do well giving her roles that are more fitting of her age."

"Gracious me, Oliver! Don't you ever let her hear you talking in that way, or we'll have no leading lady," Charles puffed as he took a seat to catch his breath.

"If Margaret is not capable of developing into a role more suited to her age, then I will most certainly replace her," Oliver snapped back. At the same time, he pulled up a different set of pants, that had the look of shabbiness about them.

"I see that you're pretending to be a commoner again," Charles remarked, rubbing his podgy hand through a few greasy golden curls on his balding head of hair. "Where is it that you go this time? Some crude street play that's performed by rogues, and has rabble for an audience?"

Oliver wagged his finger at his company manager, tucking in a shirt that was two sizes too big for him. "You underestimate the skills of the traveling theatre groups, my man. Their blood is invested in their trade."

"Their blood is dirty if you ask me," Charles mumbled, furrowing his brows in a scowl. "Well... perhaps I overstep the mark, but you were the one who brought in their blood. Truly though, Oliver, they really are quite crude people."

"Tonight, I will be watching one of the touring theatre's perform 'Forced Marriage,' and I understand they have a new leading lady in it," Oliver explained. "And I'm always on the lookout for good actors."

"Why would our theatre need to take on such unprofessional performers? I have no understanding of why you have this need to watch street shows. Not when you can sit in the comfort of your own glamorous theatre, alongside nobility?" Charles asked, still not happy at what his employer was about.

"Because I appreciate art in all its forms, Charles. If you have nothing to compare, but one set of actors, how can you know you have the best?" Oliver said, putting on a cheaply tailored earth-brown jacket. It would keep out the cold while he mingled among the outdoor audience of commoners.

"You are a duke, not a commoner!" Charles pointed out the obvious with a raised voice, which caused him to cough into his grubby hands. "You don't know what might happen out there. These crowds can get mighty rough if they don't like what they see."

"Then it is well that I can take care of myself, isn't it, old friend?" Oliver said politely. "You should get something for that cough," he added, patting Charles on the back to help clear his lungs. "I bid you farewell, and I'll see you on the morrow."

The small cough that rumbled in Charles' chest was now a full-blown fit of heaving coughs. It meant that Charles could no longer complain over his employer's actions. As he attempted to clear out his airways, he stood up to follow Oliver, but to no avail. The coughing fit had rendered him incapable of following, while Oliver made good his escape.

Leaving through a back door of the Grafton Theatre house, Oliver knew that his common disguise was sufficient to keep him out of trouble. He had done this many times in the past and considered it worthwhile. All he wished to do was watch and learn, as his father had taught him this was the way to find good talent.

Oliver was glad to see that the rain had held off. It had been threatening to ruin the evening, all day, as well as make the roads slippery and unsafe. But he always preferred the evening shows, it meant he could hide better among the crowds. But even in the dark the narrow streets of London soon became congested. Horses rattled by with their carriages in tow, and drunken louts wavered around threateningly. All went about their business, and none cared about anyone who might happen to get in their path. At least most of the street vendors had taken their wares home, allowing more open spaces on the cobbled lanes.

Trundling through the foul-smelling passageways, Oliver dodged broken glass. As he looked down, he pondered on other indescribable, offensive offerings that were underfoot, and did his best to pass it all by.

Finally, he arrived at the inn he had been searching for. The Wooden Keg had a large courtyard where they allowed traveling entertainers to perform. Though it surprised him at the large size of the crowd that night. It seemed that all the commoners in the district had come to be entertained by the outdoor performance.

The wooden stage was set up in front of the crowd, and the play had already begun. Oliver didn't mind as he'd only missed the first scene, so it meant there were another four to go. Making his way to the front, all faces were staring at the stage, so no one gave him a second glance.

Instantly, he recognized the scene and smiled once he realized that the leading male role was played by a woman. Quite the opposite to what they often did in the larger theatres, whereby a man would often play a female role. But then he did not expect a traveling theatre to stick to any rules. They played to a different clientele, and that dictated a different set of guidelines.

Towards the end of scene two, the leading lady finally appeared on stage, and Oliver was struck by her beauty. She was young, so he doubted that her acting skills would match her standard of attractiveness, but how wrong he was.

From the first word that passed her lips, he knew she was perfect for the role of Dorimene. *The play was about a noble woman forced into a marriage. Later, she was to catch her new husband embraced in another woman's arms.* Oliver watched in awe as the scene played out and the leading lady won over the audience. They were completely enthralled by her performance. *All were entranced as she portrayed her suffering at finding such a scene in her own parlour, set upon the stage.*

The commoners *booed*, but not at the excellent performance of Dorimene, no, *they caterwauled at her sufferance and called out in support of her.* She had won them over in an instant, and the crowd loved her. As the second scene came to a close, Oliver witnessed how enraptured the audience had become in only two scenes. This was theatre at its very best, capturing the audience in such a way that his own leading lady was not doing of late.

Scene three opened, with the leading lady weeping under a tree prop. Who should happen to pass her by but her childhood sweetheart. A man she had been forced to spurn because of the arranged marriage. Throughout the scene, he comforted her, and the crowd cheered for him. As they kissed at the end of the scene, the crowd was delirious with enthusiasm, happy that Dorimene had found comfort in someone she trusted.

Charles's words of referring to this audience as savages returned to his mind. Oliver knew they were not refined, but they invested such rich emotions into their entertainment. These people were far more passionate about a play than any of the nobility. His wealthy clientele, dressed in all their colourful regalia, were far more concerned about how they looked to their peers. Few showed a true interest in the show. Their purpose for visiting the theatre was merely to show off their rich silks and other refinery. Who had the grandest carriage and finest horses? Who had the largest feather hat, or the most colourful gown? That was their only ambition when they entered his theatre house.

But the honesty invested by the commoners as they watched the show play out, was unbeatable. That was why he loved the traveling theatre so much. Traveling actors played their characters as if their lives depended on it, and that resulted in a true and raw performance.

Of course, he knew how the story ended in this play, but he found himself filled with great anticipation whenever Dorimene took to the stage. He knew every word she would speak, so when she strayed off the lines, he applauded her courage to improvise with even better prose. She not only looked the part, but she gave her own take on how it should be played out. The young actor was marvellous, and he didn't want the play to ever come to an end.

As expected, it finally comes to its inevitable tragic end with the husband murdering his bride. Oliver thought, almost wishing it was the other way around, for she deserved to live on and find happiness.

He roared with the crowd as they shed their tears. The murder scene sent a wave of anger through the audience, mixed with other raw emotions that they were not afraid to show. *Never have I seen the crowd so enraptured by a scene in a play.*

The commoners might wear dull greys and browns that were shabby in appearance, but they were true to their cause. Compared to the well-dressed nobility in his classy theatre building, he would choose the commoners any day. None were out to impress the other, all they wanted was good, honest entertainment. *The character of Dorimene has given them all that they hoped for when they paid their coin to watch this play.*

The crowd roared; but this time for an encore. They were demanding more, and Oliver shouted along with them, though there were no more scenes to be played out. Their shouts for Dorimene echoed around the inn's courtyard. *They adore her.*

Right on cue, the entire cast came to take their final bow. Dorimene was forced to stand forward as they continued to yell her name at the tops of their voices.

Some are shouting themselves hoarse, for they want so much to see Dorimene alive and well one last time. It shocked Oliver as he found himself joining in, so emotional was the moment. His hands ached with all the excessive clapping he had been doing, along with everyone else. He even whistled as he put fingers to his mouth to ensure the shrill noise rose above everyone else's.

This is a night to remember. I have to come back for more, for I am hooked.

"And now, for one night only," the leading lady called out. "Here is the ending that should have been."

The crowd hushed at the sound of her voice, all wanting to hear her words. Oliver was as mesmerised as everyone else in the crowd. The actors took to the stage and an unknown scene was enacted. *In the scene before them, Dorimene's lover came upon the stage to murder her husband. The scene ended where he saved her from the inevitable death scene. As he embraced her in his arms, he told her that she was safe from the monster.*

The entire crowd had pushed forward in their eagerness for the unexpected scene. Oliver found himself squeezed against the wooden frame of the stage from his standpoint at the front. Loose splinters from the wood threatened to pierce his hands but he had no care, like everyone else, he wanted to see the play. It seemed that the audience had grown, as more had joined at the back. Oliver turned to look at the growing audience, he knew that word must have spread like wildfire about the extra scene. *A scene never before played out, and a scene that everyone wants to witness, including me.*

He knew that this was an experienced traveling show. *How they came up with such a brilliant idea as this is beyond my understanding. Was it the new leading lady's idea? Maybe she did not like the fact that she dies, and so she's giving her audience a better ending. She is indeed a force to be reckoned with. I have to meet with her. I must know if this was her invention, her doing, for if it was, then she is gifted indeed.*

At the end of a play, Oliver would usually leave early so that he could return in time for his own theatre ending. But not on this night. This night he would stay behind and watch every second of the leading lady's performance. He would join in with the crowd and feel their emotions as they all enjoyed a night of stupendous entertainment.

Read it now!
http://abbyayles.com/AmB060

3

*A*s Oliver mingled among the crowd, he was pleased that the entertainment had not stopped at the close of the play. Not normally one to hang around after a performance, he had no idea that the inn continued to distract their patrons from the toils of their day. The innkeeper had found a way to encourage them to drink more of his ale, with continued entertainment. The aroma of meat lingered in the air, as patrons tucked into the innkeeper's meals. But where was Nelly he wondered.

The stage might have emptied of its actors, but they had soon been replaced with musicians. Not the usual orchestral groups that Oliver was used to at a soiree or a ball, but more of a gathering of commoners who shared their love of music. A fiddle player strummed out a little dancing ditty, while another man joined him, playing his flute. They were skilful players and just as good, or so he thought, as any professional orchestra he had the pleasure of listening to. Still, he looked around the crowds for Nelly.

Before long, a drummer joined in. All that was missing was a harp or even a pianoforte. Whether they were a regular band, or individuals coming together, he did not know. Only that they were soon strumming together in perfect harmony.

Making his way in all corners of the courtyard, he searched to see if the actors had joined the crowd. Passing the corner, a woman dressed in a scraggy, long dress that revealed her bare shoulders, jumped upon the table to dance. She lifted up the skirt of her dress to show her ankles and cheers sounded out as the patrons gave out a rhythmic clap to the beat of the drum.

All the while Oliver's mind was thinking about the charming leading lady of the play. Where was she? The actors would return to join in the celebrations, he was sure of it. He must seek her out and tell her how much he'd admired her performance. Oliver could not help but compare her to his own theatre's leading lady, but there was no comparison to be made. She was far superior to Margaret, in looks, acting skills, and dare he suggest, energy and vivacity.

The actress in the traveling theatre was exactly what his

own theatre house needed. Exciting new talent such as she was, would breathe new life into his shows. The vivaciousness of such an actress as this one could only lend a new spirit to his plays, taking the entertainment value to new heights. Here was a young actress who had her entire crowd entranced with her performance, and completely under her spell. He had to have her in his shows, at whatever cost it might endure. If only he could find her.

The lively music lifted his spirits even further if that was possible. Oliver had not felt this good in such a long time. He continued to observe the crowds in search for Nelly. Many had stayed behind and serving trays were ladened with ales and stews, served by the buxom barmaids of the inn. If the inn could garner such profits from hosting this traveling troupe, then so too could his theatre house. But the world of acting wasn't only about business, it was a deep passion that only few understood well. And when he found Nelly, he would discuss that passion while he fawned over her, for this was more than an interest in her skills; he adored her.

Filled with a renewed enthusiasm, he started to join in the festivities, unable to resist the cheer surrounding him. There was even a bard now going around the crowd, filling his hat with coin as he called out his verse. The crowd embraced all the arts, especially so after copious amounts of ale.

Workers from around the area, farmers and pickers still wearing muddy tunics. Unwashed factory workers, and even women of the night in their low-cut ragged dresses. All had ventured to join in the fun. It was so very different from his establishment, and he loved every minute. He would love it even more if only he could find Nelly among this rowdy lot.

If only he could get such a reaction from his own patrons. Immediately after one of his plays came to an end, the crowd would gather in the large hallway as they left. Their only concern was to show off their gowns, or even their mistresses, as they made their way to their shiny carriages. They did nothing but gossip about one another; whereas here, he could hear the chatter was still about the play. People debated over the ending; whether it should be changed or remain a tragedy. Never would the nobility show such passion over a mere show.

It was one of the reasons why Oliver loved to attend the street plays. He was giddy with excitement, likened to when he was a child at Christmas. The people who gathered to watch such shows embraced the art of acting. Commoners were not bound by the rules of high society, and he had a sudden feeling of pity for his wealthier clientele. Theirs was a life ruled by directions and expectations, with no room for pure let-your-hair-down joy. Now, where was she? The beautiful woman who lit up the entire stage when she appeared. Where was Nelly?

As the night wore on and the ale flowed, many were getting up from their seats to dance. Completely unabashed, they created their own dancing steps. Even laughing at themselves for their foolish behaviour. They did not care what their neighbour thought, for they were laughing too.

Oliver went inside the inn's common room in search for Nelly. Both inside and out in the courtyard, people of the lower class were having fun. They spilled out through the front door and onto the streets of London, loud laughter ringing out into the night sky. Older children ran around in little gangs, some sneaking the dregs of ale from the bottom of glasses. While others joined in the dancing with their inebriated parents. Age was no barrier in an evening's entertainment of this calibre.

And it was all sparked from the enjoyment of the play. Had the play been a dreary one, the mood might have been different. But Nelly had given them a renewed hope in their life, with her raw, salacious performance. Her appetite for acting had entranced the audience and left them all feeling good about themselves. These people, despite their rough edges, embraced the art form to its fullest and were better for it. *Is that not what true entertainment should be about? But where oh where is she?*

Again, he looked upon the stage, longing for the leading lady to show her face again. But if he wished to see her then he would need to attend tomorrow's performance.

Traveling actors were always a tight-knit group, guarding each other against prying eyes. Getting to speak with her would not be easy. Not even coin would buy his way through the protective outer layer of such a team.

Instead, he decided to join in the dancing. The ale in his belly was beginning to affect his judgment. It was time to join in with those around him and have fun.

Just then, he spotted one of the cast members dancing in the crowd. By her side was the leading lady, out in the open and being one with the crowd. He could make out her features by the silvery moonlight, along with the yellow glow of the oil lamps. Her face was flushed with energy. As he got closer to her, she looked more beautiful than he had first thought, if that was even possible.

The lines of an old sonnet came to his mind, for poetry was his second love. He had not realised that he was standing still and quoting one of his favourite love poems of Edmund Spencer:

"But looking still on her, I stand amazed

At wondrous sight of so celestial hue."

Blinking, he became alert and walked over to the group, offering to pay for a round of drinks. Cheers erupted at the proposal, and he waved over for one of the servers to deliver five large jugs of ale to the party. Experience told him there was no better way to ingratiate yourself with an actor, especially following a performance. By seeing to their needs with alcohol, it helped to dampen their highly strung nerves. Performing on a stage took a lot out of them, and after a show, they loved to unwind.

Wasting no more time, now that he had infiltrated the circle, he soon found himself standing by the side of their leading lady. She was already swaying to the rhythm of the music, and he joined in. He was thankful that he knew the steps to the dance she was enjoying.

"You dance well, my friend," she sang out to him, giving him a most gracious smile. Her voice was soft, yet it rang out to him as if she were still on stage.

"I find dancing almost as entertaining as watching a play. It soothes the soul," he replied but found he had to speak quite loudly to be heard over the rowdy noise around them.

Dancing beside her was indeed an unusual pleasure; never would a lady of the nobility allow a man to dance by her side in such a way. Being among the common folk brought with it a certain level of freedom. And so, he would cast off the shackles of high society and make the most of it. Even if his reasons were selfish; to get close to the talented beauty.

Whilst she did not speak again, she had accepted him silently as her partner in the dance. Oliver was not one to miss out on such an opportunity and felt no shyness, being of a confident nature he made haste to open up a conversation.

"Your performance tonight was superb," he told her

while she passed under his arm as the dance steps required.

"Why thank you kindly, sir," she replied, smiling as she carried out the dance moves. "Believe it or not, it was my debut performance, so to speak."

For a short while, they parted, following other dancers in the group as the moves dictated, but they soon came back together again.

"May I be so bold as to ask a lady her name?" he asked as soon as he took her fingertips in his hand to finish the move. By now he was panting slightly, for this was a vigorous set of dance steps, making conversation quite difficult.

Her face was already flushed and she glowed with the energy of youth. But beneath, he could sense a certain shyness in her soft brown eyes as she glanced back at him, and then quickly diverted her eyes to the floor.

"You are kind, sir, to praise my performance," she thanked him. "My name is Nelly."

Straight away he liked the way her name felt on his lips as he mimed it when she looked away.

The dance ended and all the dancers hugged one another. It was their way of saying well done, it had been a good dance. Oliver took advantage of the gesture and immediately embraced the delightful woman before him. She offered no resistance to his move and felt so perfect in his arms. It seemed that she did not mind lingering a moment longer than necessary, as he held her tight.

"It was most refreshing to watch you enact Dorimene with such perfection. And the alternative ending was a delightful surprise for all," he said, as he reluctantly let her go.

"I wanted something special for my debut, and so I rewrote the ending that I know everyone wanted to see," she told him. As she spoke, she leaned into him at a close angle to make herself heard over the raucous behaviour of her fellow actors. "It was easy. All I did was play to their hearts."

"Well, I wouldn't say easy, I would describe it as brave," he replied, enjoying having to lean into her ear so she could hear him. "We all love a tragedy."

"That is true, and that's why it was for one night only," she smiled back at him.

"Then I am so pleased that I didn't miss it. Otherwise, I would not have had the pleasure to witness a most creative performance," he said. And he was thankful that he had attended that evening.

As he had been accepted into the circle of actors, he spent the rest of the evening in their company, and they soon became friends. He met her mother, the owner of the traveling theatre, though he did not let on who he was. Nelly had many close friends and family, and she was as delightful offstage as she was on it.

She meandered away from him to dance with other people she knew, but she never ventured far from her troupe. Her shyness surprised him somewhat, for her stage performance was so full of confidence. She was indeed a born actress. And it was a woman he felt drawn to, not only because of her talent, but she also stirred his heart in very strange ways.

He watched her in wonderment as she danced with others. It seemed to Oliver that everyone was a friend in her eyes, she was fond of them all. Sometimes she spoke with an outsider to her group, but always in the company of someone from the touring party. Many commoners wanted to speak with her, dance with her, and praise her, but he was the one that she kept returning to. Whenever she was away from him, he would hover close by, showing as much security as her own family did.

She had captured something inside of him, something that he had never felt stir before. Because she had accepted him, so too did the rest of the acting circle. This was a good opportunity to talk about life with a traveling theatre. Many had assumed him to be interested in such a life, perhaps even being an actor himself. Not once though did he give away who he was, other than his first name.

It was getting late into the night and the crowds were starting to thin out. After all, many of the revellers would need to rise at the crack of dawn, with a long, hard days graft ahead of them. Oliver took the opportunity to stay with Nelly longer, now that there were fewer distractions since the music had died down.

"May I ask you a question, Nelly?" he dared a different approach.

"Of course, Oliver, ask away," she sang out, always speaking to him with a smile on her lips, that shone in her eyes too.

"Can I speak with you alone?" he continued, knowing that she might find his request unusual.

"Of course," was all she said as she took his hand and led him inside to a quieter corner in the common room of the inn. Outside, they could barely hear each other's words, and so Oliver was pleased at her idea to go indoors.

Though he had not expected the close touch of her hand, and it evoked a warm glow in his chest, as well as made his heart race. Although he knew that she meant nothing by holding his hand, for that was the way of many artists, nonetheless the feel of her soft skin was a moment of bliss. Her fingers felt so delicate in his own larger palm, and he dare not squeeze for fear of hurting the slender bones.

Is she showing me kindness because that is how she has been taught; or does she think me special, as I do of her? He did not know, but he followed her like a puppy dog because wherever she went, he wanted to be with her. *Now that I have found this shining gem, I hope never to lose her.* Whether she felt the same about him, he did not know, but he intended to find out, one way or another.

Read it now!
http://abbyayles.com/AmB060

SCANDALS AND SEDUCTION IN REGENCY ENGLAND

Also in this series

Last Chance for the Charming Ladies
Redeeming Love for the Haunted Ladies
Broken Hearts and Doting Earls
The Keys to a Lockridge Heart
Regency Tales of Love and Mystery
Chronicles of Regency Love
Broken Dukes and Charming Ladies
The Ladies, The Dukes and Their Secrets
Regency Tales of Graceful Roses
The Secret to the Ladies' Hearts
The Return of the Courageous Ladies
Falling for the Hartfield Ladies
Extraordinary Tales of Regency Love
Dukes' Burning Hearts
Escaping a Scandal

Regency Loves of Secrecy and Redemption
Forbidden Loves and Dashing Lords
Fateful Romances in the Most Unexpected Places
The Mysteries of a Lady's Heart
Regency Widows Redemption
The Secrets of Their Heart
Lovely Dreams of Regency Ladies
Second Chances for Broken Hearts
Trapped Ladies
Light to the Marquesses' Hearts
Falling for the Mysterious Ladies
Tales of Secrecy and Enduring Love
Fateful Twists and Unexpected Loves
Regency Wallflowers
Regency Confessions
Ladies Laced with Grace
Journals of Regency Love
A Lady's Scarred Pride
How to Survive Love
Destined Hearts in Troubled Times
Ladies Loyal to their Hearts
The Mysteries of a Lady's Heart
Secrets and Scandals
A Lady's Secret Love
Falling for the Wrong Duke

ALSO BY ABBY AYLES

The Keys to a Lockridge Heart
Melting a Duke's Winter Heart
A Loving Duke for the Shy Duchess
Freed by the Love of an Earl
The Earl's Wager for a Lady's Heart
The Lady in the Gilded Cage
A Reluctant Bride for the Baron
A Christmas Worth Remembering
A Guiding Light for the Lost Earl
The Earl Behind the Mask

Tales of Magnificent Ladies
The Odd Mystery of the Cursed Duke

A Second Chance for the Tormented Lady
Capturing the Viscount's Heart
The Lady's Patient
A Broken Heart's Redemption
The Lady The Duke And the Gentleman
Desire and Fear
A Tale of Two Sisters
What the Governess is Hiding

Betrayal and Redemption
Inconveniently Betrothed to an Earl
A Muse for the Lonely Marquess
Reforming the Rigid Duke
Stealing Away the Governess
A Healer for the Marquess's Heart
How to Train a Duke in the Ways of Love
Betrayal and Redemption
The Secret of a Lady's Heart
The Lady's Right Option

Forbidden Loves and Dashing Lords
The Lady of the Lighthouse
A Forbidden Gamble for the Duke's Heart

A Forbidden Bid for a Lady's Heart
A Forbidden Love for the Rebellious Baron
Saving His Lady from Scandal
A Lady's Forgiveness
Viscount's Hidden Truths
A Poisonous Flower for the Lady

Marriages by Mistake
The Lady's Gamble
Engaging Love
Caught in the Storm of a Duke's Heart
Marriage by Mistake
The Language of a Lady's Heart
The Governess and the Duke
Saving the Imprisoned Earl
Portrait of Love
From Denial to Desire
The Duke's Christmas Ball

The Dukes' Ladies
Entangled with the Duke
A Mysterious Governess for the Reluctant Earl
A Cinderella for the Duke

Falling for the Governess
Saving Lady Abigail
Secret Dreams of a Fearless Governess
A Daring Captain for Her Loyal Heart
Loving A Lady
Unlocking the Secrets of a Duke's Heart
The Duke's Rebellious Daughter
The Duke's Juliet

A MESSAGE FROM ABBY

Dear Reader,

Thank you for reading! I hope you enjoyed every page and I would love to hear your thoughts whether it be a review online or you contact me via my website. I am eternally grateful for you and none of this would be possible without our shared love of romance.

I pray that someday I will get to meet each of you and thank you in person, but in the meantime, all I can do is tell you how amazing you are.

As I prepare my next love story for you, keep believing in your dreams and know that mine would not be possible without you.

With Love, Abby Ayles

PS. Come join our Facebook Group if you want to interact with me and other authors from Starfall Publication on a daily basis, win FREE Giveaways and find out when new content is being released.

Join our Facebook Group

abbyayles.com/Facebook-Group

Join my newsletter for information on new books and deals plus a few free books!

You can get your books by clicking or visiting the link below

https://BookHip.com/JBWAHR

ABOUT STARFALL PUBLICATIONS

Starfall Publications has helped me and so many others extend my passion from writing to you.

The prime focus of this company has been – and always will be – *quality* and I am honored to be able to publish my books under their name.

Having said that, I would like to officially thank Starfall Publications for offering me the opportunity to be part of such a wonderful, hard-working team!

Thanks to them, my dreams – and your dreams — have come true!

Visit their website starfallpublications.com and download their 100% FREE books!

ABOUT ABBY AYLES

Abby Ayles was born in the northern city of Manchester, England, but currently lives in Charleston, South Carolina, with her husband and their three cats. She holds a Master's degree in History and Arts and worked as a history teacher in middle school.

Her greatest interest lies in the era of Regency and Victorian England and Abby shares her love and knowledge of these periods with many readers in her newsletter.

In addition to this, she has also written her first romantic novel, *The Duke's Secrets*, which is set in the era and is available for free on her website. As one reader commented, *"Abby's writing makes you travel back in time!"*

When she has time to herself, Abby enjoys going to the theatre, reading, and watching documentaries about Regency and Victorian England.

Social Media

- Facebook
- Facebook Group
- Goodreads
- Amazon
- BookBub

Printed in Great Britain
by Amazon